Raves for

"Denise Little has put together some really nice collections in the past few years, and it's gotten to the point where, if I see her name as editor, I know I'm in for a worthwhile read."
—*Chronicle*, for *The Magic Shop*

"Given the career of an English boy named Harry, the creation of an American school for magic-workers was inevitable. Not inevitable was that the place be a fount of intelligent entertainment. Editor Little's judgment helps make it such, and the comprehensive folkloric expertise she displays."
—*Booklist*, for *The Sorcerer's Academy*

"Exceedingly well done."
—*Booklist*, for *The Valedemar Companion*

"*Familiars* is a load of fun to read for the fantasy fan or anyone who wants a good escape. Little has gathered fifteen highly original short stories that deal with magical companions." —*Kliatt*, for *Familiars*

"After finishing this anthology, readers will never look at magic shops and new age/methaphysical bookstores the same way again. Little aptly describes the anthology as a 'collection of stories of the changed fates and challenged minds of the amazed consumers—both mundane and magical—who dared to shop at a Magic Shop.' Buyer beware!"
—*The Barnes and Noble Review* for *The Magic Shop*

COSMIC COCKTAILS

Edited by
Denise Little

DAW BOOKS, INC.
DONALD A. WOLLHEIM, FOUNDER
375 Hudson Street, New York, NY 10014

ELIZABETH R. WOLLHEIM
SHEILA E. GILBERT
PUBLISHERS
http://www.dawbooks.com

First paperback printing, December 2006
1 2 3 4 5 6 7 8 9

DAW TRADEMARK REGISTERED
U.S. PAT. OFF. AND FOREIGN COUNTRIES
—MARCA REGISTRADA
HECHO EN U.S.A.

PRINTED IN THE U.S.A.

ACKNOWLEDGMENTS

CONTENTS

CONTENTS

Introduction

by Denise Little

I LIVE IN GREEN Bay, Wisconsin. Up here in the frozen north, there are bars or pubs on every block that is not a solid residential enclave. Some blocks have three or more bars. Other than Lambeau Field, it's the first thing you notice about the town. Lots of nice churches—but there are *way* more bars. They range from high end to total dives, but an amazing number of them function as neighborhood hangouts, shelters from the storm, gossip hives, religious facilitators (much of Green Bay is Catholic, and the local bars are legendary for their superb fare at Friday night fish fries), hubs for fundraising, and even tavern league sports venues. It's customary around here for wedding parties to leave the wedding ceremony and go barhopping around town in full bridal regalia for a couple of hours before the reception takes place. Imagine sitting around watching the game with a bunch of friends when two or three satin- and tuxedo-clad bridal parties of strangers burst in to join the fun. Happens every weekend in Green Bay.

Bars are central to the city's social life. If you want to watch a game with a bunch of friends, play anything from volleyball and basketball to darts and tiddly-winks, catch up on the local news or just chill, in Wisconsin you head to your corner bar to do it. The bars aren't just linked by roads and sidewalks to the community—in winter the snowmobile trails run from bar to bar, with parking lots for the mushers right alongside the regular parking lots. That was an eye-opener for me—those things can go upwards of a hundred miles an hour. And another eye-opener for me was that many folks bring their kids along for the fun to the bars. Some bring their dogs. One lady used to bring her pet monkey, until it ran away. That caused *big* excitement in town, because Green Bay is not famous for its feral primate population. Beer and bratwurst and football, yes. Monkeys, no.

So all of this was quite a shock to my Southern Baptist system when I moved here. I had to wrap my head around the phenomenon. And it finally hit me—bars in Wisconsin are like Dairy Queens and YMCAs in small-town Texas, and diners in New York City. The hub of local life. Like Cheers, only with a lot more camouflage-patterned insulated jackets.

There's a certain logic to it—around here it's too darned cold to hang around outside for five months of the year. So the parks are out as a meeting place.

And the get-together place has to be within walking distance so that access isn't at the mercy of snowplows and salt trucks. Not to mention the whole issue of getting home in one piece. On a snowy night, you can tell who has had a few too many by the meandering footprints in the snow on the pathways. Thankfully, the bar patrons are generally walking—though I did see the tire tracks from a car running raggedly through the snow on the front yards on my block last winter.

A Green Bay winter brings with it a certain isolation—a whole lot of people here don't see the light of day except on weekends for months. It's dark in the morning when we leave the house. It's dark by four in the afternoon, long before we return.

I started to think about how living in Green Bay in the winter was almost like living in outer space. It's dark outside. We're trapped all the time inside artificially heated shelters sealed against a hostile climate. Whether it's to make a sense of community, set up a communal area for grown-ups looking for a little release from the enforced isolation, or simply ensure a safe place to get wasted until the season finally turns, the bars are the hub around which a good part of Green Bay organizes itself.

Which naturally led me to think about what bars in space would be like. In far-flung outposts of civilization scattered across the space-time continuum, bars will undoubtedly still serve the same purpose as they do here—they'll be a place where just about every kind of entity can find a place to sit, kick back, and toss off a cool one, or whatever constitutes a cool one for that particular entity.

And, like bars everywhere, they'll be the place where any stewing conflicts between the various populations of a place come bubbling to a head. Green Bay is about the safest place on the planet to live, but if you want trouble, the best place in town to find it is in a bar parking lot at closing time.

Having started to think of bars as the Outer Space version of a societal United Nations, only with spirits, hallucinogens, and aphrodisiacs on offer, I thought about what amazing tales would come out of interstellar watering holes. What kind of cosmic cocktails— and tales—would be told in the many and varied saloons, pubs, and bars in the depths of outer space? What would it be like to swagger into a frontier dive and belly up to the bar when half the species in the galaxy were staring at you? How would happy hour shake out when your whole civilization might be dug in inside an asteroid?

So now you have in your hands the result of my philosophic meanderings on a cold winter's night, while I watched the northern lights and thought about shelter from the storm. You'll find tales of people stuck at the end of the universe and at the end of their ropes. You'll find rogues and saints, con men and criminals, aliens and humans, interspecies love and cosmic misunderstandings. It's all inside *Cosmic Cocktails*.

I hope you enjoy the brew!

Drink, Drank, Drunk

by Loren L. Coleman

HI AGUADO!
   Silvered bottles tip and bounce on the wide
ferro-titanium shelf, clinking and chiming together in
a musical, if off-key, greeting. Tall bourbon-fifths spin
through drunken pirouettes I can't help admiring. The
short, squat fellas make up for it with enthusiasm,
bodily lifting themselves off the shelf's pitted and
laser-scarred surface, cracking back down hard
enough, in the case of safety-plastic containers, to chip
away colored splinters of deep green and whiskey-
brown.

A slender Orion Cabernet preens in the long bev-
eled mirror backing the shelf, then gives me a rolling
shimmy that chimes soft and pure.

It's the ring of *real glass*. Delicate, and precious.
Especially this deep into LV-824's Kuiper Belt.

"Settle down," Black Mike orders as he glides by.
Skating for the far end of the bar and a pair of wide-

5

eyed, touring Terrans. You can spot their type so easily, the plastic sheen of their cosmic ray shielding turned a waxy green under the saloon's dim light.

The bottles, though still full of sloshing spirits, calm, rocking back into their resting positions. I have to admit, their welcome melts me into a small, warm puddle. Which is fairly close to my natural state, as a gel-form biote of Saggitaire VI. Not much larger than three deciliters, or four when I'm flowing heavy. Semi-translucent. Amorphous. Rigellian poets have often referred to us gel-forms as "soft cloudbursts," or "silver silica symbiotes (went silently sliding)."

I've heard worse in this last standard year while traveling; *swimming the stars*, as we like to say. "Puddle of goo." Or, "Gummi-form." I think that's one of my favorites. Most recently, "Looks like something I stepped in once, in the Saggitaire system."

Probably sleeping off a drunk. We actually spill across the floor pretty fast when we need to.

Just now I'm not spilling anywhere. I've puddled myself in a small, silver urn, kept polished and vacant for weeks. And I ignore the expectant thrill jumping around me from bottle to pitcher to ewer. Follow Black Mike as he steps off the Fullerene slide, reaches out with slender arms to catch up two bulbs of faux-blow dropping from a dispenser. A pair of fifteen-minute highs. Rolling the milky-white bulbs through long, triple-jointed fingers, like a magician's conjuring trick, he presents them with a final spin across the bar's green-glowing brightmetal surface.

For that simple flourish—and because Black Mike's *other* two arms bulge with more muscle than a K-miner—he earns a good tip.

All part of the experience at Black's Saloon and Hostelry.

I watch. The Terrans toast each other with bulbs, pinch through each membrane, and put the nanite-laced powder right up a nostril. Four-point-seven seconds to the first rush. Maybe an outside chance at psychological addiction, but no bleeding. No system-shock. Just a rush of machine-stimulated endorphins (and, of course, the heavy thirst programmed in by Black Mike's supplier) all timed to the nano-cycle. Never an ounce of danger. Right?

Denial is a wonderful thing, I say to my captive audience.

I know.

My first time in Black's. Just passing through LV-824's system (or so I thought then), on a layover while the *Celestial Walker* refueled in the local Kuiper Belt. A hostelry catering to every life-form from megapedal to matrix—it really wasn't anything more than an old, grounded crew-hauler which just happened to have a working vacuum-source generator for power and the best selection of exotic beverages to be found in the entire system. "From Kuiper to Oort, here's your port."

I pour into the saloon with a splash of attitude and barely constrained curiosity. I'm too far below the haze of yellow-and-purple smoke clinging to the ceiling to be bothered by it, but I taste the acidic solvents used on the metal decking around the threshold and approve. Black Mike keeps a mostly clean place.

Music, which belts out of overhead speakers once used as the ship's public address system, was strong and atonal. A mix of hull-stress groaning and Old Earth jazz. I don't mind it so much, and a few bipedals—Terrans, I guess—swing each other around an area of cleared tables, hard enough they seem to be testing the artificial gravity. A small pod of Saurian Weavers skitter and skip atop a metal table. A large feloid clamps paws to the side of her furred head, covering her ears.

No one pays me any attention, so I quickly stream toward the bar, which runs the entire back wall of the long, narrow room. Different sets of track lighting beam down on tables, on straw beds, on a mud-caked trench capable of holding an entire nest of Sslyth. Some ultraviolet and a bit of infrared as well, with warm, massaging fingers, but mostly subdued levels of good, old-fashioned spectrum.

The bar itself is a single piece of ship's brightmetal. A strong, durable alloy, currently charged for a soft, green glow which washes out the natural colors of most anything nearby. Except for Black Mike, of course, who presides over that long, laser-scarred shelf of liquors, fermented juices, and acidic, dry cell batteries of varying charge.

Black Mike has a tall humanoid build, with a large head, shaved bald, and a bared barrel chest. And the four arms. He also generates an inner radiance of his own which fights back against the wash of soft emerald green—a deep, dark violet, nearly indigo. But not "black" at all.

His voice. *That* is dark. And dangerous.

"What will you have?" he asks as I boil up onto the bar's flat, well-polished surface.

"I'd like a drank."

How often does the saloon tender hear that? Delivered by vocal chords or projected thought or, in my case, from a synthesized voice generated from the speech-trodes studded along the outside edge of the green, brightmetal bar. Touch any two 'trodes, let the current course through you, and the power of audible speech is yours.

Apparently, not as powerful, or as clear, as I thought.

"A drink?" he asks. "Or a drank?"

"Drank." I moisten the tendrils making contact with the speech-trodes. *"Like one."*

Needed one, actually. But I won't admit that. I don't travel well with baggage.

Soft cloudbursts, I remind myself. The water of life.

Which is when Black Mike pulls out a beautiful silvered urn. The shallow bowl and wide, round lip. A few dents in it, but still with a delicate, expensive feel. He rubs a white polishing cloth around its rim, and

9

the bowl is left ringing with a long, hollow peal. The kind of calling sound that makes a gel-form want to curl up and hibernate inside for a good long time.

Except I don't have a good long time. The *Celestial Walker* is due to depart again in two days. Which leaves me just enough time. Doesn't it?

"No. Just a drank," I say through the synthesizer.

He shrugs, which is a rather complicated gesture for a being with two sets of shoulders. The powerful muscles of his second pair ripple like molten. "One drank," he agrees. "Still counts as living quarters."

In the most literal sense, in fact.

"Fine."

Another of those complicated, threatening shrugs. "Suit yourself."

He sets the urn behind him, one long, slender arm reaching back to nest it among tall chrome bottles and a few plastic jugs. Another hand selects a wide highball from the clean rack and tips it down near the bar's brightmetal surface. I pool into it. About half full.

Black Mike picks up a mixing gun and shoots a long blast of cold lime soda in with me. The carbonation tickles, running through me in an effervescent rush. But I'm not a fan of lime. It interferes with my surface tension, puckering me up into a stippled ball.

"On the house," Black Mike says, then steps back onto a dark path in the decking which runs the entire length of his bar and pushes off with one of his muscular arms. A near-frictionless Fullerene slide, it lets him move quickly and with little effort from one end of the room to the other.

I'm less a fan of the large, reptilian species Black Mike plops me down in front of than I am the lime. The reptoid has a long snout full of sharp teeth and an obsidian glaze darkening coal-red eyes. It's just one of those times when I know the pain I'll suffer later. But that's later. And I came in for a drank.

"Good for what ails you," Black Mike promises.

The green-scaled alien leans down *very* close. Sniffs me. "Look like glass of snot," is its opinion.

Well, that's a new one.

"No complaints," he tells the reptoid. The way he says it, the way he looms above with those second arms flexing, you know the discussion is over. "One swallow, and don't chew."

I appreciate that. And it's the last coherent thought I am allowed for a time, as a scaled hand grabs the glass and, with a practiced toss, dumps me into the back of a tight, constricting throat. And I am no longer myself.

Getting drunk is a different experience for a gelform from Saggitaire VI than it is most other lifeforms. Though humanoids talk about it quite often. Especially Terrans.

For the longest time, I wondered where they ever found another being large enough to swallow one of them whole.

There is an initial rush of trepidation, as we contemplate the wisdom of what we are about. I understand that part, at least, is common. But then comes the pulsating, constricting *squeeze*—being drank, getting drunk—and the sensation one is no longer fully in control.

It is a long, dark ride at first, with only the pounding of an alien heart (or hearts?) drumming in my mind. Then a scent—a taste—of sour acid, which burns wonderfully against my flesh; but too quickly I am past that rush, being absorbed into the bloodstream and spread to the thinnest consistency—and yet, the fullest *connection*—I've ever known.

The opening of the universe.

A sense of a larger, encompassing consciousness.

Which is the reptoid's, of course. I am he, for a time, and share everything there is about him. The pleasures and the pains. The itch developing between the scales on my right foot. Wet-rot. The warm glow in my stomach as Black Mike serves me another shot of prime Blood Brandy to chase whatever it was went down my gullet like raw, congealed egg.

At least, I trust it is prime Blood Brandy. The cataracts clouding my vision are only getting worse, and this Black Mike who smells like old, toothsome meat could serve me out of a clutchling's wetsack for all I can tell. I know only the bottle is dark—certainly not a petrified egg casing, but something just as brownish-red.

And in the right shape, I see now. A half-ovoid,

resting inside a cradle with three legs. The haze rolls back, as if washed away by a cleansing water. Safety-plastic! How long has it been, I could recognize something at half the distance?

New strength floods my body. Euphoria! And I shove my way down the bar, spilling others away from their seats. No pain in my foot. No haze clouding my vision.

Rejoicing, and ready to take on the galaxy!

Ill, and about to dissolve into a puddle of regrets.

I wake in a quivering pool, dumped into a rusting pail which has been kicked into a corner behind Black Mike's bar. My whole body tastes of bile and . . . congealed blood? . . . and alcohol. So I know I was sicked up rather than passed through. That happens, occasionally, when my host refuses to let the party end.

I ache everywhere. Parts of me have hardened, almost to a solid, and those areas not ropey with congealed mucus feel delicately brittle. Even the soft green light washing over the rim of the bucket is painfully bright.

Symbiosis isn't perfect, but it's a life.

Two of them, actually.

A groan escapes me like a bubble rising to the surface and popping with a wet, sloppy sigh. Black Mike's face appears overhead, peering down. A slender hand scoops me up, finding a grip around the poison inside me—the cataracts I drew out of the reptoid—letting

the rest dangle between those triple-jointed fingers.
He slops me onto the pitted back shelf, next to the
silver urn he polished up so nice, and leaves me there,
baking under the overhead lamps and barely keeping
my surface tension above the dissolution point.

I feel them watching. Hear an occasional twitter
of energy at my expense. When I decide I'm not
about to drain away, I take a blurred look around.
Avoiding the mirror, I concentrate on the silvered
bottles and a set of plastic containers made to resem-
ble old-style earthenware jugs. A small egg-shaped
cask, which I recoil from as if it might be something
heavily absorbent. And a long row of thick square-
bottomed flasks looking like they were cut from old
waveguide runs.

You look terrible, one of them sings in short pulses
of energy. The song jumps from one of those flasks
to another, and back again. *Both of you.*

Damn cataracts. They *are* old waveguide runs. Con-
verted into liqueur flasks and doubling as tiny apart-
ments for beings in need of basic energy matrices.
Black's caters to all kinds, and room is always at a
premium in space travel. If I'm not mistaken, in fact,
there are harmonious energies camped out in most of
the shelved liquors, and at least one Batavian djinn—
a smoke-form—swirling around at the top of a tall
brandy decanter. Very agitated.

Me, I can hardly summon up the energy to harmo-
nize, but I managed a low-amperage whisper. *Both?*

Reverberation and regenerative feedback. I get a

*strong echo when the flask is half full. I see more of
what is when it's half empty. So, yes. Both.*

The song jumps around, back and forth, between at
least two waveguide flasks. It's a one-two punch I
don't feel capable of dealing with just now. *I'm just a
pair of sight for sore eyes.*

My laugh is forced, and I'm not even sure if my
word play translates, but it lends me a bit of strength.
Enough to draw Black Mike over, who steps off the
Fullerene strip and leans down to eyeball me close.

"Rough night?" he asks.

There are some speech-trodes riveted in nearby, and
I find them, feeling my way around. *"Water under the
bridge. And I would prefer to rest somewhere else.
Your reclamation system?"*

"You'd soil the filters."

I'd take exception to that. But his dark, deep voice
warns me not to.

"You know what you need, right?"

I do. And if it gets me away from my new neighbors, perhaps I can live through it. *"Be gentle."*

"Not likely."

It is the larger, muscular hands that scoop me up
this time, slapping me hard against the brightmetal
surface of the bar in a weighty splat. The hardened
areas in me poke out in curdled lumps, and it is these
that Black Mike works on first with those heavy, ham-
merlike hands and thick muscles. Beating the poisoned
areas until they become softer, more pliable, and the
poison seeps out of me like a black, inky sweat.

Cataracts. Wet-rot. I think a venereal disease or two. Hard to say what I bring out the other side of being drunk. Black Mike pokes and prods with those slender, stabbing fingers of his, and pounds at the brittle areas with his large fists until I am soft and pure once again. The rag he wipes across me wicks up the inky poison, and while I feel wrung out and left to dry, I can't deny I feel a bit better.

"The urn?" he asks.

"Just pour me into a seltzer until I have to leave."

He takes enough time to answer that I suspect the news. Maybe had an inkling when I first slid into the highball glass he'd held for me. "You missed ship's call four hours ago," he says. "Urn?"

Back to the shelf? The crowd of bottles and the big mirror. Not voluntarily. *"Seltzer."* A little carbonation to pick me up. That's what I needed. After all, I wasn't staying that long.

Right?

When do the lies get easier to tell? Easier to believe?

Of course I missed the *Celestial Walker*, plastered in filth and poison in the bottom of an old bucket. I also miss the next two star-burners passing through, both of which are making layovers for fresh Kuiper water and He-3 and will be passing on through the Saggitaire system. Home. I never hear ship's call.

Yeah, plastered again. The second time, Black Mike has to scrape me of the wall in the refresher station

16

where, apparently, I was overlooked for several days as a very poor patching job.

No more, I promise myself later, sweating out under the pummeling of Black Mike's huge fists, the taste of fin fungus clouding my senses. No more getting hammered like this. I'll rest up and catch the very next call. Or the next. Or . . . LV-824 doesn't have a lot going for it, no habitable planets—not even by the loose standards established by the plethora of galactic life-forms—but it sits astride many heavy shipping lanes and has one of the richest outer system reaches ever prospected.

And it has Black's Saloon and Hostelry. Which isn't quite a dumping ground for the flotsam and jetsam of the space lanes, but it's not exactly a destination attraction either.

It wasn't where I planned to end up, swimming the stars. Not when I started out, at least, after a three-day drunk and no longer content with the calm tidal pools of Saggitaire VI or even a long-term commitment to one of the local amphibioids. They seemed so stale. Barely a ripple in the great pond. I didn't know then what I was looking for. I'm not sure now. But I went looking, and I still resist the idea of returning to Saggitaire.

Was it the Rigellian poets who said, "Once you've been yakked, you never go back?"

It should have been.

Four standard days drag out to five. And one week into the next. I'm in high demand. Not only am I supposedly "good for what ails" most patrons . . . the high, one of the rented whiskey bottles lets slip in a kind of jealous accusation, apparently ranks up there with Olympus Mons Cognac. A stratospheric buzz.

I don't believe that. And I refuse any kind of catchy, saloon name. No Bilge Bomber. No Black's Bender. Black Mike is very clear on this, on my behalf. Has to be, since he can only sell one of me every night. Patrons learn to ask for a "Simple Saggitairian Water." Or, for *Aguado*, my new name which, after I learn some Terran Tagalog on a long, rare ride in a fairly clean body, means something very similar. I think.

I also convince Black Mike to let me rest a few of my worst days puddled near the mixer canisters, nursing a sponge soaked in carbonated sweetwater. A little artificial freshening.

It helps, as I rarely revert to best form anymore. No soft, translucency for me. A pale, milky white is the best I can do, and I'm all right with that. I am. It's temporary. A few weeks back on Saggitaire VI and I'll be right as rain.

Still, I never look in the large mirror backing the bar, and I stop talking at all with the many bottled spirits and passing thoughts, even when slopped onto that back counter for a spell. Eventually, they stop tapping, or clinking, or singing for my attention.

Except once, when a djinn nested inside some rare Caprica ambrosia spins his ancient bottle back and forth in greater and greater agitation. The dark brown

18

glass is hand blown and extremely valuable in itself. It's also very light, so Black Mike has it anchored to a slab of K-belt ore. No smoke-form would be levitating off with it. But the djinn manages to drag the ore several centimeters along the slab of ferro-titanium, and then in one last, violent tug, jumps bottle and anchor forward. The bottle teeters very near the edge of the shelf, but does not fall. The K-belt ore rolls up against it, however, giving it a good, solid *tap*. It cracks the blown glass from stem to seat, and sets the ambrosia weeping onto the pitted shelf.

I hear later Black Mike had the djinn drawn through a high-efficiency filter. I have no idea how to feel about that, but he doesn't even try to put me back on the shelf anymore. So I'm not bothered to protest. Not even for form's sake.

Life-forms who live in glass houses should not tow rocks.

That night, I'm swinging from the ceiling fixtures in a simian form, and its bleeding ulcers sting at my consciousness like a nest of maddened water scorpions. Black Mike scoops me out of a pile of dung the next morning and beats the crap right out of me.

I'm two days in recovery, spending a great deal of that time doused in seltzer and sweetwater.

. . . *tiny bubbles* . . .

I'm never going home.

19

Realizing that takes a lot out of me. It doesn't come easy. The hard-hitting thought pounds through my mind, such as it is on another morning after when I wake once more in the rusty bucket covered in sour vomit and matted in coarse, black fur. I'm stiff and brittle with new poisons—poisons no Saggitairian gel-form was ever meant to absorb—and I think I've been partially chewed on by whatever sicked me up the night before.

Stupid mutt. I knew better than to tie on with a Dober-man.

I've known better many times, in fact. With every new poison I take in, my chemistry changes. Getting drank, having been drunk, among alien life-forms is a life-altering experience. We're warned about that, aren't we? Warned that so many of us can't handle it. But still, we try. Some of us keep searching, even though we tell ourselves that it's only temporary. We can quit any time we want to. Denial, again.

But I don't want to. At least, I don't think so. And I intend to prove it to myself, summoning up desperate reserves and pouring myself out of the bucket before Black Mike comes for me again. It's not as hard as one would think, flowing against gravity. Water *can* run uphill—when it is very, very motivated.

I hit the floor with a weighty plop, quiver in place a moment, then spill across the Fullerene glide Black Mike uses to skate from one end of the bar to another. The surface is very near frictionless, and it's only by keeping a tendril anchored that I can reach over, grabbing for metal deck plating on the other side to pull myself fully across. Even then, I feel a moment of weightlessness, as my surface tension plays games against the Fullerene cages, wanting to pour out in every direction.

Good thing I have a purpose in mind. Because it's tempting, tempting. And getting onto the bar takes about every last ounce of strength I have left. My stiff parts ache like deep bruises, but at times they help me grab onto a new hold to hoist myself along. Up the kickboard, and then from rung to rung of some brass railing. Finally, crawling up the cord of one of the mixing guns, where I hang out for a time to recover my strength for that last, long push up onto the bar.

I've no idea how long it takes, but when Black Mike finds me, I'm half pooled in an overturned glass, part of me still spilling out onto the soft, green brightmetal. The glow stabs at me like a hundred tiny flares. The music, pounding down from the smoke-shrouded ceiling, thunders and rages, almost unbearably loud.

I imagine I look like something needing to be cleaned up and poured down the drain.

"Again," I tell Black Mike. *"This morning."*

"You sure?" Despite his dark voice, Black Mike can sound almost kind. Less threatening, anyway. Cautiously dangerous. He reaches into me and plucks out several coarse strands. "You do not look well, Aguado."

"Hair of the dog."

21

In fact, I've already broken down a few of the thinner strands, ingesting them, adding a new flavor to my gel-flesh, so that next time the poisons will be easier to deal with. It isn't something I have to think about doing. It's just a Saggitarian thing. I recall everyone ordering a "Simple Water" and burble a laugh. Yeah, right.

"Get me a drank," I tell Black Mike. *"And hold the carbonation."*

Say what you want about Black's Saloon, you aren't kept waiting when you really need something. And Black Mike never raises a concern more than once. Sand! He hardly raises them the first time. Just to regulars.

That's me, now. A regular.

However I look, Black Mike has no trouble finding a willing patron. He carries me down the long slide, with a few of the silvered bottles on the long shelf looking on, some of them moaning on my behalf. A few bounce jealously at the edge of the dropoff, but one of Mike's slender arms is always ready to reach back and prod the container back to safety.

I'm set down on the bar with a forceful tap that shocks me right through the safety-plastic highball. A determined offering.

A Terran. Large one. K-Belt mining is not for the faint of heart, but this guy looks like he's got the chops for it and has that ready look in his eye that I've noticed with most space veterans. He's even given up his cosmic ray shielding, living with the open sores

22

on his arms, his face. And who knew what kind of damage inside.

I'd know. Very, very soon.

"Looks like something I stepped in once." His voice was raspy and raw. "In the Saggitaire system."

Yeah, that was the guy. A real conversationalist.

But when Black Mike puts a drink in front of you, you don't complain. Much. He puts up with a lot, from an occasional brawl to swabbing out the back rooms when a pack of blooddevil-forms have been through. As near as I can tell, Black Mike does not sleep. Or eat. Or take smoke breaks (except with that one djinn). But he will not—ever!—be second-guessed on what he serves.

So the Terran grabs up the glass, and swirls me around hard inside until I'm feeling dizzier than when I started, and finally swills me down in one quick, violent toss.

It's a long drunk.

Thick blood, and surprisingly delicate brain chemistry for such a strong specimen. And the poisons! Bleeding ulcers and a ruined liver. Damaged nerve endings, fried by the local cosmic radiation. And cancers. A veritable buffet of skin lesions and tumors growing in the brain, in his lungs, and ballooning up one testicle as well.

A very long drunk, which is a good thing.

The guy needed it as bad as I did.

*   *   *

Excrement!

If I were to have a preference, a strong urinary system capable of passing me from the body is usually best. A hard, warm splash, and I'm free. Colons—especially Terran colons—are difficult to navigate, and there is that heavy constriction that, in my brittle state, always threatens to suffocate me.

I reserve enough strength, borrowed from my host, to make that necessary mad dash from the refresher station bowl, slipping up and out to spill onto the decking. I manage to slide out from the stall, right on the heels of my host, before my vitality flags. I can't say for certain yet what I look like after a second drunk, but another patron entering the station sees me as I crawl along after my previous host and does a double-take.

"Man. That is so wrong."

He should try it from my side.

Still, a steaming pile in the middle of the floor is a dangerous state for any gel-form, so I manage to crawl over near the door, finding a safer place tucked behind a waste can. It is here Black Mike finds me a few hours later, rinses away the easy muck under a nearby tap, then carries me out and slaps me onto a deserted stretch of the brightmetal bar where he beats the living shit out of me. I feel like I've gained a solid deciliter, and the cloth he wicks across me comes away black and sopping with poisoned sweat.

"Best I can do," Black Mike finally says.

I find two nearby speech-trodes. *"Best I can ask*

for." He turns to leave me for a time, but I stop him. *"Set me over on the shelf,"* I ask.

He makes no comment. He simply does as I ask. And as I lay in a quivering mass on the long, cold slab of ferro-titanium, I watch him glide up the green-glowing bar to serve a pair of tall insectoids while taking stock of my own condition.

I've mentioned it before—getting drunk is different for gel-forms like me. It's how we've evolved. It may seem like self-destructive behavior, for a time, but what does not kill us always leaves us stronger. And home, in the tidal flats of Saggitaire-VI, I'd only know a great emptiness and longing to return. To swim the stars. I know that now.

Denial is common to all life-forms. So is the desperate need to seek out your own place in the great, wide galaxy. Saggitairians are no exception. And I've avoided the obvious for far too long. Slipping up the side of that bright, silver urn Black Mike has kept polished for me these several weeks, I pool down into a comfortable puddle after only a glance at my milky-white complexion in the large mirror. It's not so bad. Now that I've accepted it.

The silvered bottles surrounding me tip closer. Jugs and ewers and pitchers of safety-plastic scratch and scoot around, wondering why I'm here, now, after all this time, and waiting. They've been waiting for me for weeks.

Used, abused, and rung out; I've survived it all. I know now I can take anything the galaxy has to throw at me, and I do not even make a pretense of planning to catch the next star-burner, returning home.

I'm already there.

A Simple Saggitairian Water. Ri-ight.

Hi. The offer is tentative, but well-meant. I slip up to the side of my silver bowl in a cautious, hesitant wave.

My name is Aguado. And I'm an alcohol.

With Unconfined Wings

by Sarah A. Hoyt

"WHAT IS A NICE nun like you doing in a place like this?" the man said as I sat the dark red tumbler of liquor in front of him.

He was a tall man, red-headed and tanned with the bronze tan of fair people who have worked outside a lot. However, judging by the faded dark blue uniform he still wore, with the stars of the Alliance on his shoulders, he hadn't worked outside, only in an insufficiently shielded space ship.

"I hope God's will," I told him, my eyes piously lowered, as I wiped the dark brown ceramite top of the tiny round table at which he sat. Of course, inside I felt a lot less pious than that. Oh, it was true that I was a novice in the order of St. Lucia of the Spaceways—the entity that owned Light of the Spaceways, the bar at which he sat.

Throughout the known space, in low dives, miner colonies—or even poorer worlds, such as this, where pirates and outcasts disguised themselves as scavengers and legitimate spaceship repairmen—the image of St. Lucia of the Spaceways, with her unfurled star-spangled cloak, her crown of stars, crowned hospitals and creches, and bars, too, because their motto was "Go where the sinners are."

The dangers inherent in this were the reason I didn't feel nearly as pious as I had, five years ago, when I'd entered novitiate on the crest of an altruistic feeling. Take our Mother Superior, for instance. Judy, her name was. Professed these twenty years, and, to hear her, as pious as they came. But she wore her blue wimple askew; her gluttony had made the blue one-piece of a professed nun fit her like a stretched second skin. She kept a hand on the gun underneath the bar, an eye on the liquor, and the other eye on the customers' hands and the girls' bodies. The other two nuns in the order, in this forsaken outpost at the very edge of the galaxy, were older than I but younger than Mother Judy. They'd told me stories that others had told them when they'd first come in, of customers—and girls—shot by Mother Judy. I didn't find it all that hard to believe. She smoked. I was fairly sure she drank. I wouldn't put it past her to be intemperate enough to shoot one of us either.

This was in my mind, very clear, as I started to step away from the table, and the customer reached for my hand. "Stay," he said. "I need to confess."

I shook his hand from my arm. "I am not a priest," I said. I knew that it wasn't a sin for him to touch

28

me. It wouldn't even be a sin for me to sleep with him. I hadn't taken my final vows. Wouldn't take my final vows until I professed in three months.

If I professed . . .

The man smiled. "No. But stay. I must talk. I am dying, sister. I'm not joking about that. Dying and I have no one . . ." His voice trailed off.

There was enough pain in it, enough sorrow, to make me look at him, full in the face. His eyes were intense, zeal burned, and—I thought—chased by something like pain. "My name is Octavian Urban," he said. "And I was a Catholic once, when I was young, on Mars, in Mare Cimmerium." He looked up, the desperation in his eyes. "I don't want to die without the consolations of the faith."

"Lyra," the Mother said behind me, in a voice not to be gainsaid. And I spun around, on my heel, and headed for the bar.

"Bring me another," Octavian said, behind me, and I could hear him slam the—presumably empty—tumbler back on the table. If he was a pilot, if he was dying of liver failure, this would only hasten his end. But then again, when the end was a matter of a few more days or less, who could care. Perhaps it was better to die sooner, with the pain dulled.

I didn't turn back, and walked straight to the bar counter. It was late and the bar, which had been bristling early in the evening, was now deserted. The only living people in the place were Mother Judy, myself, and Octavian.

The Mother's arched eyebrows questioned me, and—as usual, before she even asked anything—I found myself babbling, "His name is Octavian Urban. He says he's Catholic or was."

"Was, perhaps," Mother said, her eyebrow still raised. "He's not now. The pope himself has declared that all those who use Lifto are excommunicated, since it destroys the body and the soul with it."

I nodded, without saying anything. This was not the time to get in a theological argument. The hypocrisy of the pope in decreeing Lifto banned while using spaceflight and, in fact, having moved the center of the church to the world of New Rome in orbit to a strange sun, was part of what I learned in my five years of novitiate. Part of the reason I was not sure I could profess and keep my soul.

"And what does he want, this excommunicated space pilot?" Mother asked.

"He says he wants to confess. Before he dies."

"Um . . ." Mother said. "Look, he has more on his soul than using Lifto," she said. She spoke in a sort of half-vocalized whisper that wouldn't be audible at his table. "No one comes to this outpost of Hell without having slipped through all the rungs of life. From the look of him, he's not just a pensioned-off pilot with a failing liver. At a guess, he did something that got him kicked out of the force. I would guess graft taking, or piracy, since everything else tends to be forgiven to pilots." She turned around while she spoke. The counter behind which she stood—in fact all of the bar, the two dozen or so small tables included—was made from one giant blob of extruded ceramite in unfashionable brown, probably purchased at a discount from a construction company. While the ceramite was still semisolid, someone had taken the trouble to punch a series of holes behind the bar forming niches that now housed a collection of bottles.

This was all ancient by Terra Madre standards, or even of the old worlds, like Mars, where drinks were served by AI's, never touched by the hand of man. But, here, Mother Judy reached up for a dark red bottle. The sparkling blood-red liquor within was known as Agian Poison, and it came from a prosperous second-wave colonization world which owed its prosperity in no small measure to the sale of this. It wasn't wine exactly. It wasn't even alcohol, exactly. It was the result of the mutations that had affected Earth grapes when meeting with alien soil and light. One of the most addictive substances in the universe, it was banned in most worlds. Except here. Where it didn't matter.

As Mother Judy turned around, to pour it into another small tumbler, I smelled its sweetness, its hint of minty scent. It mixed with a thousand other floral and chemical smells in the place.

I looked at her, uncomprehending, not sure what to make of what she'd just said. "But then," I said, "he needs confession more, does he not?"

Mother Judy leveled her gaze at me. "You are not a priest," she said. The same words I had told him.

Why did they seem like such a passing of responsibility now?

I put the tumbler on my small tray.

"Get rid of him," Mother Judy said. "Tell him no more drink. It is time he was going. We should be locked in the compound by now."

I knew this was true, but it seemed curiously callow to throw a dying man outside, into the night where the cold winds howled—audible even through our door. The winds were the least of it, at least that was what I heard. It wasn't as though in the last five years I'd had much chance to go and inspect the surroundings at night. Or even during the day. My life had been circumscribed by the confines of our compound or the confines of this bar, day in day out. Prayer, and kneeling, holy service—though not mass, as such, because we didn't have a priest within light-years—and serving drinks. It all ran together over the years.

But from Mother's stories, from the stories of our customers, I'd gathered that this outpost, known only as Port, was kept under a semblance of order during the day by the members of rival pirate gangs and the punitive authority of the various worlds who, more or less knowing they weren't legitimate, yet bought our "scrap" and our "scavenged parts" with a clear conscience. But at night . . . ah, that was different. Those who could afford to locked themselves up in secure compounds. And those who couldn't afford to braved streets infested with robbers, murderers and—to believe the rumors—crews from ships that landed in the dark of night and which traded in everything from weapons to human slavery.

"And think about what name you'll take at your professing," the Mother called, louder, at my back.

I gritted my teeth. I think it was those casual words that put me over the edge. This callous woman, this creature who had lived for so long among criminals that she could no longer tell right from wrong wanted me to think about professing. Even as she meant to throw this man who was unprotected and possibly dying out into the dark of night to fend for himself.

I set the liquor down in front of him. "You will have to go soon," I said. "Do you have a way to get home safely?"

He grinned at me, a reckless grin that must have been quite impressive when he was younger. "I'll manage," he said. But then the serious, grave expression came to his eyes again. "It's not the body that worries me. It's the soul. Look, I know you are not a priest, but if you knew the sins I have committed, if you knew . . ." He shrugged. "I know I'm dying and I don't fear death so much as I fear what might happen afterward. Even if what happens is nothing but eternity alone with my sins. And, you know, I was raised in the church. I heard the vision of the mystics, their descriptions of hell. The souls tormented for eternity with what they found most pleasurable of the sins in life."

I had heard it, too. Though I had not been raised Catholic—my parents were free traders and given to the sort of easygoing Protestantism that such engaged in. They paid lip service to the religion, but living a nomadic life in tiny family groups in non-AI ships amid the stars, they lived as they could. If this meant group marriage or the occasional blood feud, then that's what it meant.

I thought perhaps it was that lack of structure in my upbringing that had brought me to the Catholic church, made me convert in the later years of my apprenticeship at college, and then brought me here, to novitiate. It had seemed, then, as if the Catholics had an answer for everything. And as if the Lucias, in particular, cared more for the poor, the abandoned in our glittering society than just about everyone else.

It wasn't until I'd started studying that I'd heard of hell and seen the paintings with which, throughout the centuries, mystics and artists had tried to depict the eternal punishment. And even now, even without my fully believing in it, the idea that this man believed in it and feared made me shiver. "I can't give you absolution," I said.

"I don't ask you to," he said. "But I've read enough, and I know that in the earliest days of the church it was permissible, in the absence of a priest, for a dying man to confess to another of the faithful. That it was enough."

I nodded. I, too, had heard of that tradition.

"Lyra," Mother Judy said, and I could almost feel her aiming a gun at my back or his front.

"But how do you propose to talk to me?" I said. "And can you do it tomorrow?"

He smiled, this time a slow smile of deep sadness. "We can try tomorrow," he said. If I live that long."

And if he didn't, he would die knowing that endless and imaginative torment awaited him. I swallowed. "We can't talk here. Not now. Mother Judith wants to close."

"My berth isn't far," he said. "Just a few steps away, down this street. We could go there." Again, the rakish, disarming smile. "You'll be perfectly safe," he said. "The last thing I want to do is add to my sins."

"But the street . . . " I said.

"Is not so dangerous as you've been led to believe," he said. "This is the way they keep the little lambs at home."

I nodded once. This seemed to make sense to me, to tie in with the nest of deception and hypocrisy that the Lucias appeared to be from within. Back when I was at college, I'd thought that my parents were detached and materialistic, too interested in the good things of life to help anyone. From that distance, the Lucias had seemed saintly. But now I wasn't so sure. This whole thing of helping the sinners seemed to be more a matter of looking good while pretending to help the sinners.

"I'll see," I said, and walked back to the counter, thinking it over. I'd more or less decided I was going to abandon the novitiate, anyway, and message Mom and Dad for fare home. But I hadn't intended to do it tonight.

Mother Judy was leaning on the counter, on her thick arms and her expression had that expectant look of someone who expects to hear a good story. "So?" she said.

"Look, just today, can I talk to him here?" I asked. "Can we stay open a little longer?"

Mother Judy bit her lip. "Child. If we stay open longer, if we don't lock the pressure doors from inside, then any of the marauders who land tonight—or all of them—might decide to break down the door and get at the liquor."

"We could lock with him within," I said.

"Him?" She shook her head. "I don't think so. We don't lock the wolf in with the sheep."

"There's just one of him," I said. "What do you think he'll do?"

"Oh, you'd be surprised," she said and smiled, a disquieting smile that convinced me she knew a lot more of what she called the perils of the world than she would share with an innocent novice.

But I'd grown up in a free trader family. We knew how to shoot, we knew how to defend ourselves, and I was no exception.

"Look," Mother Judy said. "Throw him out, or I will."

I nodded, and reached up. In one smooth movement, I tore off the white wimple that would have become a blue one at my professing in a month. I handed it to Mother Judy. "I can't give you back the suit," I said, gesturing to my gray one-piece, "as I don't have any of my normal street clothes after five years here. But I will ask my parents to pay for it when I get back home."

She didn't seem surprised. She took the wimple and folded it, with her pudgy fingers. "If you get back home . . ." she said.

"Oh, I will," I said.

"Listen, Lyra, even if he is what he says he is, a dying space pilot with a shredded liver, there are dangers that—"

I shook my head. In retrospect, every word I'd heard for the last five years seemed like a lie. I didn't want to hear any more of them. I turned my back on her. I had my idchip in the inner pocket of my jacket. It was all I needed to message home pay on delivery. And then I could go home. After I heard what Octavian had to say. After I absolved him. Just because I didn't believe in hell, it didn't mean he didn't. It didn't mean he wouldn't die thinking of it.

Octavian had drunk his liquor and was standing up, extending his arm to me. He smiled, but looked slightly puzzled. "No wimple?" he said.

"No wimple," I said. "I've had enough of this. I will message home tomorrow."

"Oh, sure," he said. "You can message from my berth. I have a lynk."

I nodded and waited for him to start ahead, then followed him. He opened the door to the outside, and I went after him.

Outdoors, it was as windy as I'd expected—having long heard the wind howl outside our locked compound. But, strangely, it wasn't cold. The air itself was cold, but the wind blowing past was warm, almost heated.

"It blows from the desert at night," Octavian said, gesturing with his head in the direction the wind came from. "They say that it's something to do with the equalizing of temperatures and that's why the wind blows every night."

Other than the wind, the street outside didn't look inhospitable. Oh—it was nothing like the worlds I'd visited with my parents on vacation, when money permitted. Its flat, unbroken landscape had nothing to the rock spears of Mars, and, unlike Luna, it was not clustered with the mansions of the wealthy who'd immigrated there upon first terraforming. Even Ganymede, though it was mostly an industrial world, looked better than this. It was, after all, filled with warehouses and factories. Civilized. It didn't look like the worlds on my parents' one-solar-system route either—the thriving colonial worlds filled with farms and stores.

Port was empty, howling wasteland, save for some mushroom-shaped compounds. Ours—the one of the Lucias, I should say—was one of them, and there were three others on the glistening, black dimatough road that snaked past it. I imagined that Octavian's berth, as he called his lodgings, would be in one of those. In fact, he set off toward them cheerfully. He walked well for a dying man, not that I thought he shouldn't. I wasn't sure of the effects of a failing liver, but I was almost certain none of them involved broken legs.

The stars looked distant here, glinting above like pinpoints on a vast, dark blanket. From far off came the sound of rockets taking off and landing. The spaceport. From when I'd arrived, I remembered that it was quite distant, but sounds carried in the night. From other places came shouts and calls and the sounds of drunken laughter. But here, there seemed to be no danger at all.

Why was it, then, that as I followed Octavian's swaggering figure, I felt as if I were threatened? As if I were walking to my doom?

I pursued the thought in my mind and thought of Octavian's face when I'd told him I intended to abandon the novitiate. He had looked . . . happy?

Of course, why shouldn't he? He wanted to have someone to confess to, didn't he?

Yes, but didn't he need to confess to a Catholic? And he'd never asked me if I was abandoning the habit but keeping the faith. And then . . .

And then there was the fact that he'd said he had a lynk. Oh, retired pilots were often prosperous. They rarely lived more than a few months after being pensioned off. The space forces could afford to be generous with them. But Mother Judy was right that no properly retired pilot would live on Port. They lived up on Mars and Jupiter and the other planets of the old solar system, the repentant ones in upscale hospices, the unrepentant ones in the stews of Luna city, the bar row of Europa.

Octavian looked like he was on his last string, from his faded one-piece to his living here, to the way he talked. So how could he have a lynk? Even the Lucias didn't have a lynk. When they wanted to send a message inter-worlds, they first messaged the spaceport, which was big enough to have a lynk. And the payment for the one message, as far away as my parents, was more than our take at the bar for a month. So why would he be so free with his lynk?

I'm not going to say I had it all figured out. I didn't. I had just enough to be alert, aware, as Octavian slowed down ahead of me, allowing me to catch up. And to know better, when he turned around saying, "It's just," and lifted his hand as if to point.

Now I know everyone thinks free traders are rich and pampered, living in their multigeneration ships, outside governmental authority, paying no taxes and growing their own hydroponics and hardly ever buying anything. We fly only within a solar system, unless we take commercial flights on vacation, so we pay no tariffs, and we don't need to pay the high wages of a pilot on Lifto.

And I'll admit that it is true, to a point. Which was why the Lucias had seemed so altruistic to me. Free traders are a pretty closed system.

But that doesn't mean people don't try to rob us.

Even in the backward, pioneer worlds in the solar system my parents covered. People who think you're rich tend to try to even things. Which was why we all learned to fight. Even the girls.

Before Octavian could bring his hand near me, in his seemingly casual gesture, I'd reacted, lightning fast, hitting his wrist with the flat of my hand. I heard whatever had been in his hand fall to the road with a metallic sound, echoing mingled with the crack of a bone breaking, and with his howl of pain.

But even as he howled, his other hand was digging into the pocket of his one-piece. I wasn't so stupid I couldn't imagine he was going for a gun. Instinctively, I dove toward the road surface, grabbed the metallic cylinder that had fallen at his feet, and jumped away, to run. Though where I could run and where hide, with the Lucias' compound closed and only the bare road behind me, I didn't know. The other compound was no nearer. Which was, I think, why he'd decided to try his luck here.

"Stop," he said from behind me, his voice no less menacing for the edge of raw pain behind it. "Stop, and I won't kill you."

I turned around. He was facing me, gun in hand. "Idiot," he said. "What do you think you're going to do with that? It's just a syringe with a soporific. I wanted to make this easy for you."

"Make what easy for me?" I thought. Wild reports and exaggerated legends of people abducted for their usable organs flew through my mind.

41

But he grinned. "Taking you to the spaceport, to your ship."

"My ship?"

The grin that had been charming and reckless now had an unhealthy edge of gloating, like the smile of a little kid who has pulled a particularly nasty trick. "Your ship out of here, at any rate. How much," he said, "do you think some rich men in other worlds are willing to give for a healthy, full-grown virgin? I mean, sure, you can get the diseased and the weak ones from the poor colonies all the time. But someone like you? It could set me up for life."

I swallowed. He was coming closer and closer to me, his smile the smile of a tiger. "So you're not dying?" I asked, sure he'd lied, sure now that I'd been a fool to believe anything he said.

"Oh, I am dying," he said. "For now. But you see, once I sell you I can get money to buy a new liver in any of a hundred hospitals throughout the galaxy, from legitimate to illegitimate, whatever I feel like paying. When I ended up in Port I couldn't imagine I'd come across such valuable goods. And pretty, too, which can't be said for any of those hags you live with. So I messaged some people of my acquaintance, and soon you'll be on your way to some glittering world. If you cooperate, your life won't be all that bad. Being the toy of a rich man is not a bad thing. If you don't cooperate . . ." He shrugged. "Then they'll erase your mind and program you."

"But mind erasure is illegal," I said stupidly.

He cackled. "So is kidnapping. And white slavery. None of which has stopped it. As long as there are humans, pretty women can be sold. I'm just glad I came upon a gullible one."

As he spoke, he'd come closer, so close I imagined I could smell the liquor on his breath. I could feel him starting to reach for me, as I lifted the metal cylinder. An injector, as I now understood it to be. And everyone knew how to use injectors. "If you come closer," I said, "I will put you to sleep."

He sneered. "It's not instantaneous. Before I fall asleep, I will have time to shoot you."

"If you shoot me, you'll have lost your merchandise and condemned yourself to death," I said. "And I wouldn't advise you to try to be faster than I. As you saw, I am pretty fast."

He hesitated. Just enough to stand at bay, holding his gun, staring at the cylinder in my hand. "You won't be alert all night," he said. "I've had experience of standing watch through the night, manning the AI. You haven't. Eventually, you'll fall asleep, and I—"

Stopping, he looked puzzled and frowned. I was so surprised I didn't realize there was a hole in the center of his forehead, before blood gushed out, as he fell, backward, still looking surprised.

I turned, looking over my shoulder, sure that some other rogue had come to claim me as a prize. And saw Mother Judy, her wimple askew, her figure looking more blobby than ever, standing behind me and holding the gun. "Rest in peace," she said to my would-be captor, before holstering the gun. "And you, Miss Davenport, can I convince you to come and stay in the compound before you call your parents in the morning?"

I wanted to scream, cry, or run to her. Instead, I blinked in the brisk wind. Mother Judy was patting herself down, looking for something, before pulling, from a concealed pocket, a packet of cigarettes, and knocking one of them against the back of her hand, to light it. "Well," she said.

"I . . . Yes. How . . ."

"I'd noticed him sniffing around you for a few days. You didn't, of course, being all worried about your professing and all. But I'd noticed and I didn't think it was just a wish to confess. He could have come to me for that. Heaven knows that's why the Lucias run bars. Bartenders have always been confessors of a sort."

"Why . . . Why didn't you stop me from going with him?"

"Would it have worked?"

I shrugged. My own mind told me it probably wouldn't. I wouldn't have believed her.

"But . . . " I said. "You killed him."

She tried to take a drag on her cigarette, then looked at the tip with an expression of extreme disappointment and said something about the wind which I was sure was not a prayer. Dropping the cigarette, she stomped on it, just in case. "Sometimes," she said, "to guard the sheep you have to kill the wolf. Doesn't mean I'm judging him, mind. That's not for me to do. After all, who knows what he faced and what Lifto does to a man's mind? No one who hasn't gone through it can know, and most who've gone through it are dead. Which is why we leave judging to the one who knows us all."

"But . . . " I said. "What are we doing here?"

"Humans?" she asked. Was she laughing at me?

"No, we, the Lucias?"

'We're . . . bringing light to the spaceways. We deliver babies, we serve liquor, we listen to the talk of lonely men, we raise children, we comfort the dying, and sometimes we kill the predators. It's all part of bringing light. We are human. We are flawed. None of us flies with unconfined wings." She thought for a moment. "And we pray. A lot. And hope we're doing what we're supposed to." She started to reach for her cigarette pack again, then stopped, as though remembering. "Did you say we?" she said. "Are you one of us again?"

"Can I be?" I said. "Didn't I resign. Wouldn't I need to do the novitiate all over again?"

She grinned. "Oh, there is not a single good nun who doesn't throw at least one tizzy before her final vows," she said. "You are tired. It's late."

I caught up with her. We walked back.

"Only," she said, "we should hurry because I left Sister Theodora in charge of the door, and Thea is such a horrible shot. I won't feel safe till we're back in and the compound is locked."

45

We walked three more steps, and I could see the open door of the bar, and Sister Thea beneath it, silhouetted in the light, burner in hand. Above her, bathed in light, the statue of St. Lucia of the Spaceways, serene and calm, with her star-spangled cloak, her crown of stars. And above that the glowing words "Light of the Spaceways."

I felt tears drip from my chin, before realizing I'd cried at all.

"Speaking of which," Mother Judy said. She'd fished another cigarette from her packet, but wasn't lighting it. "What name were you going to choose?"

"Judith," I said. "Judith."

Rachel

by Steven Mohan, Jr.

THE VERY FIRST MOMENT I saw her sitting in that bar, she broke my heart.

Oh, not like that. We're not talking Captain Kirk and the Orion Slave Girl here. That's just not the way the universe works.

She was a Hershin Trader: waxy blue-gray skin, twenty or thirty shiny black eyes sprinkled around a fist-sized sensory node set on a slim neck stalk, quarter-meter tendrils tracing a line down the back of the stalk, all of it ending up in a spidery jumble of legs. No, the emotion that stirred me wasn't lust.

It was pity.

She perched on the bar's rimward bulkhead, drink bulb clipped to the metal grill of her table, neck stalk drooping, perfectly silent, perfectly still.

Everything about her screamed victim.

That's what touched me.

Which was a very, very bad thing.

See, there are two kinds of predators. There's the cheetah that looks at the gazelle with the broken leg and thinks, "Nature is a cruel master, red in tooth and claw. Why must this creature die so that I might live?"

And then there's the cheetah that looks at the gazelle with the broken leg and thinks, "Lunch."

Guess which one nature favors . . . ?

And never mind that there are no more cheetahs. Or gazelles, for that matter. It's a *metaphor*.

So it's not about morality, it's about ecology. Sometimes the herd needs to be thinned and carnivores perform a vital ecological service. There are predators and prey, and everyone is either one or the other.

And if you can't make yourself believe *that,* guess which one you are.

I peered into the darkness looking for someone else. Slim pickings. Aside from Honxhi, the hive mind that operated the bar it/they had named Star Death Burst, there was Gherten, the bilious green amoebic whose obnoxious prattling had probably driven off most of the other patrons. There was Ko, a silicon-based lifeform whose slow metabolism and short attention span made it immune to obnoxious prattling.

And there was the Hershin Trader.

Gherten shifted my way; I turned my back on him, kicked off, and tucked my legs up under me.

I didn't like Gherten. Aside from all the obvious reasons (he smelled like rotting maple syrup and stored his tools *inside* his body) he noticed me. He was always coming up to me and offering to buy me a drink bulb. And since he was a loudmouth, when he noticed me, others did, too, sophonts who would have been perfectly willing to ignore my existence given half a chance.

And since being noticed was bad for business, I avoided Gherten at all costs.

I drifted across the space, careful to avoid the bar, a gnarled darkwood tree that stretched from deck to overhead, clusters of drink bulbs tethered to its naked branches, bobbing randomly in zero gee. Parts of Honxhi, looking a bit like cat-sized beetles, scurried from branch to branch. Doing inventory, I assumed, since there weren't many customers to get drinks for.

I drifted toward the Trader, but she didn't turn to look at me, even when I took the perch next to hers.

"Excuse me," I said softly.

Nothing. Like she was carved out of stone.

"Is there something I can do for you?" I asked.

That got me a high-frequency buzz that my translation software rendered as bitter laughter.

"Look, my name is Jordan Dart," I said. "What's yours?"

The stalk came up a little at that. I could see a dozen tiny reflections of me in the lustrous black of her beady eyes.

She said something that hurt my ears: static mixed with the chirp of a bearing going bad.

Untranslatable, murmured my translator. Not surprising—the software often had trouble with proper nouns. *Tagging sophont as Hershin Trader One.*

I studied her closer, picking out details I'd missed in the bar's bad light. Her grasping claws were crimson, which made her highborn. She smelled of cinnamon and freshly-cut grass.

And she wore a golden ring at the base of her topmost tendril.

What she was wearing so casually on her person was a few grams of the Hershin's principal trade good: nanogel.

I shuddered. I didn't like the thought of dealing with nano-anything. Not at all.

But nanogel was fabulously valuable. Twenty kilos would buy the entire Far Violet Arcology, a thousand would get the planet it orbited.

She was flashing enough wealth to set me up for life.

Nanogel was rumored to be wondrous, transcendent. It went beyond normal designer drugs, beyond even a trickle current to the brain's pleasure centers. Its use was magical, sensual.

There were whole religions built around the use of nanogel as a sacrament.

And the Hershin controlled the only source.

I suddenly realized that she'd taken a perch just a few meters from the bar's linkserv. I drifted back so that I could see both her and it at the same time.

Flashed an order to my implant.

I tried again, "Do you need something, Hershin

Trader One?" My translator would insert her actual name.

Her sensory node leaned toward me. "What are you?"

"I am Homo sapiens."

"Homo sapiens," she said slowly, as if trying the words out, "I have never seen another."

I shifted uncomfortably. "Yes, well—"

"Where are you from?"

I shrugged. "Here and there. Listen, perhaps there is something I could do for you."

She made a scratchy sound that the translator turned into a sigh. I caught the rich smell of anise and wondered what it meant.

"Hershin Trader One," I said softly.

"I think you are a cruel sophont seeking advantage. I want nothing to do with you."

"And if you're wrong?"

She moved her sensory node very close to my face. "*Then* you should know I am a disgraced fool, discarded by my subcaste. You will find no profit in knowing me."

I didn't need the translator's tricks to hear the despair in those words.

My heart twisted.

But I said, "Very well," and kicked off.

And that was that.

Except later I awoke in the middle of the night for no reason I could discern. I rolled over and slipped back into sleep, but not before instructing my translation software to retag Hershin Trader One as Rachel.

Six years ago, I was part of a small group of Homo saps that traveled to a star called Sail a thousand light years from Sol system. We were there to promote Red Line Nanotech. Humanity was hungry for the secret of FTL travel and Red Line was the only bargaining chip we had. Our nanotech was more streamlined, more ef-ficient, than anything the Galactics had.

And I was humanity's chief negotiator.

I waited. And watched. And listened. Most so-phonts have never seen a Homo sap. They don't know what I am.

Sometimes they don't even realize I'm sentient.

It's easy to learn things when you're invisible. After a single day-night cycle I discovered that Rachel's dis-grace was the result of a disastrous bargain she'd struck with the Z-4 Trade Consortium. After that it only took me three more day-night cycles to learn the name of the sophont behind her undoing.

Nanotechnology is the science of building nanometer-scale machinery. Single-molecule devices. Magical machines that can be used to cure illness, ex-tend life, transform matter.

But here's the thing. All the instructions have to be contained within that single molecule. All it takes is a single high-energy photon to cause a mutation.

And then nanotech becomes a cancer. An unstoppable cancer.

Exar was a Cube, a gelatinous mass of plasma gen engineered by some advanced race that had long since passed the Milky Way by. He was big, two meters on a side. His flesh was colorless and perfectly transparent at visible wavelengths.

I could see the random collection of eyes scattered throughout his body, each one connected to his pink-gray brain by a filament. I could see the dark network of blood vessels that branched out through his flesh like wisps of mold growing on bread. I could see his lunch, which apparently he'd ingested live, some kind of reptile, its body frozen in a twisted rigor, one desperate eye peering out at me, wide and terrified.

My God, I hoped it wasn't still alive.

I could tell Exar was a data factor as soon as his assistant admitted me to his K-level office. The room was a large cube, painted off-white. No images marred the walls, no holos fluttered through the air. There was no music, no furniture, not even an *odor*.

It was as if Exar understood the value of information so well that he wasn't willing to give away any of it about himself.

Which didn't mean I knew nothing about him.

I opened a black leather folio and pulled out the image I'd captured in the bar: the black linkserv centered nicely in the frame, about a third of Rachel's body visible.

I dropped the image. It fluttered to the deck.

Exar's multitude of eyes followed the paper down. "What is the meaning of this, Jordan Dart?"

"It is my business to know things," I said.

"As is mine," said Exar smoothly. I saw nothing moving when he spoke, wondered how he was doing it. Some kind of modulated sonar? Now which organ would that be?

"Yes, well, I'm sure the things you know are much more valuable than the things *I* know. Still, perhaps I can offer you something."

A whiplike tentacle shot out from the Cube, snared the photograph with a small blob of natural adhesive. Exar brought the image up to his near side

For a long moment he said nothing. Then, finally, "Say it all. From the beginning."

"You will pay?" I asked.

"Say it all."

"There is a mixer bar up on S-level called Star Death Burst. Do you know it?"

"Go on," said Exar, who gave the appearance of saying yes, though in reality he had yet to answer even one of my questions.

"This is an image of the bar's linkserv. All data transactions have to run through this device."

"It certainly must be encrypted," murmured Exar.

"Of course. But it is a wireless microwave connection and it is *not shielded.*"

Such a lapse would never have occurred on most of the levels, but this was S, where the zeroes lived their lives shoved up hard against polysteel and the cold of vacuum.

My home.

Exar was silent for a long moment. If the linkserv wasn't shielded, an observer in the bar could listen in on the crypto handshake between the bar and the arcology's net. Break in.

"I am sure there is little of interest in the bar's data stores," he said.

I shrugged, though the gesture was almost certainly lost on him. "The cost is low."

He dropped the image and once again it fluttered to the floor. Exar's office was near enough the rim that we were under noticeable acceleration. "You will go and take this image."

I knelt and snatched it up.

There had been no discussion of payment, and yet when I pulled out my comm an hour later I found that the very nice sum of ten thousand marks had been deposited to one of my numbered accounts.

I'm quite certain that Exar's office *was* shielded and swept regularly for listening devices, too. But even if someone had managed to eavesdrop on our little talk they wouldn't have learned anything.

The payment Exar had deposited in my account wasn't for the linkserv framed so lovingly in the center of the image. It was for the half-image of a Hershin Trader accidentally captured in the shot.

And the golden ring banding her topmost tendril.

*　　*　　*

So I made the kill. Hooray for me. I saw the gazelle with the broken leg and managed to fill my belly. End of story.

Except something jerked me out of a sound sleep in the middle of the night-cycle, the sleeping bag twisted around my body, my tiny cubicle sour with the stink of sweat.

She'd been tossed aside by her subcaste. Everything and *everyone* she'd ever known and loved had been lost to her. What was the word she'd used?

Discarded.

I flicked on the side lamp, which focused a cone of watery yellow light on my rack. The cube wasn't much to speak of. There was oxygen and there was running water and 64 cubic meters, all for me.

But that was fine. I didn't care about living in a closet. What I did need room for anyway? It wasn't like I had a lot of knickknacks to display. I mean, all I had were the contents of my suitcases when the Galactics set quarantine.

And really there was only thing that mattered to me. I reached over to the holodisk bolted to the little table. Candace, on the trip to San Diego, a strand of blond hair torn free by the cold ocean wind, her eyes closed, Rachel cradled in her arms, both of them laughing.

Rachel would've been three.

I always kept that holo running, In homage to treasures lost. I once paid a month of oxygen debt to have replacement batteries custom made. Tonight, I looked at it and felt blackness sweep over me.

Guilt over things discarded.

I reached out and touched the button on the smooth, cool base.

My wife and daughter flickered out of existence.

While my team was at Sail, we heard news of some kind of disaster within the Sol system. Details were sketchy and difficult to verify. But it was clear it was something big.

My team voted eight to one to remain at Sail where it was safe.

I was the one.

I just kept thinking of Candace and Rachel. I had to know they were safe. So I left.

I got as far as Far Violet Arcology before I ran into the quarantine.

The next day, I purchased fourteen separate treatises on Hershin Trader law and culture and spent fifty hours poring over them.

They all said the same thing.

Once a subcaste had passed on an individual's honor, there was no appeal, no rehabilitation. If Rachel had been discarded, her name could never be spoken again.

There was nothing I could do for her. Nothing the cheetah *can* do for the poor gazelle. I mean, if you don't run her down, someone else is just going to do it, right?

The smart thing was to go back to my closet and forget all about her.

Instead I went to see her father.

The Hershin Trader consulate was located all the way down on the D-level, midway between axis and rim. So the Hershins were rich enough to afford the most wondrous luxury of all.

Gravity.

The habitat was immense, blue sky arcing overhead, golden sun bringing the day. If you looked close you could see the sky's curvature at the edge of the faux horizon, but you did have to look close.

The space was filled with a tangle of carbon nanofilament cables. Traders leaped and danced along the slim lines, chittering and touching each other with their grasping claws.

Even a creature born and bred on a world a hundred light-years away could see they were family.

After a time, one of them dropped to the ground and skittered toward me. He was big, a good sixty centimeters taller than Rachel and thirty kilos heavier. Royal-blue grasping claws told me he was highborn male.

His tendrils were covered with golden rings, five or six apiece.

"You are Jordan Dart," he said. "Come to sell information."

"More like give it away," I said.

"I do not understand."

"You are father of Rachel."

He froze. "I do not know that name."

I sighed. "Please, then, tell me how I should address you."

He said something and of course the translator said, *Untranslatable. Tagging sophont as Hershin Trader Two.*

Tag as "Bob," my mind whispered to my implant. *Done.*

"Fine," I said out loud, "I will call you 'Bob.'"

The Trader executed a kind of bow.

"You must take Rachel back," I started, "or she—"

"I know of no one with that name."

I rubbed my eyes. I could see I would have to approach this from a different angle. A hypothetical angle. "What if a Hershin Trader were cheated in a deal? This would not be cause for disgrace, would it?"

The Traders were strict merchants with no tolerance for dishonesty. If I could show him that Rachel had been a victim rather than a fool . . .

He crouched down. "You have proof of this?"

I blinked. Proof? Well, no, who needed proof? The rumors I'd heard about Exar were enough. He'd devoured her whole the first time and now that he'd found her and learned she still possessed something of value, he was back for dessert. I should know.

I'd set the table for him.

"Listen—" I began.

"So there is no proof." Bob slowly rose out of his crouch.

I puffed a breath of air past my lips. "Would it matter if there were?"

He was absolutely still for several long moments, then his whole frame sagged. "No. Once a subcaste has reached its decision, it may not be reversed."

"But—"

"There is no more to say of this," he barked at me.

I opened my mouth, but he was already skittering up one of the cables, leaving nothing behind but a powerful odor: anise. This time I thought I knew what it meant.

Grief.

That close to the emergency zone, I learned the truth. Red Line had gotten loose. It turned out that our great technological marvel was more streamlined because it had fewer safeties.

The first bloom erupted in a field just outside of Paris. After ten hours there were a thousand sites. After twenty, ten thousand. After thirty, France was gone, dissolved into a sea of molecular goo.

Earth was doomed.

So I was making my way along the main arc of D-level, working back to the elevator banks, thinking that there are some sins that are unforgivable. Who knew this better than I? And if Rachel had to live with that hard truth, well, it wasn't like it was my fault, was it? I mean I'd tried.

And just as I was trying out one rationalization after another, I happened to glance in the window of a D-level mixer bar and who do you think I saw?

Gherten.

The bilious green amoebic extended a pseudopod and picked up a drink. (An actual *drink*. Where there's acceleration, who needs bulbs?)

What was he doing here? More importantly, if he could afford to drink down on D-level, why did he spend so much time up on S?

And suddenly I understood.

Everything.

A grim smile tightened my face. I turned around and went back the way I'd come.

Thousands, millions, of Homo saps tried to flee. Sometimes I wonder if Candace and Rachel were among them. It doesn't matter—no one got past the quarantine.

There's no way to be sure a ship is really free from infection at the molecular level.

Well, there's one.

The hell of it is I understand why the Galactics did what they did. Given the same situation, I would have done the same. I guess morality is all about which side of the line you're on.

They destroyed every ship fleeing the bloom, and

when they'd secured the border, they used the energy of our sun to fold time and space in upon itself, utterly obliterating the entire Sol system and any trace of humanity.

In their paranoia they even vaporized my team back on Sail.

Near as I can tell, I'm the only one they missed.

If anything, I felt worse the second time I saw her. She was no longer just a picture of tragedy, now that tragedy was my responsibility.

She occupied the same perch in the same bar, as if she hadn't moved since I left her. Who knows, maybe she hadn't.

Star Death Burst was full of the usual night-cycle crowd. I noticed Gherten in his usual corner, holding forth to anyone who would listen.

Exar and I made our way toward her.

If I'm any judge of Trader body posture, she looked at the Cube with mild alarm, legs taut, sensory node pulled down and back.

"There is no need to be afraid, Rachel," I said soothingly. "He is here to help you."

"I thought we might deal," said Exar.

For a long moment, she did nothing but look at me with all those lustrous black eyes.

And I did one of the hardest thing I'd ever done in my life. I said, "It's okay, you can trust him."

And for some reason I will never quite understand, she believed me.

Slowly she came out of her defensive posture. "What do you want?" she asked. Suspicious.

"The Hershin Trade Continuum isn't the whole universe," said Exar smoothly. In the darkness I could only see the shadows of the things within him. "I might be able to use someone with your skills."

Rachel sat very still.

"Surely you must know of some opportunities."

Slowly she reached down, pulled up her comm. Started to make her way through her business contacts. After a moment she said, "Perhaps . . ."

"Of course," said Exar, "on this first deal I will need some collateral."

She froze. She had to know exactly what he meant. Her ring.

She glanced down at her comm again, knowing the deal was sour, but desperately trying to find a way to believe it would work.

And that's when Exar looked at his own comm.

There was no reason for him to do it. He *had* her. But in the end Exar could not resist his essential nature. He was a cheater.

He had to cheat.

Unfortunately for him that was all that Gherten was waiting for. The amoebic formed a sphincter and extruded a nasty-looking energy weapon.

Question: what kind of people live double lives? Answer: undercover cops.

He launched himself across the room. "You are both under arrest for pirating encrypted data."

I suppose Exar was startled. With a Cube, it's hard to tell. I calmly put my hands up.

Bob stepped into the bar.

Rachel's sensory node came up. "Father," she whispered.

I looked at Bob, and he looked at me. "Here is your proof that Rachel was cheated," I said.

She looked at me and shivered. "It doesn't matter. I have been *discarded.* My name can never be spoken." She reeked of anise.

"This is the truth," said Bob. "Which is why you must have a new name. Daughter." And then he reached out and touched his claws to hers.

So Rachel would get a new identity, a legal fiction that no one would believe, but everyone would choose to accept because she had been shown to be a victim rather than a fool.

And the laws of the Hershin culture would be preserved.

Bob laid a claw on my shoulder and turned to Gherten. "I have no quarrel with this one. You will release him."

"But—"

"That is my final word," he said sternly. Bob pulled a golden ring from one of his tendrils, pressed it into my palm. And then he and Rachel were gone.

I looked down at the nanogel. My hand itched where it touched my skin. I could spend it and retire to a life of comfort and luxury. Or I could ingest it myself, dive into an ecstasy that just might wipe away my memories.

Somehow I knew either way was a form of running away. And I was done doing that.

It is true that some sins are unforgivable.

But that doesn't mean you don't have to try.

I tossed the ring to a startled Gherten, who caught it with a pseudopod. Then I pushed off and drifted out of the bar, whistling softly to myself.

Crossing the Road

by Phaedra M. Weldon

"WHY DID THE CHICKEN cross the road?" The stranger's voice was even, strong, assured. And quite audible through the bar's low hum of conversation.

"The other side?" said the bartender as he polished a glass.

The stranger frowned and waved his hand, disturbing a tendril of smoke just expelled from a patron two seats down. "Not you. Her." He pointed at me. "I want *her* to answer."

Oh, for crying out loud. The guy was obviously drunk. "Tell me why the chicken crossed the road."

His eyes refocused on me then, and a crinkle formed between two salt-n-pepper eyebrows. The ambient bar noise stopped. The voices of several regular customers diminished, as if the universe knew I was about to be given the key to the question of why.

With a shallow breath he leaned toward me, the

veins along his neck protruding like the roots of a tree. "Buttons."

That's when I stood and pulled out my gun.

Tomorrow was the expiration for the body I'd used and abused for the good of the universe. Unlike most of those that'd given their lives for the Protectorate, I chose to spend my last days drinking myself into oblivion.

Seemed like a good idea at the time, too. I was tired, depressed, and thinking back over a childhood I never had. My mother I never knew, and my father had died when I was three. I was raised by the state— fed, clothed, educated, and housed. So when I grew up, the Protectorate wanted repayment. I became a Prefect, signed on for eighty years recompensation, sworn to protect the people from evil aliens.

Whup. Dee. Do.

Nobody really explained out the little clause in that contract. About how if I were killed before the contract came up, I'd be downloaded into a different body, over and over again, until they'd gotten out what they believed they deserved.

And after ninety years of living, I was tired. And depressed. And wondering what my life would have been like if I'd lived here, on this planet, in this bar, with real parents and no Protectorate for a light-year in every direction.

Nice dream. Really nice dream.

Before the stranger disrupted my misery, I'd been

sitting beside him, on a quiet stretch of road, on the furthest terraformed planet known to civilized races, in a bar of memory. I call it memory because though I've frequented the establishment often during my less than savory career, there exists not one written locator to its position. There are no advertisements. No billboards. Not even an ad in a newspaper or magazine anywhere I've ever seen. Finding the bar relies on memory. Which is a bit troubling, since most who frequent the bar leave drunk, their memories pretty much cold-cocked.

And the more I think about it, I can't even remember the bar's name. I can remember where it sits, nestled between two purple palm trees. They're that color because of the ocean nearby, where the water's red all year long because of the rich ore deposits beneath the surface. The weather's always mild, with only a minor rain or wind, and the air always smells like rotten eggs.

The sand that clings to your shoes looks brown, but I learned if you look at it under a 'scope, the colors are pure and dazzling, as if someone shattered a rainbow and spread it on the ground.

The place itself is downright ugly. A flat silver building, pieced together from scraps of metal from a nearby shipyard. It always looked to me as if it started out as a fort built by a group of kids, and each piece was added as their club grew in size. Company logos, eclectic paintings on personal businesses, and even a few government seat paint jobs, all cobbled together to form a hideous, if not fascinating, miasma of modern art.

It's that mess of color that makes it hard to find the door.

But once inside, it boggles the senses.

The smell of rotten eggs disappears, replaced by the friendly odor of urine and smoke. The air moves and caresses your cheeks. There's always the sound of conversation, even when it's empty. Neon sculptures of popular drinks decorate the walls which are dark and practically invisible. Round wooden tables litter the smooth gray floor where a three-inch-high autobot moves silently around picking up peanut shells and beer can tabs.

The bar isn't much—a high wall outlined in stools of varying heights. The side is decorated with the scuff marks of millions of shoes pressed against it. The bar's top where we place our elbows is wood, made from the bark of the palm trees, or so I was told. It shines nicely when cleaned, and when I rest my elbows on it, it almost feels as if the wood bends and shapes itself to my arms. Quite comfortable when feeling a bit poorly after a zero-g landing.

"Hey, Jane, what'll it be?" The bartender was one of the native-born. A human birthed in this atmosphere, whose DNA was adapted for life on a forced atmosphere. He was medium height, with skin the color of a permanent sunburn. His hair was a soft blue, one of the effects of drinking the red water, and his eyes were the color of a puppy's, liquid brown and so dark I couldn't see his pupils.

His name was Cornelius, and I'd gotten to know him pretty sweet over the past two years. "Oh, the usual, I guess. Unless you and Moad finally imported in some other nonalcoholic swills."

Moad was Cornelius' partner. Life partner I should say. Each of the governments on independent worlds developed different rules and different customs. And here, on this planet whose name escapes me, the locals find life mates, meaning once promised, one looks after the other till death. It's not so much a marriage as having a mom or a dad around all the time.

If Cornelius was Cupid in disguise with his good looks, Moad was far from Psyche. She was one of the Average, not born here. She never changed her body, or traded in enhancements for a little less humanity. She could have used a nose job, and some skin-scrapes, but Moad believed she chose the body she was born with and stuck to it. She could easily afford enhancements—only those with wealth could, or those who chose a life of service like me where the Protectorate made extensions mandatory for the enlisted—but Moad didn't want them.

Neither did Cornelius.

What they wanted was a child. But, sad to say, Moad was behind her child-bearing years and wasn't about to have anything implanted. She preferred to adopt, and the two had talked about it in front of me, several times. I'm apparently a good listener.

Moad tolerated me, and that was about it. "We got a new beer in, imported from Terra. I'm pretty sure it tastes worse than horse."

"I'll try it." My previous body had been allergic to alcohol. I wasn't sure this one wasn't. I didn't care anymore. I was going to get rip-roaring drunk.

He gave me a white toothy smile and set a blue bottle on the counter, a glass, and an opener. Self-serve all the way.

"So, are you here for a stay? I hear the new luxury Premiere hotel is up and running."

I popped open the beer's top, tossed it over the side, and watched the little bot race over and suck it up off the floor. After tilting the glass and pouring the amber liquid along the side, I glanced up at Corn. I liked him. Lots. "I'm done, Corn. I'm retiring. Finished."

His eyes widened. He didn't look happy. "Jane . . . you're retiring? Expiration?"

"Yep." I sipped the swill. Not as bad as horse, and it still had a kick to it. "Decided to enjoy my last hours here at my favorite bar." I smiled and then belched.

Cornelius looked stricken. "Shouldn't you be at the Protectorate headquarters? I mean, aren't you sup-posed to get a new body for retirement?"

I shook my head, sipped again, and pulled air

through my teeth. "Not in the contract. Oh, I could buy one. But I'm tired of stealing lives, Corn. You see this body? You know what it did before it was reformed for my use?" I looked down at my thin frame, at the age spots along my left arm and at the boney knuckles clutching the glass. "She was a mother, Corn. A real mother with real children. Two of 'em."

"A mother?" Corn's voice was filled with awe. "Where are her children?"

I took another sip. "She killed them. Just up and decided one day she wasn't going to be a mom anymore and drowned them." I sighed. "Damn shame—with all the advancements we've made through the centuries, we still can't weed out the whackos."

"Jane." Corn reached out and touched my hand. His skin was warm, and young, and I was filled with regrets. I wanted Corn and Moad to have children, and I wanted those children to look like him, with ruddy skin and blue hair, and I hoped they bartended here at the end of the world. "I don't want you to expire."

I squeezed his hand. "I don't want to either," I sighed. "But I don't have money for a new body, much less the life code to this one. I guess in a few hours I'll know the answer to the greatest question in the universe."

That's when the stranger opened his mouth.

A few seconds after that, I stood over the stranger, the butt of my gun to his forehead, the side of his

face smashed against the bar, my thoughts a jumbled
mess of system analysis. I was programmed to track
and destroy Buttoniers, humans who worked for the
evil aliens. And here was one, a day before my
expiration.

And here was I—asking the very question of re-
cruitment for the enemy I'd been sworn to destroy.

So the big hooey was—what did I do now?

By law, I was supposed to restrain him and bring him
in. But I wasn't bound by that law anymore, was I? If
I disobeyed, what was the Protectorate going to do?
Revoke my license on this body? Take away my gun?

Wah.

Trained reflex had brought my gun out, and I
glanced around at the expressions of the patrons.
There weren't many—Corn and Moad simply looked
bored. And as for the Buttonier? He looked about as
frightened as an eagle on an updraft.

Nada. And who could blame him. I'd done it—I'd
gotten the answer to the world's oldest question. I'd
been taught that code, conditioned to listen for it, instructed on how to apprehend those who used it—all
for the protection of humankind against the atrocities
The Grays had done with their abductions.

"Jane," Corn said in a tentative voice. "You gonna
shoot him? Or arrest him?"

Well, that sounded like as good as any line to back
out of my reflex trained drama. I pulled the gun back
and released his neck before stepping away. "No—
guess not."

The Buttonier straightened up, adjusted his shoulders, and moved his jaw back and forth. "I really thought you weren't going to accept the gift, Prefect."

I was impressed he knew my title, but then again, I'm sure any of the traitorous humans that worked for the very scum that tortured our race for centuries knew about the Protectorate's Buttonier special force.

Which led me to my next question. I reholstered my gun and sat back down again. Corn refilled my drink. "You knew I was a Prefect before you offered up the question."

He nodded and shot back the tiny glass of fire-red liquid that had survived my attack. His eyes rolled back in his head, and he stopped breathing for a few seconds before he could hiss and take in air. Mr. Brave here had just swallowed Moad's special blend of rocket fuel and acid. "Yes . . ." His voice sounded abused, and I was sure the drink had singed a few vocal cords. "Which is why I made it."

"Why you made it?" Corn asked the question before I could.

"Yeup." The Buttonier nodded and took a few more deep breaths. I was sure I saw smoke wisp out of his ears. He leaned back and looked at me. It was then I realized this guy was young. Way young. Though he carried himself like an aged farmer. He wore the usual tan pants and cotton shirt of the locals, which is probably why I didn't take him for a fugitive. "Part of my contract, Prefect Jane Knowles. It states if I meet someone whom I believe deserves to have their dreams come true, or I—at least—think they're worthy, I ask the question. If they ask for the answer, I give the answer, then I'm free of my duties to The Grays."

I cringed at the sound of their name. And then I thought about what he said. "So you actually made a contract with them?"

"As did you, with the Protectorate. And it's up to you how long you work it, and when you retire. But—" he held up his hand "—I think before you start your work, you need a little enlightening on the history of your new employer."

I shook my head, entertained as well as miffed at this guy's lack of embarrassment. "And I think you weren't listening to me. As of tomorrow, my license to this body expires. I will cease to exist. Nada. So, any little contract I made with The Grays is void."

There. Chew on that, Mr. Smug.

I was surprised to see him shake his head. "No. 'Fraid not. Oh, you can choose to lay down and die if that's what you want. Accept the Protectorate's version of immortality in a body that was never yours. Or, you can deliver the cargo I've collected and buy an extension."

Someone laughed in the back of the bar, and I glanced that way. The windows showed the sinking of the suns outside, and the water a few meters away resembled blood. "You can't buy an extension on a government body."

"The Grays can."

No, he was wrong. The Grays and the Protectorate of Terran Ecologies were enemies. For centuries they had battled The Grays and their unlawful abductions. The Protectorate would never sell extensions to Buttoniers.

Unless The Grays had stolen codes. DNA triggers that would allow the body to remain active. No shutting down.

I glared at him.

And he knew he had me.

He admitted the codes were illegal. "But they'll keep you alive long enough so you can achieve your dream."

"My dream?"

With a nod he reached inside his jacket, careful to let me see every move lest I draw on him again, and pulled out a black bag. He set it in front of me. "Rules are simple. Get them buttons, and they give you a new life. Your life."

Buttons. I thought he'd been kidding.

I took the bag. The fabric was velvet and caught against the rough patches of my fingers. I lifted it. Not so heavy. But I sort of figured I already knew what was in the bag.

I opened it up and wasn't surprised. Buttons. I'd almost venture to say there were hundreds of buttons inside the bag. Every color of the universal rainbow lay inside that black recess of ridiculousness. I looked up from it to find Moad and Corn looking at me.

"So—there *are* buttons in here. What do I do with them?"

"You deliver them."

"Deliver them where?"

The Buttonier shrugged. "They'll contact you and tell you where to make the drop."

"The drop?" I narrowed my eyes at him, aware that Moad and Corn had grown very silent.

"Where to deliver them." He smiled at me, and it was a surprisingly warm gesture. "They're good aliens, Prefect. Yeah—they have a little quirk with their attachment to buttons, but it's harmless and a whole bunch of nothing's been stirred up against them because the Protectorate wanted more from them and they refused."

Okay—that was more information than I expected. All at once. I had to cipher through a few pieces to the weirdest one. "Uh—attachment to buttons. They pay you to bring them buttons?"

He nodded. Moad placed a new drink in front of him, though I noticed it wasn't the fire-water.

"Why don't they just buy them?"

"From where?" The Buttonier raised his arms. "How often do you see a button nowadays? Think about it, Jane. You don't. Because the Protectorate made them dangerous. Remember all the labels and warnings from our childhood, and our parents' childhoods? Ooh, beware buttons. They'll choke little ones? And the fashion magazines poo-pooed them? Saying they were garish and so yesterday?"

I had a vague recollection of this—but I'd never really cared. I liked Velcro better, and zippers. Not to mention melding fasteners.

"Well, that was the attempt by the Protectorate to make it harder for The Grays to find buttons. That way they controlled the market."

"Buttons." I lowered my chin and looked at him through my eyebrows. "It's all about buttons."

Nod.

"So—" none of this was making sense to me, "—they never abducted us for sterilization?"

That statement brought a laugh from the Buttonier, as well as Corn and Moad.

"No, Jane. That's what the Protectorate *wants* everyone to think—The Grays been collecting buttons since Greek history, when they first noticed them. Well, they collected them themselves—before they had to resort to hiring mercenaries like us. Look, you'll learn it all when you go in for orientation."

"Orientation?" I felt stupid. Was he for real?

"You don't think they expect you to swallow everything I tell you, do you? No." He shook his head, knitted his eyebrows. Jane had to admit he seemed a lot more animated than he'd been since she sat down. "They want you to know the truth. If you still say no, then they'll let you live out the code they acquired for your body just for listening to them."

"That's that?" I leaned back in my seat. "They'll just let me go?"

"Yeah, but I'd pay attention to what they say, Jane. I've seen a lot and done more than I care to admit. But don't let the travel and recreational benefits blind you. Buttons are not easy to find. They're impossible. And the only place they're still somewhat plentiful is on Earth."

"Earth." I pursed my lips. Home of the Protectorate itself. I'd been there once—for training. It was built like a fortress with instant death to those found trespassing. And for expired Prefects? Well—I wasn't sure I knew the precedent for that crime, or even if it was a crime.

All of this over buttons. It was going to be interesting to hear what The Grays had to say. Some people were just dumb enough to pay more than something was worth, unless it meant more to them than life itself.

And that—boys and girls—was why the Prefect beat the chicken across the road.

The buttons my predecessor collected were enough to buy me the code to my body. The Grays were actually kinda nice—if not a bid creepy. Graceful movements. Slow blinks of their enormous eyes.

And buttons everywhere.

They decorated the walls, the furniture, and even the food! Though, of course, you didn't eat them. It was like walking in on that part in Mary Poppins with the guys dressed in button-covered clothing.

Everything seemed on the up and up. And they offered me something my own people wouldn't—a longer life. And not with someone else's body.

But with my own.

Apparently, The Grays had samples of DNA from every known Prefect since the Protectorate turned on them. Three hundred buttons had bought me the code. Six hundred buttons would buy me my DNA. And a thousand buttons—I could get a copy of my own body back.

Oh, yeah, I took the job.

I returned to the bar several times in the next ten years, and I told them the truth about The Grays. Corn was fascinated. Moad didn't seem to care—as long as I paid in cash for my swill, she was tolerable.

Moad was too depressed most of the time. Their petition for adoption had been turned down twice.

"So they never abducted us for sperm?"

I smiled at Corn. He was just as cute and dopey as he always was. He'd cut his blue hair and lost a few pounds, but all in all, he was still handsome as ever. "Nope. Apparently a group of them found Earth at about our Greek period. They chose us for observation—primitive species and all that. The story goes that one of the members chanced upon a couple in the woods, doing all sorts of non-PG things. Being observers, the scientist watched, and found herself fascinated not with the humans and their medieval foreplay, but with the gold buttons on the lady's sleeves."

Moad made a nasty noise and disappeared into a door behind the bar.

I ignored her.

"So they abducted the humans, stole their buttons, erased their memories and then put them back. Now, these scientists didn't wear clothing—they really didn't need it. Their skin is as thick as an elephant's hide and they've never had any real need for covering. So the idea of buttons was as alien to them as their existence was to us."

A small female at the bar turned in her chair. I'd noticed her when I came in, as I'd noticed her the last time I'd visited. Dressed all in black with stiletto heels and shimmering panty hose. Her hair was as dark as her suit. She frowned at me. "Are you saying the first alien abduction caused a fashion craze?"

I smiled. "Uh-huh. They made a sash of satin that draped from left shoulder to right hip, and along that satin they attached the golden buttons."

"I don't see why they didn't just make their own buttons." Moad was back in the room, and she eyed the petite woman coldly.

"They didn't know how to make them. It wasn't something known to their culture, and through the centuries, it was more thrilling to collect these buttons from Earth. So thus began a fad among the race known to us as The Grays for wearing button-decorated sashes. The abductions continued with more frequency, but The Grays established a better system of collection. What I found funny about the whole thing was that they never—not even once—considered knocking off a button factory."

"It has to be worn by a human?" the petite woman asked.

I nodded. Who was this person? "And this is where it gets sticky. Eventually, the governments caught on and they reached a settlement with The Grays. Buttons for technology. Which explains the huge technology boom we had in the twentieth century."

"But they took that technology away from us," the petite woman said. It wasn't a question.

I looked at her more closely. Noticed the creases along her eyes. The slight way her right shoulder pulled from her side. She was slim and petite, but not graceful. No—she moved as if she weren't familiar with the body. As if it wasn't hers.

Prefect.

I leaned toward her, my left hand on the stunner in my pocket. Nobody expects me to use my left hand— I'm legally a rightie. "No, we got too greedy. We asked for cures to cancers and we got them. We asked for space travel and we got it. We asked for terraforming technology and we got it. We asked for faster than light, and wow, we got it, and the buttons flowed." I held up my right index finger. "But then we asked for something they knew we didn't have the moral fiber for. We asked for their cloning technology. And that time they said no."

Corn and Moad blinked. I assumed it was the first

time they'd heard that. It wasn't the petite woman's first—I knew that by the lack of reaction.

She said, "They had no right to deny us that."

"Oh? Look at you. Is that your first replacement body?"

The petite woman narrowed her eyes. "I don't know what you mean."

"Look, stupid. I was a Prefect for over eighty years. I know how it works. You bang up your own body protecting the masses, and they give you a new one. They figured out how to transfer consciousness, but not how to grow a new one. And what happened to the person who owned that body? Did you know her? Or what it was she'd done to have her own soul erased?"

I sat back on the stool. "And you're here to arrest a Buttonier, aren't you?"

She reached for her gun, but I was faster. I shot her through my pocket. Stunned her. She slumped forward and then hit the ground with a thud. Several of the patrons at tables stopped what they were doing, and then continued on.

Move along, nothing to see here.

Corn came around the side of the bar. "She was a Prefect."

I nodded and checked the hole in my suit. "Damnit. I'm gonna have to patch that."

"You didn't kill her." Moad leaned over the bar and watched Corn lift the Prefect into his arms. "How come you didn't kill her?"

"Because it's not her fault. She was fed the same line of bullshit we all were. It's easier to believe there are things out there to hurt us, but how can we believe our advances in this universe happened because of a simple, plastic circle?" I smiled and watched as Corn carried her around the bar to the back. I knew he'd secure her for me, until I left.

When he returned, Corn was oddly quiet. It wasn't till after the lunch crowd died away that he finally moved to stand in front of me. "Why did you come back here?"

"You and Moad still thinking about having kids?"

Corn smiled. "Yeah. We've looked into two orphanages near New Gaza, over the yellow mountains. But we're just not qualifying."

"Well, that's why I'm here." I reached into my pocket and pulled out a slip of plastic. I held it up in front him as Moad stepped closer. "This is the written deed to three accounts on Pluto. Terran system. There's close to six million when combined. I've deeded it all to you with only one condition."

The couple looked at each other, and then Corn reached out and took the plastic. "How did you . . . ?"

"The Grays pay nicely, Corn. And I knew where to get some nice buttons. Not on Earth, but on the first settlement. Mars. I'd met a nutcase about twenty years back that collected them. He passed away, and his estate was up for bid. I bought it all." I smiled at them. "And I also bought myself a second chance."

Moad frowned. "What's the condition?"

"You adopt me."

The vein on her upper right temple throbbed. "Say what?"

"You adopt me." I smiled. "I want to live here. I want my hair to turn blue. I want to swim in the red sea—" And with that I nearly choked on the images of home and comfort and a loving family. "I want to be raised by you."

Corn shook his head. "I don't understand . . ."

But I couldn't explain it all to him. Not now. They'd heard my words to the Prefect, but they hadn't understood them. In three days I'll be reborn, cloned from my original DNA. But unlike the process the Protectorate used, I'll start from the beginning. As a babe. Growing into my body experiencing the joys of life all over again.

I won't know who I was before. And I didn't think I'd want to.

They agreed to the deal and signed the dotted line. Once I had the contract with me, I set up the delivery for a month from now and took the next ship back to The Grays home world for the very last time.

It took four years to find that damned bar again. She was dressed in black again as she stepped into the bar whose name she couldn't remember. What she did remember was the smell of rotten eggs, the red color of the sea, and that she'd found a Buttonier here, the one that got away. A famous one who'd once been employed by the Protectorate.

She assessed the patrons. Only two this time, seated at tables and watching a soccer game on one of the wall monitors.

The same man stood behind the bar, his blue hair cut short and his reddish skin glowing. He wiped the bar and with a smile offered to get her something. If he remembered her, he gave no sign.

She ordered the local swill and looked around. "Quiet today."

He nodded and set the bottle, the glass, and an opener in front of her. "For now. At least till my family gets back from town."

She sipped the swill. Not as bad as she remembered. "So, any strangers in lately?"

"No, just you."

Before she could answer, the door flew open and a blue-haired child of four ran in screaming, "Daddy! Daddy! Mommy gave me a new prize today!"

The bartender stepped around the bar and scooped the child up in his arms. The woman in black watched the two of them, and felt a slight cold in her chest as he hugged and kissed his daughter. She was beautiful with her sky-colored hair and bright green eyes. Her skin wasn't as ruddy colored as her father. She looked like one of the natives.

The child's mother stepped inside then, smiling. "She got all high marks, Corn. Jane's quite the little speller."

The little girl, Jane, squirmed to get down and ran around the bar to where the woman dressed in black sat. She climbed the stool beside her and smiled up. "Hi. My name's Jane. What's yours?"

"Hannah," the woman dressed in black said. "Well, Jane, you were in a spelling bee today?"

"Uh-huh." She beamed. "You're still very pretty."

Hannah frowned. "Still pretty? Jane, have you seen me before?"

"Yes. It was in a dream, though. And you needed an answer." She scrambled down and ran behind the bar. In a few seconds she came back with a black bag, climbed back up, and then set it on the bar. She frowned and then looked at the bartender who'd come to stand in front of Hannah. "Daddy, what was the question again?"

The handsome man looked Hannah directly in the eye. "Why did the chicken cross the road?"

She blinked. It was *the* question.

The very question she'd waited for. But she didn't draw her gun. She didn't move. She simply stared at the bartender, and then at his wife, and then at the little girl named Jane seated on the stool beside her. She swallowed bile as she realized who looked out of those beautiful green eyes back at her. "Do you know the answer?"

"If you hear it, then you have . . ." Jane frowned. She looked at her parents. "How did it go again?"

"You have to take the responsibility in the knowing," the mother said in a rough voice. "And you have to promise never to come here again."

Hannah was sure she recognized her. Just as she recognized the tiny girl seated beside her.

But was it possible? Was this *her?*

"Right," Jane said. "And the answer is—" She straightened up. "Button. B.U.T.T.O.N." She grinned again and tossed her pale blue hair back from her glowing skin. "Button."

I'm Not Ashamed

by Greg Beatty

"WHERE TO, SIR?"

"The Spaceport Bar."

"Ah, dude." The cabbie's eyes found mine in the rearview mirror. "I'm so sorry. Hop in—I'll make sure I get you there on time."

I didn't correct his misunderstanding. I just pulled the door shut. As the maglocks secured it and the engine whispered into life—no, we were already up to freeway speed—I looked around the cab and thought about how much had changed since they'd arrived, and how much was still the same.

The nearly silent doors and nonpolluting engines, and the very fact that there was a spaceport where there used to be an airport, those were new. The string of fast food joints, empty lots filled with detritus, and all the titty bars we were passing, those were unchanged, as was the inside of the cab, which still

smelled like fatigue, Fritos, and feet. *They* don't care
about the smell.

And the cabbie, he was the same. He handled every
curve the way he'd probably handled every change in
technology and social structure, leaning into the transi-
tions and handling them with body English and low cun-
ning. He was using both of these as he made near-record
time past the homeless and the crazies that lined the
road to the spaceport. Their existence was as old as
urbanization, but their specific slogans, curses, and af-
flictions were new. I saw familiar faces among them.
People who had been trained professionals, before.

The cabbie'd driven this road many times, but I'd
known that by the basset eyes that had accompanied
his apologies. He understood shame. He'd driven
enough humans to The Spaceport Bar, and more
importantly, home from it, to know what it meant. Or
thought he did. In response to his continual stream of
consolation, I murmured noncommittal responses that
could be taken as agreement or excess pain. Either
way, they kept him from realizing until we were finally
there, and he started to pull the car into the alley that
led to the employees' entrance.

"No," I said. "The front door."

"Oh." Sympathy fled his voice. He squealed the
tires getting away from me. I didn't think that was
still possible, but I guess he'd developed the skill when
driving gas engines on rubber wheels, and wasn't going
to give it up.

"I'm not ashamed," I called after his retreating window. As if he'd heard me, I saw my damn generous tip being dribbled out the driver's side window.

I sighed, pulled myself upright, plastered a broad smile on my face, and headed for the door. The doorman gave me the look of one servile damned to another. You know the look. It's the look a field slave gave a house slave, or the look a devil laboring in the flames of hell might give an incubus who was putting the moves on Gabriel. The mask that smiles and damns as it says, as the doorman did, "Welcome to The Spaceport Bar, sir!"

He bowed and opened the door to damnation for me. I entered willingly, tasting bile and feeling my balls tingle like they used to when I was seventeen and the next door neighbor's mom used to sunbath with the back of her suit untied.

The Spaceport Bar. If you're human and alive, you know what it looks like, no matter where you live. What's scary is, if you lived in what used to be the United States, the damn thing probably looked familiar to you even before you saw it. We used to make movies about humans in space. When we did, we sometimes included scenes set in the spaceport bar, in which a zany array of aliens drank, smoked, buzzed, and in general recreated in a display of interspecies camaraderie that was modeled on endless pulpy stories of spaceports that were modeled, in turn, on pirate stories that were themselves about as realistic as the world toured in Disney's "It's a Small World After All."

Everyone got along, or if they didn't, it was a clash of individuals that served as a kind of interstellar head butt contest, in which brash younger races face down complacent aliens with spunk and light sabers. Of course, for "humans" read Americans, which really meant white guys, which made this particular space-port bar especially depressing. I might expect this in Lebanon or Vietnam. Not here.

We have it rough. We're still young enough to remember these dreams. They make The Spaceport Bar sting more than they will in twenty years. When the new generation grows up, it will be used to having them around, and The Spaceport Bar will seem, if anything, just like a symbol of the way things are. God fucking save us all.

Now, see The Spaceport Bar through my eyes. It's only half-lit by human eyes, because our alien lords and masters see things differently. For them every-thing is luminous. Booths, the·bar, and stools—all of these are in deep shadow. From where I stand, my back to the door, I can't see any aliens. I can only see the waitstaff in glimpses, and, more frequently, only hear them stumble into the tables or a casually sprawled tentacle. When I hear the drinks spill, I close my eyes, because every mistake is always followed by punishment, and the arcers hurt my eyes. I can't close my ears, though, and a few seconds after the foot-long spark stalls a human nervous system, causing its owner to fall to the ground in spasms, the screams start.

I can't not hear, but I can try to distract myself. I

look away. My eyes find the light, and I look there, until I can't. You see, the only dependably lit spots are the holos. Did you ever visit one of those bars near an airport that caters to flight fanatics? Catered. Or one that was just trying to cash in on the cachet air travel used to have for some people, where they set propellers out for women to stroke to get men to buy them drinks?

At first glance, the holos at The Spaceport Bar are like this. Each lit area portrays some major milestone in humanity's rise to the stars. If you've seen them, you know that these, too, are familiar, but just a little bit off. There's the Wright Brothers at Kitty Hawk. From above. There's the Hindenberg. The holo's taken from within the flames, and if you step close enough to get a better look, you'll trigger the sound and hear skin cooking. And people screaming. Across the room, there's the *Challenger* explosion. If you squint, you can see their faces, and see that they're looking at the holocameras when they blew. On that one you can hear the ablative tiles clicking and popping in the heat, and then the blast. And alien laughter.

I can't keep looking at it too long. It hurts to know that every step of the way the aliens were watching, even when we died, but I always look. I look to remind myself, and to try to figure out where the aliens' holocams were and speculate on why the aliens don't show up on our cameras. That made the initial invasion especially disturbing. People only saw them if they saw them with their own eyes. The news cameras only showed things blowing up and melting, like the whole world had rebelled against us.

By now my eyes have adjusted to the screaming dark, so I look back at the room again. Now I can see the humans. And their masters.

The aliens look the same as they always do. No matter how strange their faces, or technically, facades, were to us when they first arrived, we've had strong incentive to learn their expressions, at least for the emotions we can recognize. When they're first decanted and deployed, the younger aliens look alert. They scan spaces regularly, and every time a maglock clicked into active mode, they spun toward it. But even then, it's not fear, but mostly a kind of eagerness to do a shitty job really well. I always think of a new recruit snapping into attention or parade rest with a kind of crispness when I see it. Once that settles down—a few days, for most of them—they relax, and the only emotions you ever see on their facades are confidence and a sense of smug entitlement. Now they are garrison troops, and showpieces, and assholes. If this were an old movie, that would be the cue for me to wipe that expression off their facades. It's not an old movie.

The humans, well, it's how humans have changed that really gets to me. We used to come to bars from work, and stayed in our jeans to knock back a beer, or we dressed to impress the opposite sex, or we wore matching shirts and little tags with our names on them, because we worked there. Now, it was like Mardi Gras. No, scratch that. Mardi Gras was a carnival, a time when the normal values got stood on their heads. This was a carnival of carnival, if that made sense.

All the humans in the bar—serving drinks, serving zash, serving sex—were dressed in the most outrageous costumes you could ever want to wear for Mardi Gras. There was a young guy who was naked except for a huge array of feathers that were shaped into wings and affixed to his body by means of candle wax. He looked almost buff enough to take wing if he flapped his wings. And if he weren't crying. Over in the corner there was a guy who was stumbling along with a tray of drinks clasped between thick mittens. There's no way he could feel the tray through them, since they were meant to withstand vacuum. Sure enough, he dropped the tray a moment later, and was himself dropped into a pile of pain, his shrieks somewhat muffled by the shiny dome of his helmet.

I looked away, letting my eyes glide over someone dressed as a trapeze artist, a stewardess, someone dressed as a giant beagle who was muttering "Curse you, Red Baron," someone else apologizing continually for dragging an open parachute behind him . . . it would have been comical if it weren't for the way the humans continually flinched, apologized, and bowed. And if it weren't for the scars, and the fact that everyone knew that if there were too many individual mistakes, they might be treated like Portland.

No one knew what the humans who lived in Portland had done, and no one knew precisely what the aliens had done in response, but my eyes found the largest hologram in the bar, which showed three aliens cavorting in the low pool of water the Willamette River made as it poured onto the smooth, featureless plain that used to be Portland.

"Man!" Boy, I heard, and I was in motion before I could even tell which alien was speaking. So was half the room, the cost of even accidental disobedience being so high.

"Man!" This time I saw the call was coming from the far corner, and knew it was for me. I rushed to answer it.

The other humans got out of my way. Some of them watched me with pity; some humans were queer for the aliens and came to The Spaceport Bar to bow before them. Others watched me with hatred; some humans were scrambling to be capos, the highest of the low, and thought this was the way to get there. Even so, traces of gratitude lined all of their faces. If the aliens were arcing me, they wouldn't be arcing them. Probably.

"Little man." Though I was taller than it was, I bowed in response to the alien's call.

"Lord and master."

He, well, call it he, nodded at my ritual response. He acknowledged me casually by bending part of his body. "Little man, what do you do?"

Their English is perfect, as is their Russian, Chinese, etc., but they sound like they're placing each word down on a tile surface. Click. Click. Click. A mosaic in the making, in which they know the pattern and we are . . . raw material.

"I pick apples, master." I did, in season, and that would explain most of the calluses on my hands.

"He picks apples." Za. Zha. Za. Even their laughs are distinct from one another.

"And before? What did you do before?"

"I was a helicopter pilot." No human ever had to ask what "before" meant.

"A pilot!" Zha!

It rippled one of those intricate flipper limbs to flick one of its companions, which nodded. "A pilot. What do you know about flying, pilot."

"I have flown both small, single-engine planes—do you know planes?"

"We know planes."

"Are they like what you first flew on your world?" I made my posture as worshipful as possible.

It wobbled a flipper. "Some flying of similar planes is done, by hobbyists. Archaists. I was trained directly on landers, though, since a mature gravity drive operates largely independent of air pressures. It—" Its peer placed a flipper on the speaker, which fell silent and leaned toward me. I kept groveling as I repeated its words to myself.

"Did you avert my question, little man?"

"No, my lord and master."

"You did avert my question."

"No, my lord!" The other humans did their best to

back away while still smiling. I didn't blame them, even if three anecdotal reports had shown that proximity of other living bodies reduced the pain of arcing by about half. Half an arc still made me cry. I pushed on. "Master, I sought only to gain sufficient context to better answer your question. I swear. Let me tell you what I know about flying, my lord. At least forty hours of training time is required before a private license is issued for piloting a helicopter. I received fifty-six hours of training, in large part because I knew I wanted to fly in certain conditions . . ."

Appeased, but no longer amused, it flippered me to silence. I stood, head bowed and waiting.

"Not entertaining. Simply backward."

I no longer flushed at that label. "Backward" meant we were close enough to be on the same spectrum, but not near enough to be interesting. I can live with that. I call that striking distance.

"I apologize, my lord."

A flipper moved. A woman dressed like a giant peacock rushed up to refresh the speaker's drink and its companion's zash.

"It is not your fault your race is primitive. That is what you know. So, tell us, primitive things. You eat fruits grown from the earth?"

"Yes, my lord."

"And you gather them with bare flesh?"

"Yes, my lord, except for a few orchards that still use pesticides."

A flipper wave. "A detail. Gathering fruit is quaint. Tell me about gathering fruit."

Quaint. You mean, you won't spill any details that are against regulations. I smiled, bobbed my head, and began a well-worn tale of apple-picking that was half childhood memories polished for nostalgic presentation, half hard seasonal labor presented as character training, and all so familiar I could deliver it without full attention, leaving me free to focus elsewhere.

"Well, I guess I got back into apple picking as an adult, after you came and delivered us from ignorance, because I remember enjoying it so much as a kid, a young human. We'd watch the apple trees blossom, and the petals emerge, and move in the breeze." I waved my fingers, tracking just how attentive his facade seemed, and how smoothly he was tracking me. Not very.

I went on. "We'd play under the branches, hiding and laughing. We'd climb the apple trees, to look up to the sky. Sometimes a foot would step on a branch that wasn't as solid as we thought, and snap!" I snapped my fingers.

"It would break off. Sometimes we'd fall and hurt ourselves, but other times, we'd just break off another branch and have a sword fight. Ha! En garde." I lunged at the aliens and stamped my foot, in my best Errol Flynn imitation. They didn't flinch until my hand got within eighteen inches of a flopped flipper. Confirmation. They'd never used swords, and so military tradition did not instill those reflexes.

Back to my story. "But it was picking the actual apples that was the most fun. Us boys would climb up on ladders to pick the ripe fruit. If they were too ripe—squishy bombs, we called them—we had to throw them away, and so we threw them at each other."

I raised an arm, as if about to throw a rotten apple. By the time my hand reached the level of my ear, both aliens in the booth had shifted back on their haunches. Each had raised at least one flipper. I turned, and mimed throwing the fruit across the room.

"Pow! I'd spin and throw, and I'd hit my brother straight in the chest. Then we'd . . ."

Their spinelike hackles relaxed, and they lowered their flippers as I spun my yarn out for some time. I had covered hay rides, lugging baskets, cold ears and fingers, before I got to cider pressing. ". . . and sometimes, when the grown-ups were making hard cider, we'd sneak in and steal a bottle or two. We'd drink it, and even before we really got drunk, we'd start laughing and dancing around like nobody's business, and th—"

The alien farther back in the shadows had raised both flippers. "You find intoxication amusing?"

"Well, yes, my lord. Don't you?"

"Take care, apple picker. You deflect?"

"No, my lord. Yes, my lord, intoxication can be funny."

"Woman!" The peacock returned and bowed her trembling crest. "Bring the man hard cider. One full thoc."

"Lord, that is a great deal . . ." I knew when to stop.

The feathered beauty passed through the dim bar in silence, returned with a facade-sized beaker of amber fluid.

"Drink, apple picker. Drink and dance. Woman: watch."

I ducked my head, and lifted the thoc with both hands. I drank deeply, and heard the alien's "Zher" of amusement when cider streamed down my neck.

"Thank you, master—"

"Again."

And so I drank, again and again, until I smelled like an half-emptied barrel in the deep of winter, maybe one in which the cider's turned a bit.

"Master, if I drink any more—"

"Now dance."

I swear I could hear the thoughts the rest of the humans were glaring my way. Is it worth it? Do you want them/power/to be special this badly? Yes, it's worth it, I thought back, as I began a clumsy clog with a stomp and a pull.

I clogged for a while, the impact of my steps the only sound in the crowded bar except for an occasional alien sipping its drink. When I got tired of clogging, I started a bunch of novelty dances from the twentieth century, swimming, and running, and moving robotically.

When I couldn't think of any more to do, I started spinning like a wild dervish. I was burping apple gas by now, and I swear my head was spinning the other way from my body.

Eventually, I fell. So did the thoc, shattering into a million pieces that seemed to melt away before my eyes. "Enough!" I screamed. "That's enough."

Both aliens rose to their tetrapods. I pressed on. "Who were we hurting? We were living here, and we were happy, and then you came here with your fucking invisible ships and you reduced us to this!"

I snatched two fistfuls of the peacock and brandished them at the aliens. The one deeper in the shadows raised a flipper, arcer clearly visible between its tips. A space cleared around me again, and I ran at my lords and masters with the feathers.

I woke to the smell of burning feathers and the memory of a burst of electricity that had arced from the flipper to my chest. How long had I been out?

Not long. The peacock woman was resting in the booth beside the alien, stroking his arc flipper. I rose to my knees and crawled over.

"Zee!" The alien screamed when I bit it. This time I saw the arc coming.

I woke up to the steady patter of a light summer rain. It was washing away the burned smell from my chest, and the apple stink from my face, too. I brushed my face, wiping away mud and a couple of matted feathers. A few feet away, safely in the shadow of the aliens' protective shielding at the entrance of The Spaceport Bar, the doorman watched me coolly.

"Ca— call me a cab?" I called.

"I cannot leave my post," he said, "and that is not my job." His tone and posture added, "Besides, you deserve it, you worthless fuck."

"I'm not ashamed," I said in response.

I crawled for a while. Eventually I could stand, and then walk.

I stumbled along the road I'd driven in imported comfort. The mad and the homeless were still there with their signs. So were the titty bars and the fast food joints, all of them full of defeated humans.

Most people I passed looked away. They knew where I'd been.

But whether they looked away, or whether they looked at me, I talked to them.

"Their ships use a gravitational drive that allows them to operate independently of air currents," I whispered to the guy holding the sign reading "Exodus 6:6."

"Handheld projectiles and thrown weapons are close enough historically for them to worry about them, but swords are not," I'd mutter to another who looks quick on his feet. "We can stab them."

"Alien blood tastes more metallic than human," I say to a third, adding, "and once you've been arced more than thirty-seven times, the pain is far less intense and you don't stay unconscious even half as long."

And on and on and on, all that I learned, in this visit to this version of The Spaceport Bar, and in my twenty-three previous visits to them.

Some of them think I'm crazy. Shit, all of them may think I'm crazy. Sometimes *I* think I'm crazy. But some of them listen. I see them repeat my words, storing them away to pass on, and to test on their own.

I walk on, sharing what I learned. The road from The Spaceport Bar gets longer with every visit. But I'm not ashamed that I visit The Spaceport Bar, because with every visit, the road *through* The Spaceport Bar gets shorter.

When that day comes, when enough people know what I've learned, we'll drive them out. Until then, there's not much this soldier can do but visit The Spaceport Bar, where I drink and dance and get arced unconscious. And test their reflexes and remember their stories. And dream of the stars. And hate them.

Favio Demarco

by Michael Hiebert

E INSTEIN WOULD'VE HATED this place.
The *Well, In Theory*: for legal reasons, the bar
travels at the speed of light, which makes docking hell,
but also keeps the authorities away. Because of the
simple impossibility of the whole thing, normal regulations don't apply to an establishment in this sort of
time/space frame. At least, that's the theory. In reality,
nobody's bothered to question it and any sort of refute
would be so wrapped up in red tape that, by the time
any decision was passed down from the Intragalactic
Supreme Court, all involved would have disappeared
into the nearest wormhole never to be heard from
again.

It is here that Tara Lynn Boysienne, junior reporter
for the *Quasar Weekly Gazetteer*, has agreed to meet
Zydego. She has never met him and knows him only
from a brief conversation they shared on the Intragalactic Exchange where he agreed to be interviewed,

providing it was on his terms. Zydego claims to have not only known the legendary Favio deMarco, but also to have intimate details illuminating the recent debacle that ended his life.

Ah, Favio deMarco: adventurer, space pirate, mercenary, womanizer and—depending on who you ask, of course—all-around scoundrel. Simple mention of the name is enough to bring either chills or giggles depending upon which sort of company you keep. It can make both grown men and young women squirm for entirely different reasons. Or, if you're in the habit of keeping with members of the GLEP (Galactic Law Enforcement Police), or someone involved in BOCA (Big Organized Crime Association), it might bring eyefuls of dollar signs as hands are greedily rubbed together in dreams of collecting the huge bounty that's on deMarco's head.

But, alas, all this came to an end eighteen months ago, when Favio deMarco officially disappeared off everyone's long-range scanners. After failing in his bizarre attempt to slaughter two hundred thousand orphans at the space station Cat's Cradle, deMarco took his own life. It's an event still wrapped in controversy and littered with rumors.

Some say it was a setup; that deMarco was double-crossed in a deadly plan that resulted in his death. If that's true, someone must have truly thought he was more valuable dead than alive, and that's hard to believe considering the price one could collect for bringing him in. If this is true, whoever did it was a mastermind, and it is doubtful the culprit will ever be uncovered.

Tara Lynn set up this meeting with Zydego because Zydego's story is different than the rest. He claims to have been a close personal friend of deMarco and insists he has information that will not only illuminate exactly what happened out there at Cat's Cradle but will also prove deMarco is not even dead. Indeed, he insists that the galaxy's most revered man is alive and in hiding, waiting out the time until he can prove his innocence.

Tara Lynn, of course, believes absolutely none of this, but, hell—it'll make good copy. And so that's why she's here; standing outside the *Well, In Theory,* wondering what she should do next.

She gets the feeling this is the type of bar one cannot just saunter into, if for no other reason than because the street outside would have infinite mass when accelerated to the speed of light. But that problem she already averted by taking a Steller Cab.

Still there's the issue of *blending*; of being an invisible connection to her story. Most people in her field walk into a place like this silently screaming, "I'm With the Press," and it all goes bad. Luckily for Tara Lynn, she's not like most reporters. She has the sort of body that—when dressed up right—stops a clock (that is, if clocks actually ran in a bar traveling at the speed of light, which they don't).

So, she takes a deep breath and high-heels into the establishment, taking a seat at the bar. It's not long after she drapes one fishnetted leg over the other and hikes up her purple plastic skirt that someone plunks down on the stool beside her.

"You Zydego?" she asks.

He nods, eyes like slits, as if he's expecting someone at anytime to jump him. "That is who I am," he says. "Zydego." He speaks quietly with a heavy accent.

Tara Lynn opens her Dynamic Relational encrypted-data Wallet (her DReW, as it's otherwise called) and places it on the bar between them to digitally record their conversation. She'd already cleared this with him ahead of time, and he said he didn't mind although now it spawns a series of back-and-forth glances across the establishment.

"You okay?" Tara Lynn asks.

"I am now," Zydego says. "You just can never be too careful about who might be—" and he whispers the last word, "—listening. You know?"

"I know," she says. She is drawn to his chiseled good looks that are still evident despite his eyes, which he keeps narrow and shifty as he talks. And, my God, when was the last time he shaved? Five days ago? She didn't think she liked that sort of thing.

Or maybe she was wrong . . .

"So," she asks, "you said you know what happened to deMarco at Cat's Cradle?"

"Yes," he says as the barmaid places a purple drink in front of him. "And it all started here, at the *Well, In Theory*. Right here, at this very bar, in almost these

108

exact seats, the night Favio deMarco was asked to go on the last job *he ever did*."

Except, when Zydego says it, it sounds far more romantic. More like: "Vus asked to go on zee last job he ever deed." So romantic, Tara Lynn finds the whole package sitting on the seat beside her quite alluring and listening to him continue his story leaves her more than a little (shall vee say?) "excited." And continue, Zydego does:

"Are you the famous—or shall I make that, infamous—Favio deMarco?" the woman asked. She had beautiful legs, like a giraffe. Long and tapered. Yellow and spotted.

"That really depends on who's asking," deMarco said, lifting his cosmozitini and taking a sip. When he returned the glass to the table, the drink had left the most exquisite purple line of foam above his upper lip.

The barmaid blows her nose into her dirty dishrag, interrupting the story. Tara Lynn and Zydego stare at her standing there, puffy eyed and sad. She is chubby and wearing a red peasant dress with ties crisscrossing up her ample cleavage; the type you'd find back on Earth, in England, a long, long time ago. "He loved cosmozitinis," she weeps into her rag. "Oh, how he loved them. He would drink them by the bucket."

Zydego glances back at Tara Lynn. "Shall I go on?"

Despite Zydego's obvious embellishment and flair for the dramatic, he's a captivating storyteller, and so she nods and says, "Please."

So the woman sitting beside deMarco asked, "What if it's me? What if I'm the one asking?" As she said it, she slid her empty glass in front of Favio deMarco. Beneath it was a crisp bank draft, drawn on a Noytorian intragalactic bank account. Noytorian accounts, as you know, are completely untraceable. Pure, unadulterated mucho deniro.

Cocking a stylish eyebrow, deMarco gently pushed the glass aside and read the draft. "Five thousand credits?"

"And ten more on satisfactory execution of the task."

DeMarco's eyes narrowed. "Who are you working for? Who is asking to hire me?"

The woman tossed her head, her long brass earrings jangling against her neck. "That's not part of the deal." She smiled. "Five thousand now, ten more on completion."

But deMarco was suave, and he pushed the note back. "Two things," he said. "First, you haven't even told me what the job is, and, second, what would ever make me believe you will be around to pay me the second part?"

Ah, but the sexy, yellow-skinned, spotted woman with the most intriguing bustline was relentless. She pushed the check back to deMarco. "First," she said, "you will be given cargo to be delivered to a specified location. Just drop off the cargo, and return. The cargo will be sealed in a carbozantium box, and its contents will be unknown to you or anyone else you might encounter. This is for your own safety as well as ours. You will be given the coordinates of the drop point upon acceptance of our agreement."

DeMarco nodded, with a grim smile. "And what about my second point? How do I know I'll ever see you again?"

Her auburn lips spread into a smile. "Second, I know without doubt that this five thousand credits is at least a magnitude larger than any other payment you've ever received for any job. You would be a fool not to do the job for just the first payment alone."

And this was absolutely true. "So, why don't I just take the money and run?" deMarco asked.

"Because you're greedy. You're a pirate. And besides," the woman said, uncrossing her legs and recrossing them the other way. "If you did that, you would never get to see me again." She leaned over, her wet lips brushing gently against his cheek, and whispered, "Do we have a deal?"

DeMarco thought for a beat and then took the credit note, folded it once, and put it in the inside pocket of his syntholeather heavily buckled flight jacket with the studded collar.

"Good choice," she said.

"Where's the cargo and the destination?"

"The cargo is, in fact, ready to be loaded onto your ship outside. The coordinates for the destination, you *will find etched into that drinking glass." She pointed at her glass, the one she had pushed over atop the cashier's check. "When you have completed your mission, I will contact you again."*

DeMarco lifted the glass and held it up to the light, unfortunately the wrong way, and the final few drops of Gargarian Ale inside ran down into his eye, momentarily blinding him. He wiped it clear with his wrist-studded-leather-gloved finger and tilted the glass the other way. Sure enough, as the neon and acytologen lights of the bar reflected off the glass, he could make out a map etched delicately on the bottom. "This is absolutely amazing," he said, turning back to the woman.

But she was gone.

Two men approach the table, pulling Lynn from Zydego's story. One man is tall and skinny and, judging by the double mouth, probably Karëësian. The other might be human; it's hard to tell because his ears taper into a subtle point that may or may not be a birth defect.

"You mind if we listen?" the tall one asks.

"We *love* Favio deMarco," the short one says. And as he says it, they both put their hands on their chests and look at the bar's ceiling. Tara Lynn follows their gaze to find nothing there but black light effects and a disturbing red stain.

Tara Lynn picks up on the verb tense. "Love?" she asks them. "Love and not *loved*? So you believe he's not dead? You think Mr. deMarco is alive still somewhere and can still be loved?"

The short ugly one looks straight into her eyes, well, as straight as he can given the slight penchant one of his has for wandering. "We don't *think* it, toots, we know it. Favio deMarco *is* alive." The other grunts in agreement.

Zydego considers the two newcomers and then to Tara Lynn, says: "I don't mind if they stay. Providing you don't, Miss Boiseemantalatitipickijun . . . ?" He trails off and Tara Lynn gets the feeling he's completely forgot her name. But she doesn't care, she just wants the story. And so she shakes her head and asks him to continue.

And Zydego does.

DeMarco paid for his drink, flipping the barmaid a hundred giba-cent tip.

He left the bar to find two men in the shadows waiting beside his ship, The OverAchiever. *Beside them was a square metal box, measuring maybe a meter in all three directions. Upon seeing deMarco come out, the men folded into the darkness and disappeared.*

The crate was heavy. It was made of carbozantium— one of the strongest substances known to—well, to anyone. The crate alone was worth a small fortune; probably a good percentage of the value of his ship, he observed while dragging, pushing, and prodding the thing up the loading ramp and into The Overachiever.

Strangely, the bay doors were unsecured, but de-

*Marco's memory of activating the ships' security proce-
dure upon landing was fuzzy at best. He had imbibed
a few interesting beverages onboard before docking.
And this wasn't the first time he'd forgotten to lock
her up.*

"I heard he'd had an entire barrel of Yintok Polar
Wine before docking," the tall double-mouthed
stranger standing at the table says, yanking Tara Lynn
out of Zydego's entrancing cadence and back into the
reality of the bar around her.

"What's that?" Zydego asks.

"Yintok Polar Wine? Why it's simply the most
expensive—"

"No, I mean what is it you said just now?"

"Oh, that Favio deMarco left his craft unsecure because he had drank an entire barrel of Yintok—"

"Are you *sure* it was Yintok?" the other interjects.
"I'm quite certain I heard Grayland Port. *Bottles* of
Grayland. Four dozen of them."

"It doesn't matter," Zydego says.

"Well, it matters a little," the first man says.

"It matters quite a lot, I'd say," the second man
says.

"Does it matter to you?" Zydego asks Tara Lynn.

She shakes her head. "Not in the least."

Zydego narrows his eyes even more than usual at
the two newcomers, warning them against more
words. "Shall I go on?" he asks Tara Lynn.

She checks her DReW—everything's recording fine. "Please do."

So, DeMarco quickly laid in a course with his shipboard computer. He had the new cargo strapped safely to the bridge deck floor of The OverAchiever. *He spent most of the trip through lightspeed using the carbozantium crate as a foot rest. His destination? The Quee Lo Quee.*

Now, in case you don't know, the Quee Lo Quee is one of the nastiest areas of the galaxy—a good area to stay away from unless you happen to be in the market for something you can't get anyplace else. Or, of course, if someone offers to pay you fifteen thousand Noytorian intragalactic credits to fly into it and drop something off.

Favio deMarco was not that unaccustomed with being in the Quee Lo Quee. It wasn't somewhere he spent a huge amount of time, but he knew his way around.

Only this time, things were different—because this time, Favio deMarco wasn't actually in the Quee Lo Quee at all. It was a fact he knew almost immediately.

You see, he hadn't left the ship's entryway unsecured at all. While he was in the bar being given his mission by the yellow-skinned enchantress, someone had broken in and reprogrammed the shipboard computer's entire telemetry system to make him think he was in the Quee Lo.

"Computer," he said. *"Report current position."*

The computer came back with coordinates matching those transcribed on the bottom of the drinking glass. All available information coming from the ship's computer showed him to be exactly where he needed to be to drop off the cargo: a few parsecs out from the central rim of the *Quee Lo Quee*, in perfect geosync orbit around a small moon belonging to a midsize gas giant planet, 800,000 kilometers from a yellow dwarf star that was the centerpiece for a five-planet system.

But when he actually checked outside, through the realtime viewscreens of The OverAchiever, *he saw only a background sea of stars and an ancient space station that looked as though it spent the last three millennia being bombarded by stray comets. The moon, the planet, the star—everything he should be seeing—were disturbingly absent.*

Being the expert computer systems engineer that he was, deMarco quickly discovered someone had not only tampered with his telemetry systems while he had been courting the yellow-skinned diva in the bar, they had also hard-wired OverAchiever *to launch her entire weapons phalanx at the space station. The ten-minute countdown had begun the second deMarco pulled out of warp.*

DeMarco's gaze left the computer and snapped back to the viewscreen.

He recognized the space station. It was *Cat's Cradle.*

Cat's Cradle: the galaxy's largest free-orbiting orphanage, full of hundreds of thousands of homeless

children just waiting for a chance to be loved. Just look-
ing for a home.

Zydego takes a moment to dab a tear from his eye
with the napkin from under his glass. The tall Karëësian standing beside her has tears streaming down his
face and the lips of his top mouth are trembling. Tara
Lynn passes him her napkin. He thanks her.

"Sorry about that," Zydego says. "I just get a little
emotional at that part."

So Favio deMarco learned the truth: that he, peace-
loving, justice-upholding, morally-perfect citizen that he
was, posed an imminent danger to the lives of hundreds
of thousands of orphans. The only thing between him
and horrific tragedy was his ability to reprogram the
ship's computer in the next ten minutes.

No, nine minutes, the central system reminded him.
Nine minutes and counting.

Nine minutes to break through the security wall and
rewrite the weapons logic.

It was far too close for comfort. Almost impossible,
maybe entirely impossible. Either way, it became offi-
cially, bona-fide card-carrying completely impossible
fifty-seven seconds later at the eight-minute mark when
the ship's self-destruct procedure automatically initi-
ated.

Things hadn't improved.

Not only was he now about to kill hundreds of thou-
sands poor orphans, he was also going to kill himself

in the process. That is, unless he could break into his computer, do the reprogramming of the weapon systems and disable the self-destruct countdown all in eight minutes.

No, wait, scratch that. Seven minutes, ten seconds.

DeMarco began keying information into the terminal as though he were a cyborg. His fingers danced a vicious tango with the touch-screen entry pad as he attempted every conceivable hack combination he could think of to bypass the new security gate.

A thousand meters out, Cat's Cradle knew about his presence, of course. They even saw his weapons systems go online, and their sensors were completely privy that deMarco's targeting system had everything trained directly on them. The orphanage had no defenses of its own, so it immediately sent a distress call, shouting out in all directions for anyone anywhere to come and save the floating raft of poor defenseless parentless kids who were actually very good little children, simply victims of circumstance.

Although deMarco heard these tragic pleas, there was little he could do about them while he was trapped inside his tiny death ship.

At T-minus six minutes, the red alert lights along the perimeter of the bridge began to flash annoyingly. It made it even harder to work but deMarco was relentless. He would stop at nothing short of death to save those kids.

Unfortunately, it looked as though death was going to be the big decider on this one.

And then, things got even worse.

Whoever broke into The OverAchiever's *computer system and rewrote the entire weapons system and keyed the self-destruct initiator to kick in wanted to make sure their task would be successful. So it was now that they played their last ace.*

Three aces.

Not a perfect poker hand, but a good one.

A damn good one.

Too good in a game like this.

The straps wrapped around the carbozantium crate he was so generously paid to transport suddenly sprung free and the latch clicked open, allowing a SaX2 Destroyer Droid to pop out from the top. And this Destroyer Droid seemed particularly pissed off.

"Damn!" deMarco cursed and, in a fit of anger, drove his fist into the main systems entry terminal with so much force it shattered, sending sparks flying. It was a stupid thing to do. Now he had absolutely no way to stop the weapons from firing, no way to stop his ship from destructing.

And worse, he hurt his hand in the process.

The pointy-eared human pipes in: "It was so bad, I hear he had to get a cyber hand installed to replace it."

The Karëësian agrees. "And it cost half his five thousand credits to do it."

As Zydego reaches for his glass, Tara Lynn notices his hand is covered in a leather glove. Probably smart on his part. If half this story is true, Zydego is risking a lot divulging it. The last thing he wants to do is leave any DNA evidence or something as simple as fingerprints behind as truth. As it is, she wonders if anybody is going to believe a word of this story when it hits the press.

But then, that doesn't matter. That part rarely matters.

The SaX2 Destroyer Droid fired a high-frequency drill laser at deMarco who yanked his bloody hand from the shattered terminal in just enough time to dive out of the way and tuck into a barrel roll. The purple blast buzzed by him, missing by mere inches, but it did manage to tear a wound into The OverAchiever's *main starboard bulkhead.*

Damn. It wasn't just himself he had to worry about. He also had to worry about his ship.

Scampering quickly behind the weapons targeting system, deMarco peered out cautiously. The Droid was scanner-sweeping the interior of the bridge, mapping the environment in his neural robotic brain, something that would make killing deMarco and his ship much simpler.

And of course, deMarco's forehead jutting into view from the steel instrument panel stuck out like a toaster attached to an ottoman.

"Damn!" he shouted—this time out loud—as he ducked back, just barely avoiding a blast that would have separated his head cleanly from the rest of his

body. Instead, the energy drove into the back of the ship, making the entire craft shudder for an instant before the ballast controls automatically kicked in and compensated for the change.

The Droid went hyperdex.

Eight legs sprang from beneath its conical body and now it ran and leaped throughout the interior of the bridge, bouncing from floor to ceiling and wall to wall like some deranged flea. Too fast for deMarco to keep track of its position. He grabbed his knees, pulling them up to the fetal position, and closed his eyes, hoping for the best.

One shot roared over top of him. He could feel the heat on the top of his head and smell his hair burning. Then another missed his right arm by barely a nanometer. It was followed by yet another, laser shot after laser shot, each one barely missing and instead slamming hard into the side of The Overachiever. *And each time, the ship would jerk suddenly until the onboard systems managed to compensate and bring her to normal.*

Hold it. That's something he hadn't thought of.

The stabilizing systems.

The stabilizing systems weren't mission critical systems; they could be accessed without having to go through the weapons system. That is, if deMarco had a way to access the computer now that he'd put his fist through the terminal.

And there was: the manual keyboard—a redundant data entry system installed on the ship for contingency plans. Something put in place for those incredibly rare off chances that the touch displays on the main terminal became inoperable. When he purchased The Over-Achiever, *deMarco tried to get them to uninstall the thing so he could save four or five galactic temple credits.*

Now he was quite happy the three-headed salesman disagreed but instead threw in a pair of olive-green Jeconsta fuzzy dice.

The manual keyboard was located (very inconveniently, deMarco realized) in the back of his captain's chair. There was a corriar-plastic latch that twisted, allowing it to drop down like an old-fashioned tray table.

Another bolt of energy whizzing by his ear made him stop laughing. He ducked and ran for the seat back while the SaX2 took the opportunity to snap across the floor in a blur, as though it were being bounced off of a Sniper Pinball Banger. DeMarco watched the blur train its laser rifle straight at him as it went by.

He tucked into a roll and slammed into something hard, relieved to find it was the back of his captain's chair. The impact unjarred the keyboard and it fell open onto his head, momentarily dazing him. But deMarco would not be abated.

With rapid fire, his fingers danced over the keys, taking the ballasts offline. He looked up at the main display terminal where the weapons system were counting down in a big bold Arial Sans Serif font: Thirty seconds to engagement.

Thirty seconds until hundreds of thousands of children were murdered by Favio deMarco's ship.

He knew what he had to do.

The main bulkhead ran across the front of the bridge and it was there that a blast from the Destroyer Droid would cause the most spin. It wouldn't be easy; the whole thing had to be timed perfectly. If the computer had any time to sense a change in The OverAchiever's *impulse vector, it would simply modify the targeting vector accordingly. It would compensate for the variations and slaughter hundreds of thousands of orphans.*

Blow them into bits.

Blast them to smithereens.

Powderize them into—

The Droid unloaded another cylinder of laser blast, and this time deMarco wasn't so quick. The laser clipped the side of his leg, tearing a layer of skin and muscle from whatever that part of his leg was called. His calf, deMarco thought.

He scrambled awkwardly to the air lock, limping like an injured crab as he tried desperately to keep the weight off his hurt leg. But the Droid was already coming around for another shot, bouncing between the walls in the corner and spinning its targeting systems. And this time, there was nowhere for deMarco to hide.

The main terminal flashed down to ten seconds. De-Marco could hear the whining of the Droid's laser charger and smell the ubiquitous burnt-rubber odor of the Hi-Temp™ nuclear fusion reactors as the thing screamed toward him.

His muscles tightened, and he gritted his teeth against the pain as he prepared. His body went rigid, and his muscles wound up like springs as he waited for his moment.

And then, with six seconds to go, deMarco leaped straight over the Droid's head. The maneuver thoroughly confused the SaX2 and as deMarco landed painfully in a clump on the metal floor of his ship, he watched the countdown, menacingly blurring numbers in his peripheral vision.

5.

4.

Wait for it.

3.

Wait . . .

2.

DeMarco mustered every bit of energy he had left to dive across the front of the bridge, just as the Droid figured out what had happened and vertically spun in some strange Olympic swimmer-move. Its guns already charged, it unloaded from barely two meters away, but deMarco had already used his palm to push off the floor and send himself into a parabolic cartwheel that landed him behind the energy cell arrays. The shots missed him and instead thundered against the main bulkhead, sending The OverAchiever *into a slow forward topple like some sort of sick whale.*

The ballasts didn't right the ship this time and the SaX2 Destroyer Droid was flung against the ceiling, a cymbal crash of legs and lenses. Then it fell to the floor with a thud. Dead.

The OverAchiever *shot her entire weapons phalanx*

out into space. Out toward a defenseless floating or-phanage full of hundreds of thousands of sweet inno-cent children. The blast radius from the explosion violently shook the ship, throwing deMarco across the floor, slamming him painfully into the main bulkhead.

And then . . .

nothing.

Just silence.

Pulling himself to his feet, deMarco scanned around him as his ship slowly spun. He panicked. It was proba-bly his imagination, but in his mind he had just heard the cries of hundreds of thousands of babies being sud-denly stifled as though they had been simultaneously smothered by nuclear pillow explosions.

He had failed. Cat's Cradle was no more.

Or so he thought until it rolled up into view through the main viewscreen! The orphanage wasn't blown to tiny itsy bits, it was alive and well. DeMarco had saved every single child aboard that space station.

"Self-Destruct Module Announcement," the detached disturbingly transgendered-sounding computer voice announced, "two minutes to ship detonation."

"Oh, yeah," deMarco sighed. "Forgot about that bit." But he didn't care. He had saved those children's lives and that was all that really mattered. He walked clumsily across the rising and falling floor to the man-ual keyboard, now lying lifelessly on the floor, its cable stretched like a hangman's noose after the floorboards were kicked out.

With a few keystrokes he brought the ballast systems

back online and The OverAchiever *made a violent creak as it snapped to Fenzenzium ecliptic-normal. Behind deMarco, the Droid that was once in the crate showered to the floor like a toppled bucket of nuts and bolts. In front of him, the now empty carbozantium crate slammed down to the floor like a hammer on a spike.*

The crate gave deMarco yet another idea.

Struggling, he pushed, pulled, and dragged it to the air lock bay door and pressed the big green access button on the sand-blasted panel beside it.

Nothing happened.

The air lock was stuck. Damn. Damn. Damn! The ship was about to blow up and the air lock was stuck closed.

"Damn this ship!" deMarco cursed, fighting the urge to follow it with "Damn it all to hell!" In anger, he raised his boot and kicked the button with what little strength he had left. His foot went through it, into the wall. Electricity leaped up his legs, jarring his entire body into a frenzied vibration.

His jaw locked. Blinding blue-white that shook through him like the heat from a supernova and then, the electroshock fired him straight across the deck of his ship, slamming into the side of a bulkhead just as the Destroyer Droid's laser blasts had done a moment before.

Barely conscious, deMarco lifted his eyelids and saw the act was successful. Just as the ship's computer announced there was but one minute left before it blew

everything to smithereens, deMarco watched the air
lock door slowly dilate open four meters away. But he
couldn't move. His leg, first clipped by the shot from
the Destroyer Droid, was now so badly injured he sus-
pected it might never work properly again.

As if on cue, the two strangers interrupt the story.
Tara Lynn had been waiting for it, as that was the
longest they had allowed Zydego to talk without piping up.

The ear-challenged human spoke first. It was about
deMarco's injured leg. "I heard he'd mangled it so
bad they had to replace it with a mechanical one."

The Karëësian, of course, followed. "As did I. And
it cost the other half of his five thousand credits."

Just then, a cacophony of sound wails from the
JuKe.Di.giBox across the room. One of those horrible
Aguarina trance pieces that sound like a bunch of fish
playing the handsaw underwater. Tara Lynn glances
back over her shoulder and sure enough, the woman
(if it's a woman) standing (if she's standing) in front
of the JuKe.Di.giBox has a huge dorsal fin and four
purple antenna with bright green tops.

Beside Tara Lynn, the barmaid breaks into tears yet
again. "I am so sorry," she sobs, "but I just remembered Favio deMarco's favorite song on that box: selection number 487C."

The Karëësian nods sympathetically. "I know the
one. 'Just Searchin' For a Simple Space Girl (To Hem
This Black Hole in My Heart).' "

The barmaid looks up at Tara Lynn, blotting her tears with a dirty rag. "Do you know that one, love?"

Yeah, she knows it. One of those sappy hurting songs that are always coming out of the Borpit Constellation. They're always about pilots with old broken starships and dead AI programs lost in hyperspace somewhere, wandering the universe forever in search of their true loves or some sort of pet with a lifespan longer than theirs. *Favio deMarco liked that crap? Let me guess. On top of everything else, deep down inside was a hopeless romantic, too. Geez.*

But before Tara Lynn has a chance to think anything more about it, Zydego assumes his tale.

Laying there, amid the rubble and broken circuits that used to be his beautiful ship, deMarco was bathed in the flashing red lights counting down his doom with every tick.

His doom.

His doom.

His doom.

"Sorry," Zydego says.

With his doom anxiously pending, Favio deMarco once again marshaled every bit of courage he had left. He gathered the strength of his soul, pulling it from deep down in his gut, and rose to his feet.

Limping deathly slowly, forcing his legs forward one

at a time like one of those wounded zombies at the end of those Steller Grav Splatter movies, he stumbled forward as the ship's internal alarm rang out, announcing only fifteen seconds left between now and the end of everything.

Woop! Woop! It rang in his head as he hefted the carbozantium box, rolling it so that the top faced upward.

Ten seconds until kablooey as he leaned his weight against the box, pushing it slowly forward, sliding it on the metal floor of The OverAchiever *toward the air lock.*

With eight seconds left, he keyed a four-second delay into the main outer hull door and stepped into the carbozantium box. He squeezed his knees against his chin, making himself childlike, barely fitting into its confines. Then he pulled down the lid, sealing it.

Carbozantium. The strongest substance known to man and everyone else deMarco had ever had the pleasure of running into on his travels. But the question was: was it strong enough?

Years seemed to go by as he squatted there in the cramped darkness. An eternity of five seconds ticked off as he mentally calculated how much air the box could hold given that he was taking up most of the physical volume.

Not much, he decided.

Probably ten minutes. Maybe not even that.

Outside the box, he knew the outside hull doors had

*opened as he felt the vacuum of space suck the box
from the ship's floor. Ten minutes, he thought as he
tumbled gently out into open space.*

Ten minutes.

*When you're used to having a whole lifetime left, it's
not enough. Especially if you spend it crammed into a
one-square-meter box.*

*Only in this particular moment it turned out to be
exactly enough.*

*Nine and a half minutes later, deMarco was tractor-
beamed into the freight compartment of the Yukovean
ship* Immortal Monkey, *a space freighter that had received the distress call from Cat's Cradle ten minutes
earlier and had just come out of warp. As soon as
they saw the carbozantium crate floating listlessly out
in space, they brought it onboard.*

*It was worth almost as much as deMarco's ship, and
they would have salvaged that if it hadn't exploded into
pieces before they arrived.*

*They were surprised to find deMarco inside the box,
but he managed to negotiate his freedom in exchange
for the crate.*

"And that," Zydego smiles, "is pretty much all
she wrote."

Tara Lynn regards him for a beat and then asks,
"So, if what you're saying's true and deMarco is still
alive, why doesn't he just come forward and explain
what happened? Why all the cloak and dagger
nonsense."

Unbelievably, Zydego's eyes narrow even more. "He can't. Too many people want him dead, especially now. He can trust no one. His very name has been blemished. The public believes he purposely tried to blow up a space station full of innocent, starving orphans."

"I don't think they were starving," says the human.

"They were starving," says Zydego.

The interview is drawing to a close, but Tara Lynn wants more. The story is big, but it can be bigger. She just needs a few more facts. "So, if you know all this, can you set up an interview with deMarco?" she asks. "Where is he hiding?"

Zydego shrugs. "Nobody knows."

"I heard he got one of the galaxy's best surgeons to give him a brand new identity," says the human.

"And how did he pay for that?" the Karëësian asks. "After the hand and the leg?"

The barmaid returns, still sniffling. "Hardly wouldn't matter," she says. "Nobody really knew what he looked like anyway cuz of that mask he always wore."

Puzzled, Tara Lynn looks to Zydego. "Wait. He always wore a mask?"

"My time has run out," Zydego says. "I'm afraid I must be leaving."

Tara Lynn snaps her DreW closed and drops it into her pocket. "Thank you for agreeing to meet me and telling me the story. How much do I owe you?"

"Not a giba-cent," he says. "Just print the truth. If

131

not for me—" He lays his fist on his chest and looks to the ceiling. The other two follow suit. "—then do it for Favio deMarco."

Zydego stands and limps to the door. Just before disappearing outside, he pulls off one of his gloves, revealing a hand carved with scars. With a thud he whaps the top of the JuKe.Di.giBox with his fist, halting the warbling fish sounds emanating from the machine dead in their tracks.

Strains of steel guitars fill the ensuing silence as the music is replaced with selection 487C—"Just Searchin' For a Simple Space Girl (To Hem This Black Hole in My Heart)."

Zydego disappears out of the bar. Behind her, Tara Lynn hears the barmaid gasp into her dirty towel.

Her story, it seems, just got much bigger.

Tara Lynn Boysienne, junior reporter for the *Quasar Weekly Gazetteer*, smiles.

A Union Against All Odds

by David DeLee

THE ENTRYWAY SENSED their presence and dissolved in a shimmer of green light allowing them entry into the bar, along with a cloying gaseous swirl of the outside Altarian-atmosphere. Once they crossed the threshold the force shield winked back into place.

I watched 'em come in with a wary eye, and I knew from the start they was doomed. He was Humanoid. She was not.

With my left arms I wiped the bar down and swiped the paper credits and coins left behind by a hairy Tarantilyte into my tip trough under the bar. I selected two tumblers and set them on the bar with my right arms, filled them with ice, water, vodka and a splash of vermouth. Being quadra-limbed comes in handy when you're a barkeep at the Formex Bosh, a bustling gin-joint at the ass-end of the universe.

I slid the ancient Earth drinks across the teak bar to my Human customers: a male and a female. We didn't get many of them out here. They told me they were on their honeymoon. I didn't ask what that was.

My attention was back on my two newest arrivals as they made their way past the crowded bar. He put a furry, protective arm around her shelled carapace and she leaned into him, her compound eyes nervously reflecting everything around her.

All conversation in the joint stopped. A small pocket of gray-skinned, tri-ped Irys' in colorful ceremonial gowns scuttled back to give them room, a group of Altarastan maintenance workers playing Tingarbo paused their bets, even though the lights and bells of the gaming table continued to ring. All eyes were on the two of 'em, tracking 'em till they found an open booth at the back of the room and sat down.

This was gonna be trouble, I just knew it.

But, I thought, nothing a solid baseball bat or a laser blaster wouldn't handle. I gave a quick glance at my equalizers strapped under the bar and within easy reach. The bat came from an Earthen who passed this way several years ago, the blaster had been my brother's 'fore he was killed. I tossed the wet bar rag over my shoulder and pulled out an order pad.

An uneasy sense of normalcy slowly returned to the bar. At the booth I pulled a stylus from the back of my ear. With it poised over my order pad, I wiped down the table with my other hand and rearranged the assortment of stacked condiments with my third one. "Welcome to Formex Bosh. What can I get ya?"

The Diter-atelur, that was the he, glanced over to

the Thysanrinae with his yellow-and-black pupillia eyes. "Darling?"

She plucked at the wiry brown hair poking out like short spikes around her compound eyes. They glistened, reflecting back the bar's swirling lights in a thousand honeycombs of color. Her antennae quivered while she rubbed her top two twiglike legs together to make a low, twittering sound.

"What are they having?" she asked, pointing a jointed leg toward the Humans staring back at us.

I raised one side of my thick, graying unibrow. "They're called martinis. It's an ancient Earth drink. Don't get much call for 'em out here."

The whiskers around her bulbous brown head twitched excitedly, what passed for a mouth spread into a wide smile. "I want one." She looked at her companion. "Can I get one, Scoyn?"

"Of course, Phyura," Scoyn said. "You can have anything you want."

"They're pretty strong," I warned.

"Get her what she wants, Hye, then maybe the filthy twig will get outta here." The insult carried over the stringy *Al-tar* music from the adjacent booth. Suth, one of four Diter-nicolet hunters sitting there—regulars—had his thick, hairy arm slung over the back of his seat. His tusks gleamed wetly.

They were just in from a hunt. High from the orgy of the kill, they were drunk, mean, and looking for trouble.

I gauged the distance from there to the laser blaster

under the bar. "Settle down, Suth. I don't want no trouble in here."

He snarled. "Then don't let in the swamp maggots."

"Yeah. This used to be a respectable place." This from Suth's younger and stupider brother Jun.

"Both you, cut it out," I warned. "Or it'll be you twos out in the fog on your furry asses. Got it?"

Neither of 'em said anything, deciding instead to go back to their smoldering drinks. I turned back to the Thy and the Diter-atelur. I didn't apologize for their behavior, I drew the line at that, but I gave 'em a look that said it would be okay.

With the stylus on my order pad, I said, "A vodka martini. What about you?"

"Same," he said. "No, wait." He glanced over to Suth's table. "Those are Kuma Volcanoes, aren't they?"

I nodded with a sideways glance. Four half-finished drinks, along with eight empties and the ravaged remains of picked-apart beetle nuts, some of their little legs still squirming, littered the table.

"Strong stuff," I said, marking the order down. "Don't know many -atelur's willing to try 'em."

"My Scoyn is very brave," Phyura said.

Yeah, right. "Anything to eat?"

They shook their heads. I thought about offering to move 'em, but there was nowhere else in the crowded bar to move 'em to. Instead, I tucked my stylus behind my ear, gave the table a final swipe, slipped my pad

136

under the waistband of my apron, and gave Suth and his table another warning look before heading back to the bar.

There, I mixed the drinks—glasses, ice, liquid from tilted bottles—my four arms twirling in a frenzy. I noticed the two Humans watching me, a bemused look on the male's face, a concerned one on the female. Her eyes kept darting over her shoulder to the table of -nicolet hunters.

"That's amazing," the male said. He was referring to my four arms. I was used to that. What amazed me was how any species got along with only two.

"What was that all about?" the female asked, her interest focused across the room, not on me.

I told her I'd talk to 'em when I got back.

I delivered the drinks, took another round to Suth and his underlings, then returned to the bar, making sure the rest of my customers were set along the way. They were.

Taking advantage of the brief respite, I used the power shooter to fill a glass with water and drank it down. Idly, I wiped away the water rings on the bar, dunked a few dirty glasses in the sudsy wash water, and pulled dry glasses from the drying compartment.

"You were, um, going to tell us about those guys," the female urged. She indicated the Diter-nicolet table with a sly nod of her head. Her eyes were wide, bright, and full of curiosity.

And blue. That was creepy.

"Yes," the male said. He rose from his stool, leaned

over the bar and extended a hand toward me. I recognized the gesture, a Human offer of greeting. "Robert."

I shook his hand. "I am called Hye."

The female offered her hand. "Jane."

Humans are warm-blooded creatures, their flesh hot and soft. And while they came in many different skin shades, they were mind-numbingly similar in appearance.

"Those two?" I looked at Scoyn and Phyura while I wiped down glasses. "The male. He's Diter-atelur."

"Which one is that?" Robert asked. His two eyebrows—another Human oddity—moved together and his forehead wrinkled.

"The hairy gray one."

"Has a face like a weasel," Robert said.

The reference was lost on me.

"The other one, she's a Thysandrinae. Her people came from a planet that blew up 'bout a century ago. They had nowhere to go, so they invaded Diternia, the fourth planet in this system. They live in the soil, burrow into caves where it's dark. Like it damp and cold as a *bitych's*—" I cut myself off, my eyes sliding over Jane's form.

She wore a sleeveless, yellow one-piece, had it unzipped in front, exposing the curve of her two breasts like some deformed circus freak. I know Human females are supposed to have only two, but why did they insist on advertising their shortcomings that way?

"Anyway," I said, "the Diter and the Thysandrinae

138

been at each other ever since. The *skent* of it is they've dragged most of the neighboring worlds into their war, too."

There was a shout from one of the hangar workers. He must of scored *Tingarbo*. Several of those around him pounded 'em on the back. One shouted, "A round, barkeep."

Returning to the bar, I continued my little history lesson for the curious Human tourists. "The Diter–Thy Conflict's been going on for centuries. The first immigrants were hunted down and exterminated. Those that survived were enslaved—"

"Slavery. That's horrible," Jane said.

I nodded without comment. An argument could be made either way. "In spite of Diter efforts to contain 'em, the Thy multiplied in numbers, in swarms. They staged peaceful protests at first. Then growing in number, and discontent, they became bolder, stronger. Soon revolts broke out all over Diternia, and then, organized and with enough weapons and off-world support, they declared all-out war. That was nearly a century ago. Over time, as the conflict worsened, more and more neighboring worlds were dragged into it."

"How?" Robert wanted to know. I refreshed his drink.

"Their own fault in a lot of cases. In war there's opportunity. Not all of this system's worlds are as economically secure as we here on Altar. We can afford to be neutral. But a lot of people joined the war effort, some as mercenaries, some as gunrunners and black market profiteers, others for misguided ideological or political reasons."

Like my brother.

"Protesters."

"Sure. Protesters, relief workers, thrill seekers, others with more determined Altartarian reasons."

Jane gave him a quizzical look. "You don't approve."

I shrugged and busied myself with straightening up behind the bar. The under-counter lights appeared very bright to me, too harsh. "Ideology belongs in the classroom, politics in the Senate Chambers. Not in the streets, not on the battlefield."

"How do you effect change, then?"

She was one of *them*. I'd heard Humans were like that. They've had world peace for hundreds of years. They can afford to be that altruistic. "Who says change is good?"

"Who says it's bad?" Jane countered.

"Depends on the change, I suppose."

"I suppose." She didn't sound convinced.

Robert sipped his drink, asked, "So why do those boar-faced ones have such a hard-on for the Diter and the Thy?"

" 'Cause they're Diter, too." Jane and Robert couldn't have been more shocked. No small wonder there, coming from a single-species world.

"They don't look anything alike," Robert said.

He'd referred to Scoyn as looking like a weasel. He was gray, skinny, frail-looking. Suth and the others, they were brown and thick, dark, and mean.

"They look like gorillas with tusks," Robert said.

Another meaningless reference. "The Diter have a three-caste system. The Diter-nicolets are the warrior sect. Rough people. Violent and brutal by almost everyone's standards. They enjoy fighting. They enjoy the war. The Diter-atelur are the philosophers: the politicians, educators, and healers."

I was out of clean glasses to put away, out of dirty glasses to wash. "With the recent peace talks, and the ongoing cease-fire, a lot of the Diter-nicolets see their way of life being threatened. They're afraid," I gave Jane a direct look, "of change. They stand to lose money as black market demands dry up. They are afraid their status, the prestige they currently enjoy, is evaporating as freelance mercenaries fall out of favor."

"And cross-species fraternization like that is frowned on," Jane guessed.

"It's consorting with the enemy. Easy to see how it enflames strong feelings; whets the appetite for vengeance, for revenge to atone for fallen brethren."

Robert twisted around in his seat to look over at the interspecies couple. "So what brought those two together?" he wondered out loud.

Jane followed his gaze. "Love."

I had my doubts. "War sympathizers, more like."

"You think?"

"War brings out the eleemosynary just as it brings out the patriot."

"And because one is humane, it means he's not patriotic?" Jane's voice rose in pitch, suddenly rich with passion. Two Symrians wrapped in colorful clothes down at the end of the bar looked up with alarm, their extended tongues dripping creamy *garsh* back into their lapping bowls.

She was eager to enter into a philosophical or political debate. I wasn't in the mood. "Some people, a minority, think the two species can coexist. They encourage interspecies relationships. They think it can lead to a single, peaceful society. Some even promote the comingling of the races: natural creation of a hybrid species."

"That's beautiful."

I shrugged. "If you say so."

"You make them welcome here," she said with a warm smile. "That's seems very altruistic of you. Yet, you harbor great resentment toward them."

I shrugged. "Altar's neutral territory. Everybody's welcome or I lose my charter. 'Sides, a Thy's credit's as good as anyone's. Excuse me. Need to see if they want more to drink."

With my pad in hand, my stylus and my bar rag in the others, I made my way back to Scoyn and Phyura. They had their hands clasped across the table, hairy paws over tiny trifingered stalks. They stared into each

142

other's eyes and had silly smiles on their faces. Her antennas twitched.

"Can I get you folks another round?"

"How about a round of leaves and twigs?" Suth called out over his shoulder from the next booth. "What do the Earthens call it, salad?"

"No, Suth, the Thy *is* a twig."

The others at the table laughed and slapped each other like the lame joke was the most hilarious thing they had ever heard before. The Thy's shiny carapace deepened to a bluish-silver.

"Let it go," I warned the young Thy and her escort, Scoyn. "There's four of 'em and they're already floating in booze. I don't want no trouble in here."

"If there's trouble," Scoyn said, "it will be because of them."

Tough talk from a politician, I thought, seeing in the dim light for the first time the diplomatic emblems each of them wore on their tunics. I should've known, yet most -atelur talked of hiding, of negotiating, not fighting. Perhaps there was something different 'bout this one.

"Please," Phyura said, squeezing his hands. "It's our special night."

"What night is that?" I asked, not caring at all, but I thought it would take his attention off Suth and his stupid brother. 'Sides, An -atelur fighting against a -nicolet, much less four of 'em, was beyond ridiculous, it was suicide.

"We were betrothed today."

A union between a Diter and Thy? I wondered how good I was at disguising my revulsion. "Congratulations . . . I guess. Next round's on me."

"Hey, how about a free one for us?" Suth called out. He looked around his table for encouragement. " 'Least we don't stink up the place like swamp slime."

The others, too witless to do anything else, laughed and egged him on. He slapped the table. "How 'bout it, Hye? Another round."

"Not tonight, Suth. You've had enough," I said.

Anger filled his face, and his snout turned up into an ugly sneer, revealing full gleaming white incisor fangs. He jumped up from the booth. Diter-nicolets were all short. Suth was no exception, coming up only to my chest, but he was wide and muscular, strong. I knew in a straight on one-on-one he'd take me down ten times to two.

His gloved hands fisted. The leather creaked and the metal studs encrusted with animal blood gleamed in the swirling, colorful lights splashing across the walls and floor. "You cutting me off, Hye?"

I was three steps and a leap over the bar away from my blaster. I'd anticipated trouble, but events were escalating faster than I thought they would. "No, Suth. One more, *then* I'm cutting you off. It's late and you got another hunt in the morning."

He held me hard with his yellow-and-black eyes.

The others at his table waited, tense, ready to strike

or settle back in for another drink. Whatever Suth led them to do.

I returned his deep, penetrating stare. Only a strong stance now would keep things from exploding out of control. For the first time that night all four of my arms were still. They quivered at the restraint of movement.

And then Suth grinned. He slapped my top arm heartily and laughed. "All right, then, Hye. One more round, and then we go." He turned to get the approval of the others. "One more round."

They whooped and cheered, banging the table triumphantly and chanted: "One more round, one more round."

I went back to the bar and whistled a sigh of relief under my breath. My arms grabbed for glasses and mixed the four volatile Kuma Volcanoes in record time. It was like I was on Croten stimulus pills.

"They're a scary bunch," Robert observed. He pushed his empty glass toward me. "When you have a chance. No rush."

My blaster and my bat hung within easy reach. I completed the drink order and considered jamming the blaster into my waist belt. I decided to wait.

I made the drinks for the Scoyn and Phyura as well, and distributed the drinks all around without further incident or exchanged words. The Diter-nicolets accepted them with grunts, snatching 'em from my hands almost before I could set them down. Scoyn and Phyura were more civilized. They thanked me with furtive glances, determined not to aggravate Suth, who was now spoiling for a fight.

"Tense, huh?" Robert said, accepting his martini and sliding another stack of credits toward me.

"Comes with the job." I exchanged the credits. Robert left the change. When he and Jane glanced over at the Diter-nicolets once more, I took the opportunity to palm the blaster and jam it down my waist at the small of my back without anyone noticing.

"You don't think much of a Diter–Thy coupling, do you?" Jane commented, refusing an offer to refill her drink.

"Unnatural, ask me," I said.

"Might help unify the planet."

"Might reignite festering animosity." Proof, in my mind, as evidenced by Suth and his hooligans' behavior. I didn't say that out loud.

"Coexistence is the way to go, I'd think." Robert downed his drink and slid the empty over for another.

A Human who could hold his liquor. I was impressed. I poured him another. "What would you know about it? Earth is a single-species world."

"Been at peace for four hundred years," Robert said with pride, like he was personally responsible for that.

"Wasn't always that way," Jane said. "We were worse than the Diter and the Thy. A history of wars, fought against ourselves."

"Over what?"

"You name it." Robert banged down his drink. "Land, religion, skin color."

"Skin color?" As arrogant as the Humans were now about peaceful coexistence, they came from that kind of violent history? I couldn't believe it.

"Yep. Even enslaved our own people, just 'cause their skin was too dark. We stole the land out from under natives who worked and lived off the land for centuries. We invaded countries when we disagreed with their choice of government or their religious faith."

"You joking?"

"I wish we were." Jane had an eye on Scoyn and Phyura. "The blending of the races helped us. Eventually, people weren't so white or so black, so red or so yellow. We were just people."

Scoyn had a hand across the table, stroking Phyura's head. She snuggled into his petting, her antenna quivering and her mouth made little sucking sounds. Three of her legs patted his hairy arm.

"I had a brother. Lost him to a land mine. Don't know whose it was, Diter or Thy. Don't matter much, I guess. Blew him up so bad there wasn't enough of his DNA to identify him proper like. Don't care much for either of 'em now, tell you the truth."

I don't know why I told 'em that. Felt like it had to be said, somehow.

"I'm sorry," Jane said. Robert nodded his condolence.

"Thanks, I guess. His own fault. Him and his damned causes. Bleeding heart, he was." I wiped at my nose with the back of my hand.

"He believed in the Thy's plight?"

"Yeah. Just like I suspect you would, too, girl."

She smiled. "Probably would." She slid her empty glass at me. "Think I'll take that refill now."

I mixed her drink. "On the house."

"Get your hand off her, you treasonous, demented *elate!* What's wrong with your own kind?"

I recognized Suth's drunken slurring without having to look up. When I did, I saw he was standing over Scoyn, had pulled the young -atelur's arm away from Phyura. Scoyn twisted around in his seat to defend himself, to try and get out. Jun was halfway over the booth, holding him down.

"Shaz-damn!" I leaped over the bar 'cause it was faster, landing about a half meter away from the confrontation. Already drawing the blaster from my back, I crossed the distance between us and grabbed Suth's arm. I pulled him back.

He wasn't surprised to see me.

"You defending this *elate*, Hye?"

"Ain't my stance to defend 'em, just protecting my place of business. Take it outside, Suth." I kept the blaster pointed at the floor, hoping to deescalate the situation but wanting Suth and his cronies to see it.

"Gladly." Suth grabbed Scoyn by the tunic and pulled him across the seat.

Phyura screeched. It was so high-pitched it made my ears ring. Her legs skittered across the table as she tried to scoot her awkwardly folded thorax and abdomen out from under the table. In her compound eyes I saw fear, multiplied a thousand times.

Scoyn scrambled to his feet. His hands fisted.

"No, Suth. Not in here." I tightened my grip on his arm, raised two of my other arms to ward off blows I was sure were coming my way.

"I'll ground you into paste, Hye," Suth growled. "You know that."

"And I'll blast you, sure as you're standing there." He knew I would do it, too.

Out of the corner of my eye I saw Robert and Jane had come off their stools. Robert was behind the bar. My first thought was that maybe the pasty-skinned Human was taking advantage of the situation to steal from me; drinks or credits or something.

I'd deal with him later.

Suth was blabbering. "Jun and the others will avenge me. You will be dead, Hye."

"So will you."

"I welcome death." Suth gnashed his jaws. His fangs gleamed wet and white.

"So do I." It came from Scoyn.

It was enough to make Suth pause. He turned his head to stare at the thin politician of his people. "An -atelur with a spine? Don't make me laugh."

His throaty laugh was forced and ugly.

149

"For the woman I love, yes." Scoyn went toe-to-toe with Suth. He was taller. Suth was bigger in every other way, and stronger.

"I'll snap you like the twig she is." He pointed at Phyura.

"No!" She rushed to Scoyn's side, clasping two stickly legs over his shoulder.

He patted her limb. "Our love will live on. People will hear. Your ignorance and your anger will not stop it."

I didn't know about all that, but the kid had guts, I had to give him that. As for the rest, well the Formex Bosh wasn't going to be torn up making it happen.

"Think about what you're doing, Suth." I raised the blaster to make my point.

Jun and the others were clamoring to get out of the booth. They pulled at each other to be the first one out. Their knees banged into the table, and the leather seats groaned and squeaked with the sudden burst of motion.

I raised the left side of my brow, cocked my head to the side at them in warning.

They stopped.

Fury raged in Suth's eyes. His yellow-and-black pupils darted from me to Jun to the defiant Scoyn, then with disgust to Phyura. It was looking at her, her clutching hold on Scoyn, that moved his decision to the wrong side of stupid.

"I'll kill him, Hye. Then I'll kill you, too."

I don't know when or how it happened, but I found

150

somewhere along the way I crossed a boundary, too. Maybe it was talking with the Humans about their history, or maybe it was thinking about my brother. Whatever it was I decided I couldn't let Suth kill Scoyn. Not just in my bar, but not at all.

"Can't let you do that, Suth."

"Me, neither." I recognized Robert's voice behind me. He punctuated his statement with the slap of my baseball bat into the palm of his soft hand.

"Or me." Jane joined him.

Impressed again by the Humans, I smiled at Suth. "Evens the odds, don't you think."

A sudden stillness fell over the place, as if a new ice age had befallen Altar at that point. The only thing moving in the bar besides the swirling ceiling lights— and my two hearts thumping in my chest—was Suth's beady eyes. They bounced around looking for sympathizers. They found none.

Ideas came hard to Suth, as they did with most -nicolets I'd discovered. They were soldiers, not thinkers. Fighters, not intellectuals. But something wormed its way through that dull, thick skull of his, made its way passed the wispy, booze-induced fog, something that told him proceeding down the path he'd started wasn't such a good idea.

"Come on," he said to Jun and the others. "I'm tired of this place anyway. And you." He slammed an open hand into Scoyn's chest.

Scoyn reeled but came back strong. I put a restraining hand on his shoulder. "Let it go."

"Yeah, let it go," Suth said with as much venom as he could muster. It wasn't much. "And if I ever see you again, or your twig girlfriend, I'll squash you both into the mud."

He stormed toward the exit. Jun and the others trotted along behind him. One after the other they passed through the force shield and disappeared into the dusky, swirling soup Altar called an atmosphere.

I waited a beat or two, half expecting them to return. They didn't.

"Are you all right?" Phyura asked of Scoyn.

"I'm fine," he said. To me, and then to Robert and Jane, he added, "Thank you. All of you."

"You're welcome," Robert said, reaching out to shake his hand. His pink fleshy hand disappeared beneath Scoyn's hairy paw.

"You're welcome to finish your drinks," I said, leaving it at that.

Scoyn looked at the table then into Phyura's eyes. "We have caused enough trouble here tonight. I think we'll go."

She nodded her agreement. Her two forelegs scrapped together. It sounded like music. She bent forward, her carapace expanded like twisted conduit cable. "Thank you."

With that, they headed for the exit.

It should be okay, I figured. Enough time had passed for Suth and the others to have found another bar, to be pints deep into drowning their wounded egos in more liquor.

Figuring it was safe, I let them go.

"Think I could try one of them Kuma Volcanoes?" Robert asked. He steered me toward the bar.

"No. They're deadly to Humans," I told him as I watched Scoyn and Phyura pass through the force shield.

Through the shimmer of the shield, I watched them walk off together, her twig in his paw. Somehow, they looked good together.

A Diter-atelur in love with a Thysanrinae. I knew from the start they were doomed. But then again . . .

I've been known to be wrong a time or two before. This time, I thought, I'd kinda like it that way.

Fortin's Revenge

by Louisa M. Swann

IT WAS A QUARTER past midnight when I shoved through the door of the Broken Dreams Saloon. A quick scan of the main floor showed the place hadn't changed much in the years since I'd passed this way. Different barkeep. Different customers.

Same acrid stench of despair.

Not too surprising. The only folks that hung out on this rock were the specialists necessary to keep the mining station operational. Miners, transport pilots, mechanics, and, of course, support personnel.

Probably once a decade or so a Judge's Official Enforcer would stop by in search of someone who'd been hiding way too long from justice.

Someone like me.

Not that I'd been hiding from justice. Just the opposite, in fact. As a J.O.E. agent, I spent years in space chasing after justice. Now that I'm retired, I seek justice on my own.

154

After almost thirty days flying through space, my mouth tasted like space dust and canned air.

Long past time to wet my whistle.

The crowd blocking the doorway parted like I had some kind of disease. I didn't take offense, though. I'd splurged on a fancy new vest and tie hoping to pass myself off as a regular, but that wasn't gonna happen.

Not this time.

Most of these folks looked like they'd been around the stars a time or two. They knew an ex-J.O.E. guy when they saw one. Being shunned kinda came with the territory.

I made my way toward the bar, admiring the architecture along the way.

Hewn straight from the rock itself, the Broken Dreams wasn't so bad for being stuck on an asteroid just this side of nowhere.

Space-hardened on the outside, polished on the inside to a sheen so fine you could count your pores if you looked at your reflection hard enough, the mirror effect also made the place feel busier without all the noise and hassle of actual customers.

Tonight was busier than I'd ever 'seen the joint. Hell, with those polished walls, the place looked downright crowded. 'Course, the last time I settled my aching bones on the ridiculous fur-covered bar stools had been close on nineteen years ago.

Nice to see business had picked up.

My barward progress was halted by an ear-shattering cry rising above the ever-present roar of raised voices, bad music, and clattering dishes. No one but me paid any attention to the scream, so I casually scanned the room one more time.

A game I didn't recognize was in full swing just beyond the dicing tables. It hadn't drawn much attention, just a few surly-looking fellas who might've wanted to be someplace else. What looked like an electric containment field formed a sparkling dome over two thirds of the table.

As I watched, a spacer with long front teeth reminiscent of an ancient Terran squirrel stuck his hand clean into the middle of that containment field. The guy let out a banshee shriek as his scrawny body flopped around like a fish on a hook.

Finally, he jerked his hand free, collapsed into his seat for a moment, then shook his head and left the table.

As soon as he'd left, another sucker slipped into his place.

I scanned the crowd around the dicing tables, trying hard not to breathe too deep. A miasmic fog of illegal tobacco and burned rice husks clung to the ceiling like a cloud of hungry mosquitoes just waiting for the taste of blood.

You'd think folks with the technology to be running around in space would be able to do something about second-hand smoke. The Powers-That-Be made smoking illegal umpteen years ago, but places like this thrived on doing what wasn't supposed to be done.

Couldn't really complain much. Not in my line of work. But I'd seen the way that airborne poison could work its way into a person's lungs and stick around for years, not showing its ugly face until something happened to weaken the tissue, then blam!

Good-bye lung. Good-bye host.

The folks who patronized this joint didn't have much choice, though. Not if they wanted to get their minds off the job.

I gave up trying not to breathe and hoofed it over to the obsidian black bar lining the back wall. A quick hop parked my ass on an empty stool.

The bartender served the gal at the far end without glancing my way. I started to give the barkeep some grief, but stopped before a word slipped out of my mouth.

That guy serving drinks was none other than Gak Mitchell.

I'd come looking for the man. Only he wasn't a customer like I'd expected. Dear old Gak had switched sides in his grayer years. Now he was looking at life from the backside of the counter.

Other than that, the guy hadn't changed much. He still looked like some two-year-old kid had shaped his face out of volcano mud and left it to dry.

I kinda liked that. Always had, probably always will.

"Pick your poison," Gak said. His voice still sounded like a rock tumbler gone bad. He shoulda recognized me, but the man didn't even lift an eyebrow.

If that was the way he wanted to play the game, it was all right by me.

A groan worked its way through the crowded gaming tables, followed by rowdy laughter. I waved my thumb as the containment field claimed another victim.

"What's that? A new torture device?"

"I guess you could call that positive punishment." Gak grabbed a martini glass and the nearest dish towel and started polishing what looked like ultra-thin titanium to a burnished glow. "Some fancy, schmancy way of playing poker. Colton here invented it. Calls it 'Destiny.'"

Doesn't seem to matter whether you're sniffing Gold in the dust bars of Mars or slugging Plutonian wine in the tangled warrens of Alpha Centauri, you always run into the same kinds of people: those who have and don't know what to do with it; those who have not and will try anything to get what they think they're missing.

And those who plain don't give a damn.

Like the man Gak just pointed out. I gave the big brute sitting two stools away the once over, keeping an eye out for any telltale bulges that might indicate he was carrying. The man leaned over the bar counter, arms spraddled, like he was gonna hug the damned thing.

"Play you for the next round," Colton said.

Colton, if that was his real name, didn't even look at me. Could be the guy was talking to the fly in the bottom of his glass, and maybe he was, but it didn't appear the fly was listening.

The big man didn't say anything more, he didn't even turn to look at me, just stared into that glass, lost in silent memories. Or maybe he had some kind of psychic communion thing going on with that fly.

Psychic barflies.

Not a pretty picture.

Dim light caught the back of Colton's hand, illuminating a time-faded tattoo. I might have seen that mark before. Once. A long, long time ago.

"Sure." Not that I really wanted to know the ins and outs of a new game, but I was curious about the challenger.

"Wait here." Colton stood like someone hit him with a shockrod. The bar stool clattered back and forth a moment, then finally settled back into place. The big man disappeared into the crowd, only to reappear a moment later with the Destiny control box clenched on his hand. Colton gave me the directions as he set the box on the bar counter and played around with the buttons.

"Three cards, all face up where everybody can see 'em. Costs you three marks to get into the game. Call, raise, or fold after each draw. Three cards down and you got one chance to change the cards. Stick your hand under the game controller and blamm-o, one of those cards is something different. Could be good, could be bad. You ready to get burned?"

Colton smiled for the first time as the containment field snapped, crackled, and popped into existence. A leering, pirate-type smile, like he knew my weakest

159

points and was ready to capitalize on each and every one.

I shrugged. "You deal the cards, and we'll see who gets burned."

"With Destiny, there's chances to get ahead. Just like in real life," Colton said. He passed the controller to Gak.

Three cards and three bets later, I was staring at a major loss. Colton wasn't doing so hot either, but he had me cold. He leered at me again.

"Are you ready to take a chance, Mr. Lawman? Thing is, for every chance you take, you gotta do some suffering. Just like in real life."

Some folks seem to thrive on punishment. The harsher, the better. And it doesn't always have to be physical—the punishment, that is. Some of the worst forms of self-torture can be purely mental.

Give a man enough reasons and he'll drive himself insane.

Took only a minute for me to decide that Colton was long past the insanity stage; in fact, the guy was totally nuts.

Without blinking an eye, he plunged his hand into the containment field and held it there. No screaming, no flipflopping body parts. Just an ice-cold stare that challenged me to do the same.

So I did.

As soon as Colton pulled his hand from the sparking electric field, I plunged mine in.

"Big mistake," Gak muttered from somewhere nearby. "You had him."

I wanted to tell the barkeep that it wasn't about the cards, not anymore, but the only thing getting through my clenched teeth was air and not too much of that. I held Colton's gaze, fought back wave after wave of muscle spasms. Across my skin, over my head, even on my face, the hair rose with a not-quite-painful tingle.

"Whooeee!"

Someone slapped me on the back, breaking my concentration. Pain poured through every cell. Before I started flopping around like a dead fish, I jerked my hand out of the containment field and glanced down at the cards.

Two queens and the ace of diamonds sat in front of my left hand.

Colton held the other two queens . . . and the ace of spades.

"Well," Gak said as he reached beneath the counter. "Looks like this round's on the house."

"It's a tie," the man who'd destroyed my concentration hollered. I could hear the news circulating through the gaming tables. Gak must've seen the confusion in my eyes. Either that or the bartender had been communing with that psychic fly.

"Colton's never lost a game," Gak said.

"He still hasn't lost," I said.

"Never tied, neither. Go again," Colton said. So much for warming up. This guy was out for blood.

161

A tight look came over Gak's face. He set the martini glass he'd been polishing for the last five minutes on the back bar and slapped the bar towel over his left shoulder so hard I could hear the snap.

"I make it a policy to always quit while I'm ahead," I said.

Colton growled. Slammed his hand on the counter.

My gut tightened and my pulse skipped a beat. Exotic smoke clogged my throat. But I didn't back down.

Some folks came to a bar to forget what's happened to them outside. Some were only reaching out, looking for something to remind them they were warm, living beings.

Others came looking for trouble.

I wasn't looking for trouble, but that didn't mean I'd come unprepared. The wrist scabbard hidden inside my right sleeve pressed hard against my skin.

Gak, however, preferred to handle the situation without bloodshed. The bartender pulled a long-necked bottle from beneath the counter. Lifted the silvery container so it caught the light. Saliva flooded my mouth.

Fortin's *Revenge*.

"Like I said, this round's on me," Gak said. He tipped silver-green liquid into two fresh glasses. Shoved one glass in front of me, the other in front of Colton. "Fightin'll cost ya."

Colton wasn't going for it. He was itching to lash out—at me, at Gak, at the woman sitting in the shadows—at anybody, laboring under the delusion

162

that if he hurt someone else, some of his own pain would go away. At least for a minute or two.

Across the room, a chair skittered across the floor as a card player tossed down his cards and stomped out.

Colton and I were about the same age, but he out-weighed me by at least fifty pounds and those pounds didn't look to be all flab. He also held a pretty good height advantage.

I flexed my fingers and tried to work some moisture back into to my desert-dry mouth. I don't generally indulge in anything more than a carbonated beverage these days.

There's a time and place for everything, though. A motto that's kept me alive so many times during my career that I've lost count.

"Might as well line 'em up," I told Gak.

Revenge hugged the bottom of the glass in front of me like liquid platinum. Nothing sits a man's tongue easier once he makes it through the first shot. Takes at least two shots to cool that magma-in-a-glass to a level a human stomach can tolerate; three shots and the universe starts looking a little less lonely.

Four shots, and most normal guys'll spill their guts to anyone who'll listen.

I raised my glass. Tossed back the silver-green liquid as he slid two more shot glasses in front of me and topped them off. Without taking a breath, I slammed the glass back on the counter, grabbed the next in line, and opened wide.

163

Chasing fire with ice. Makes a man's gut feel like it's frozen in eternity.

Unfortunately, eternity only lasts until the next shot. Then everything goes numb. That's when most people quit.

When I slammed the glass into line with the others lined up like soldiers awaiting execution, I could almost feel my eyeballs rolling around in their sockets. I shook my head, turning to see how my drink mate was doing.

I could almost see steam rising from the man's ears. Tears scalded his age-dried cheeks and trickled along wrinkles the size of an ancient crevasse. This guy had been around the stars a few times. Probably been in and out of trouble enough times he should know better than to get skunking drunk in an asteroid bar.

Colton shook his lion-sized head and snorted. He gazed bleary-eyed around the room, his gaze settling on my cheek. Self-consciously I brushed at my face, wondering if maybe I didn't have some of this morning's breakfast caught in my beard.

So the guy wasn't going to keel over. Not yet.

I eyeballed Colton's tattooed hand. Wondered if maybe now was the time to dredge for information in that *Revenge*-soaked brain of his. My brain was probably just as pickled, but I'd had a little more experience with *Revenge* than he'd had. I could keep my thoughts from going down the rubbery path of intoxication.

For a few minutes, anyway.

"You ever killed anyone?" the words slipped out

of my mouth before I'd thought them through. So much for the sober approach.

Colton's head lolled in my direction. "Sure. Hasn't everybody?"

"You ever feel guilty about it?" I was slipping into interrogation mode, or someplace like it. I hoped.

Colton shrugged.

"You, see—the key is not to let guilt get the upper hand," I continued. "Guilt'll eat you up from the inside out, like a plug of bad tobacco, and piss you into the river of no return faster'n a whore slides off silk sheets."

Not a bad analogy, considering the whores I'd frequented generally came sandwiched between sheets that could rub a man's skin clean off his body. Except for the occasional dalliance, I'd relegated women of the night to the same category as incessant space travel—both were best left to naive young idiots and the criminally insane.

"What the hell're you getting at?" Colton said. He grabbed the front of my shirt and hauled me one-handed off my stool. I tried unsuccessfully to keep my feet from waving ridiculously in the air.

Not a very advantageous position, but I made the best of it. "You got something you need to get off your chest?" Colton's breath reeked of *Revenge*. Or maybe I was smelling my own breath. Either way, I tried not to breathe the noxious fumes and shook my head.

"Not really. Guess I just had too much to drink." I

threw in a hiccup to make the statement more authentic. Bad enough my feet were spinning in midair, I didn't need my head dancing around, too.

"Hell, you don't weigh no more than a sparrow," Colton said, tossing me back onto my seat in disgust. He stroked the bar's surface, stared deep into the black reflectionless counter. The counter stared back like a frozen slice of event horizon.

"Sometimes life forces a man into making decisions he wouldn't normally make; doing things he wouldn't normally do," I said, staring into the counter like it was some kind of crystal ball.

Gak frowned. He scooped the empty shot glasses along with the fly glass off the counter. Took the long-necked silver bottle away.

Too bad.

"He buries those memories deep inside," I continued, "dark secret strung on dark secret, shoved in a drawer in the back of his mind, only the secrets grow and grow until the drawer can't be closed and the secrets spew across a man's psyche, expanding, ballooning, oozing into every niche of his body, every crook of his soul. . . ."

"You look familiar. What did you say your name was?" Colton suddenly asked. He stared me straight in the eyes, his gaze steady and meteor-hard.

"You get something straight," Colton said before I could answer. "There's killing that needs doing and killing that don't. Sometimes the young and stupid don't know the difference."

Seems like I found a tender spot in the tough man's hide.

Gak gave me an unreadable look. Clanked the dirty glasses into the disinfector. Pressed his lips into a tight line.

An itch sparked to life beneath my beard and started to grow. I scratched the three thin lines trailing from the corner of my right eyebrow to the corner of my mouth. The wound had stung when it was fresh, itched bad while it healed, but a deeper wound lay hidden beneath the damaged flesh.

Suddenly, Colton lurched to his feet, yanked his shirt high, pointed at a puckered bit of flesh near the bottom of his left rib cage. I took a round during my last tour. Last day of my last mission. Back when I was young and stupid enough to believe I knew everything.

"That's when it happened, you know. When I killed that little girl. Hell, I killed a whole lot of people back then. No one'll ever pin it on me, though. So don't even try."

"Of course not," I said. "Wouldn't think of it in a million years."

Colton slumped onto his seat and tapped his finger on the counter. "Line me up another round."

Another barkeeper in another place might have told Colton he'd had enough, time to go home. Not Gak.

Gak pulled out the *Revenge* and lined up another row of shots.

Like I said, there's a time and place for everything.

167

I shook my head when Gak held up the bottle. For the first time that night, the bartender's face creased into a grin. He didn't say anything, though. Just filled Colton's three glasses to the brim.

Air hissed as the door clicked open, letting a group of spacers slide through.

"Hey, Delilah. I thought you weren't expecting another supply ship till the end of the week," Gak said to a woman at the far end of the counter. I'd noticed her—half-hidden in shadow—when I first came in. She tipped her head into the light. I tried hard not to stare. Every strand of shoulder-length black hair had been captured and drawn up into wicked-looking spikes.

"I'm not." The woman's voice was as dark and sultry as the shadowy niche she occupied.

"Gentlemen," Gak said, with more than a trace of sarcasm. "May I present Delilah Wolf, Portmaster and bar junkie, among other things."

The woman glared at Gak and shook her head. Emphasizing her point? Or delivering a subtle threat.

"No need to go getting your quills all pointy," Gak said. He refilled her glass and waved the barmaid over. "Here, Lisa. Why don't you take the contribution plate over to our new guests?"

The new "guests" had worked their way over to the hologame table. Lisa made her collections, then gave Gak the thumb's up from across the room. The bartender growled deep in his throat.

"Damned floater rig crew," he muttered. With expert ease, he slid open the keeper sitting under the back bar shelves, pulled out two handfuls of what looked like authentic Terran ale, and piled the bottles into a large bucket.

Next to me, Colton slammed down his second glass. He slid sideways—just a bit—straightened back up, arms spraddled like when I'd first seen the man. Only this time the glasses in front of him didn't have any flies for him to talk to.

He did, however, have that faded tattoo splayed out right in front of me.

I got a good look at it this time. A real good look.

Gak and I exchanged glances. The bartender turned away to finish filling the spacers' order. Kept his back turned as I slipped a thumb-sized vial out of my pocket and emptied the contents into Colton's last glass.

Back before my gig with the Judge's Official Enforcers, Gak and I served together in a small planetary militia. Our job was to protect the new colony from any marauding pirates looking to take advantage of the newcomers.

Unfortunately, we failed.

The pirates took out half the colony and two thirds of our militia on their first strike. In a suicidal rage, I plowed through their ranks, crazy with grief and fear. I managed to nail one of their leaders with my first shot. I'd watched the marauder go down. Seen his hand flop lifeless into inches of dust. A hand with a tattoo exactly like Colton's.

I managed to take out at least ten of the attackers

myself before going down in a blaze of not-so-glorious fire. Gak claimed he'd taken out more.

The militia was wiped out along with the colony. But we managed to inflict some damage of our own. Only three attackers got away and they didn't take anything but death along with them.

Gak and I were the only ones left from that militia. Or so we thought. We'd found one other survivor—Charlie Miller—still alive beneath a pirate's severed torso.

We'd seen each other exactly three times since.

A time and a place for everything.

"Got my first taste of this stuff years ago at some colony you guys probably never heard of," Colton said, holding his glass toward the light. He studied the silver-green liquid thoughtfully. "Can't seem to find it anyplace else. Tried to buy the whole stock last time I headed out on a job, but Gak here wouldn't sell."

"You're damned right I wouldn't sell," Gak said in a low growl. "Share the wealth, and the wealth comes to you."

"Whatever the hell that means." Colton slammed back his last drink.

Good thing the Broken Dreams Saloon had been chiseled straight out of asteroid rock or the place would've shook off its foundation when Colton fell out of his seat. A few customers looked around, but most were too busy watching the newcomers torture themselves to pay much attention to the man lying on the floor.

Lisa bent over the crumpled ex-customer. "You want I should call Charlie?"

"As good a time as any," Gak said. He picked up the glasses from the counter, dumped them into the disinfector, and started the machine.

Moments later, Charlie strode through the door. The third member of our little triumvirate made Colton look like a little boy. Charlie'd sprouted a beard since the last time I'd seen him, but he still had that twinkle in his eyes that made you feel like everything was going to be all right.

"Took you a little longer this time," was his only comment before bending over and lifting the body effortlessly from the floor.

I scratched my beard and hid a grin. Charlie claimed his slight accent was Earth-born, but I've been to a lot of planets in this universe and I've never found an accent to match. "Good to see you, too, Charlie."

"You need a place to stay?" Charlie asked. I shook my head. He gave a quick nod and headed out the door.

"Never trust a man who can't hold his drink," Gak muttered to no one in particular. He rinsed off the bar towel. Wiped down the entire length of the counter, sidestepping the woman at the end. Soon every trace of silvery liquid had disappeared from the counter. Everything was once again in order.

Nothing less would do.

"By the way, you two about drained my barrel dry,"

Gak said. I laughed. "If you can wait a week, I'll have another ten delivered."

Delilah slapped a credit down next to her glass. "You better get in something worth drinking. The stuff you gave me tastes like worm piss, Mitchell."

"Complain to the management." Gak nodded in my direction. I swiveled in Delilah's general direction. The room swirled with me. Maybe I should give up swirling—at least until the *Revenge* wore off.

Delilah slid off her bar stool, thumping softly on the wooden floor with both feet. "I don't believe we've met."

I held out my hand. "Eli Fortin. At your service. Would you care to spend the night with me?"

Something soft and fuzzy settled in my palm. Definitely not Delilah's hand or any other part of her anatomy. I peered at the ball of fuzz. Glanced up, confused.

"You look like you need a little tension tamer, Mr. Fortin. Corbils are great for frazzled nerves," Delilah said with a smile. "Now, if you'll excuse me—"

I should've seen it coming. The fuzzball, if not the rejection.

Somewhere between the birthdays and the *Revenge*, my lightning-fast reflexes had slowed to a pace slower than a slug on an icy moon. But my powers of intimidation were still awesome.

Weren't they?

"You just watch yourself," I said to the furball in my hand. "I'm a trained killer."

The furball started to purr. I listened for a moment. Felt the tension ooze out of places I hadn't realized were tense.

"Guess Delilah's right," I whispered to the furball. "But don't you tell anyone."

Relaxing didn't have anything to do with the fact that I'd finally nailed the last man on my list. Or with the fact that maybe I could finally kick back and enjoy the simple things in life——like brewing up gallons of my family's favorite hooch.

Not at all.

I looked around at the Broken Dreams. At the gorgeous arched mirrors and rock pillars . . . You'd think the place'd be darker than space with all this black rock, but with the reflective surfaces the overall atmosphere was kind of . . . sparkly.

Maybe I should talk to Gak. See about giving the place back its original name.

Fortin's Hope.

Finally, after all these years, the name seemed to fit.

Hanged Man

by Leslie Claire Walker

THE SWAMPY RICHNESS of burning peat settled at the back of Griff's throat. His abraded
back stung with sweat. The hearth fire threw shadows
on the walls and the wood-grained plastic floor of the
empty High Side Pub at Outpost Six. They hypno-
tized, until in the flickering fades of dark and light he
could see the face of the accomplice he'd better Give
Up or Else.

The agent who'd taken him into custody this morning had hanged him upside down from his left ankle
by tying it with a length of leather to the Last Tree
in the center of the damned pub. That's what they did
with spies.

Yes, sir, the agent hanged him, and the Maker made
him drink. Drink what? Something that made his vision blur and cloud so he could hardly make out the
swing of the front door. In fact, maybe he'd have
missed it if the hinges hadn't shrieked and a breath

174

of fresh-chilled spring humidity hadn't gusted in. The wet and the northerly breeze made him cough, and made him move so that the bark of the Tree drew blood from his back through the fabric of his shirt. The coughing would only go on since the door stayed open, and the wind never really quit.

From what he could see of the sky, the sun hovered twenty degrees above horizon on its way down. It'd be about an hour before the dusk whistle signaled the whole town to wind up their work and head over for a pint and a public spectacle (which would be him).

Maker John walked in like he owned the pub (which he did), wearing a cleaner version of the blue plasticene coat and coveralls and white pullover he'd had on earlier. His bald head glistened. He headed over to the bar and ducked under the service counter, checking his reflection in its scratched glass surface. He poured himself a big black tumbler full of bubbly water and stared at Griff.

Griff spoke, his voice raspy as reeds in the wind. Foremost on his mind: whether Maker John had delivered his message to Lu. *Sorry I missed our wedding, I was busy being hanged.* "You told her, right?"

"Wrote it all down and handed it to her like you asked," the Maker said.

"What'd she say?"

"Not much of anything. She got married." The Maker ran his hands over his head. "You know, I never been in a wedding before."

Griff's jaw dropped. Or it would've, if it'd had gravity on its side. "Who the hell'd she marry?"

"That Snow fella who works at Customs."

The one whose hair stuck up in seven different directions. Whose clothes always seemed a couple sizes too small. She didn't even know him. "Why?"

"Well, you weren't there," the Maker said, as if that made any normal kind of sense.

Just then, Lu herself came in from the cold and picked up the conversation. "Nope, he weren't."

Her blue-black hair flowed down her back in three thick braids. Her cheeks flushed like they always did when she got pissed. She wore black—not the mourning kind. The smart-looking kind.

The whites of her big, brown eyes were red, too. But not from crying. Lu didn't cry. Not under any circumstances. Not even when she realized he could've given her up as his accomplice, since she'd been in on the job from the beginning. He obviously hadn't, and she'd screwed him anyhow.

Griff bet she'd been all lovely in her wedding dress, what with the fall of the fabric to the floor and the plunging neckline that showed off her assets so well. Creamy, her skin and the color of the dress. "Sorry."

She stepped to him, nose to nose. "You should be. We had a deal, Griff."

"Plainly, I couldn't help breaking it."

The Six Corporation, who'd settled the planet in the first place, had high hopes at one time of finding anything precious beneath the surface, and certainly they'd harvested every other valuable thing they could. With nothing left except the peat, deemed not worth the effort, they were pulling out. They transported all workers and families except those in the last town; they didn't have enough ships for everyone to evac.

Enter the lottery, and his winning ticket for two seats on the last transport off this rock. With the ticket being good for a married couple only, and he and Lu being both single, they'd hatched themselves a wedding.

"Snow has a ticket like yours," she said.

He also had that good job and the prestige that went with it. Griff's experience loading and unloading transports not only didn't compare, he'd been officially out of work for months now. "I see why you married him, then."

She nodded. "The transport leaves in twelve hours."

As if he didn't already know that. "And you're going to leave me here."

"I didn't promise to stand by you through thick and thin," she said.

No, she hadn't. She'd said those words to Snow, not him. "You don't love him."

She flashed him a wry grin. "I don't love you either. What the hell did you do, Griff? What'd you steal to end up strung up like that?"

He wondered that it wasn't obvious to her, him having

spent half his life at the High Side, and for the most specific of reasons. "The secret formula for the Maker's stout."

Her eyebrows climbed slow and deliberate to her hairline. "What would you need with that? There'll be plenty of brew where we're going."

He didn't doubt that. "But it wouldn't be the *same* brew."

"You threw away your future for that?"

He guessed he had.

She apparently didn't believe him. "Might I suggest that this is *not* about the stout?"

How presumptuous of her to say. Especially since he'd had that thought on his own and done his very best not to explore it. "I'd prefer you didn't."

"Aw, hell, Griff." She raised up on her toes and planted a soft kiss on his mouth. Damn, but she tasted good. "Have the best life you can, however you make it."

She turned on her heel and walked out with a wave to the Maker. Griff watched her go—every inch of floor she crossed, every swing of her arms and slight move of her fingers, the way her braids slid across her back. He watched until the last molecule of her went out the door.

Behind the bar, the Maker sighed. "It's a howlin' shame, son."

It was. "So's the fact you wouldn't let me go."

"The law's the law."

He'd never understood that. "The only good thing about rules is all the different ways you can break them."

"Well, then I hope you can find something good come out of this." The Maker pulled a glass off the stack behind him. "You want something to drink?"

"Stout," Griff said without thinking, because it required no thought.

"You want a straw with that? No other way you're gonna get it down your gullet."

He had to be kidding. "You're not going to cut me down?"

Maker John shook his head. "Not until the Customs man gets here and tells me what to do with you. Or you give up those accomplices of yours."

Just the one accomplice. Griff didn't see how that mattered anymore. The Maker, however, would see different. "Yes."

"Yes, what?"

"To the straw."

John brought over the pint, bless him.

Griff hung there for three days before the Customs agent showed up and pronounced him free on account of time served. Seeing as how he'd never be able to leave Outpost Six, he didn't consider freedom meant all that much.

The day after that, everyone left in town gathered at the High Side after the whistle to make a plan. If they had to live out the rest of their lives on Six, best they had some common understanding of expectations.

Griff's fellow citizens tracked in dirt and water and something he didn't want to identify that looked like it'd come off the butcher's floor. Maker John poured glasses and pitchers of brew. The din of voices and footfalls and the occasional sacrilege of a dropped drink filled Griff's ears to overflowing.

He ordered himself a pitcher of stout, meaning to consume it out on the stoop while he waited for the meeting to start, but John wouldn't let him take away that much. He could have two pints. No more.

With the transport had flown any meaningful version of credit, and most of them left behind hadn't considered what would happen if they didn't have trade. It stood to reason that real goods and skills would take over as currency. Griff could offer only muscle. No way would that keep him in brew in the style to which he'd become accustomed. Maybe John knew that. Hence the rations.

He warmed the top step with his seat, hunching as far as he could and still drink to keep the wet cold from leeching through his clothes and into his bones. Even the sun folded in on itself, turning the sky bronze with the last of its shine.

The last of the stragglers wandered by. Mills and his girlfriend Sarabell, him with his thick, chapped hands stroking the loose waves of her orange hair. Dolan, scratching his beard, his hair combed straight back and pasted there with what appeared to be spit. They'd all of them been friends since he could remember.

They would never have a chance now to lose touch and wonder whatever became of so-and-sos, and did they have children, and how had their lives turned out. Instead, they'd have the luxury of knowing. The blessing of knowing. And hopefully friendships would stick, and when time started to stretch out over the generations that would never leave Six, bitterness wouldn't get the better of them.

Sara and Mills and Dol nodded at him. In they went.

Out came Maker John.

He hunkered down next to Griff. "You drink too much, you know."

Griff wondered what brought on this pronouncement. "No more than usual."

"That'd be my point."

It sounded a lot like what Lu had said. Or what she'd not exactly said. He didn't like it. "I'm still trying to see your point."

"If you're gonna spend so much time in my establishment, don't you think you should make yourself useful?" John held his gaze.

Oh. "What'd you have in mind?"

"You wanted the formula for the stout so bad you messed up your chance with Lu," the Maker said.

"I had no chance with Lu."

"You know what I mean, Griff."

He supposed he did. He supposed John would ask him to wash dishes or mop the floor, and he'd be all right with that.

The Maker chewed his lip. "I need an apprentice."

Griff couldn't believe what he'd heard—especially after he tried to steal from the man. Maybe John knew something he didn't, saw something in him. Either that or this was some new and different kind of punishment.

He let the words sink in and didn't ask John to take them back. "I accept."

Midsummer New Year arrived before Griff could poke his head out of the hole he'd dug in agreeing to work for John. The shift in season brought warm breezes from the southwest and seedlings struggling to the surface of the spent soil. Dawn came an hour earlier and dusk an hour later.

For Griff, the rising and setting of the sun were arbitrary events in light of the schedule he kept.

In the hushed stillness between moonset and sunrise, he made his way to the High Side. The best stout brewed in the morning, flavored with the quiet and the promise of something new. Hope, Maker John said.

Griff didn't know whether to agree, but besides that he learned all he could about roasting barley and the exact shade of dark John expected (indeed, demanded), the percentage of raw unmalted barley and whether cooking it or flaking it gave the best results, and how much pale malt served for the rest of the grist. He learned about vatting.

John didn't make only stout. So Griff learned about porters and ales. And about the bitter brew Maker John gave him the morning of the hanging.

The bitter contained an inordinately high percentage of the white root from the blanket mires. A little bitter turned the world on its head. You'd have hallu-cinations, elevated body temperature, euphoria.

A lot of bitter would kill.

Griff had afternoons off for sleeping and anything else he might want to do, but the former took up all his free time, and when the sun sank to twenty degrees he reported to the pub to get ready for business.

The New Year promised to be the biggest night of the year. He ought to know, but he'd spent the last several in his cups, and who knew how it was for the proprietor?

This was how:

The place smelled of special holiday cologne and sweat and brew. He felt sure he'd experienced how the pub held every single human being in town, except suddenly it seemed like twice as many people crammed in the same amount of space. Women and men and a handful of children ebbed and flowed from the bar, carrying overfull, foamy containers to their tables, arms tucked close to their bellies or raised high overhead. Despite their care, brew sloshed over the sides of the glasses and pitchers onto the floor, where it slicked and tripped up unsuspecting folks.

The noise near to deafened him. Voices raised in good humor and big belly laughs and exclamations of shock and surprise and claps on the back and the ring-ing clink of glasses. In the west corner, a quartet of women sang some old songs and some new—all cele-brating the height of the season and the sacrifice of the sun. Shorter days from there on out. A turning inward so something new could be born. Three of the women sang melody. The fourth was Sarabell, and she wove harmonies that made him want to close his eyes and block out the roar of sound—to block out everything except the notes of her voice.

Her hair twisted at the nape, held up by a pointed black lacquer stick. She wore a wide, sea-green skirt that brushed the ground, and a shirt of the same color, only a shade more pale. He couldn't see her black lace-up boots, but she'd have them on.

Sara had broken up with Mills three months ago. She'd taken to working at the swap, trading her hand-knit sweaters and scarves (more the rage now—and warmer—than the plasticene) for vegetables.

He thought about her far too often for his own good.

She glanced at him. He took the opportunity to pay a little more attention to where his hands moved and how, to pouring drinks and shaking hands. And in the case of Dol, giving a big hug.

Griff noticed she looked at him on and off all night, and wondered if she noticed him doing the same to her.

He'd never poured so much brew or worked so hard. Or felt so good about it.

Maker John hung back and let him have the stage for most of the night, slipping in now and again when Griff needed a hand with a particular customer too drunk to be reasonable, or to spell him for a few minutes of fresh air.

The stoop looked dirty, and felt like heaven when he lowered himself to sit. Someone had left an empty glass in the corner. He picked it up and set it beside him so he wouldn't forget to bring it in, and turned his sights on the moon, waxing just shy of a quarter, marching steady toward the second full moon this month. Blue moon, they called it.

The stars winked cold and distant in the velvet black. The breeze lifted the hair from his forehead and stirred the hair on his arms. He smelled rain. Gave it maybe two, three hours before the sky opened and poured a torrent.

Sara walked up behind him; he knew the rhythm of her step and the way she always stopped a few inches back of where anyone else did. Like she felt unsure. Or shy.

Griff cleared his throat so she'd know he felt her there. "Thanks for singing."

"You heard me?"

"Always," he said, laughing to soften the admission.

She sat next to him and gathered her knees to her chest. "Do you want to court me?"

Her directness surprised him. There was no dancing around the answer. And he found he didn't want to. "I do."

She smiled. "Good."

He could feel the heat of his face blushing crimson. "I agree."

Sarabell looked him in the eye. "What kind of man are you, Griff?"

185

He didn't know. "What kind do you see?"

She kept on smiling, more with her eyes than anything else, mulling the question. He wished she'd answer. He was glad she didn't when she leaned over, her breast brushing against his arm, and kissed him.

Maker John swung open the door ten minutes earlier than usual, letting in a gust of frigid air and a curtain of rain all over the freshly mopped floor. He looked older than he had in a while, his brows beetled and stone gray, some of the wrinkles on his face deepened to crags. His bare head shone, gently reflected the light of the fire. He moved as fast as he could—at a wholehearted limp.

His eyes were wide, and he got three quarters of the way to the bar before he stopped walking and poured himself into a chair. He breathed too hard. It worried Griff more than he'd let on to the old man.

And Griff saw that John's eyes were full of fear and wonder.

He froze over his stout, having just taken the first sip of the day. He wiped the foam off his lip and waited for an explanation.

John raised a hand to wave off concern. *I'll be fine.* But he said, "They're back."

That begged the question. "They who?"

"The Company."

Griff couldn't have heard that right. "You been hittin' the bitter, John?"

"Don't patronize me," the Maker said.

He had no intention to. "Tell me how you know."

John rested an elbow on the table top and leaned into it. "I saw the transport, Griff."

He thought of Lu in her wedding dress—no, in her smart black outfit with her blue-black hair and brown eyes. Immediately, he wondered if it was the same ship, the odds being worse than zero. And for her to be on it? No. Only fate would know where she laid her head, what had become of her.

He sighed. "Did it land?"

"Just outside of town. Near Dol's place."

"You see anybody?" Griff asked.

John shook his head. "We should go over there, you and I."

"Of course." They were the Makers here; they had the duty and responsibility to extend a welcome. If a welcome were necessary. Or desirable. "What do you figure they want?"

John cocked his head. "You sound like you wished they'd never come."

Did he? "Do you think they're here to evac the rest of us?"

"No way to tell," John said. "Maybe they brought tourists. See how the other half lives."

Griff laughed that off. "It'd be a profit."

The Maker coughed. "Would you go now if they offered you a place?"

Would he?

When he'd had his chance to leave, he'd screwed it up, probably on purpose. He'd had his whole life ahead of him then. Now? He and Sara had two children and a piece of land to call their own. He had his job at the pub that was more than a job. "Don't think so."

John narrowed his eyes. "You could take Sarabell and the kids. See something besides Six."

He'd thought he wanted to, once upon a time. "What about you? Can I take you?"

The Maker's silence on the topic telegraphed his answer just fine.

"That's what I thought."

"You already have the secret formula for the damned stout. What more do you want?"

"Lu was right all those years ago, what she said to me." He could admit that much. High time, too.

John nodded.

"This isn't about the stout."

The Maker held his gaze. "Never was, was it?"

"No." Griff could admit that to himself now, finally. "It was always about home."

"Same difference." John pushed to his feet, waving off help before Griff could offer even though he'd bent himself halfway over with the effort. It took a bit, but he got himself turned right side up. "You ready?" he asked.

"You bet." Griff polished off his brew and wiped the condensation from his hands on his pants. He grabbed the coat his wife had knitted. "Come on, John. Let's go see the tourists."

2 Drops of Heaven

by Dan C. Duval

WHEN ASTOR BASE HAD been built, a new wave of Temperance had been in progress and they had made no provision for a bar or tavern on Kuiper Belt Object 2009 DS133, so Harold had to go to the commissary—the *de facto* bar—if he wanted any privacy for his experiment.

He would never be alone in his quarters. There was always *someone* in there, somewhere among the bunks. They would swarm over him in an instant if he did anything that even hinted at being interesting.

DS133 should have had a name by now, but the IAU still had not settled the issue of what constituted a planet and the people who did not want Pluto to be an official planet did not want anything outward from there named as a planet either, not until the Pluto issue was resolved. The argument had been going on for over 120 years already, with no resolution in sight.

Someone once said that science only advanced with

the death of the old generation. Another downside of longevity treatments: the stodgy old bastards just would not die.

The commissary could have been any cafeteria anywhere on Earth: cheap metal tables—rounds and squares—with too many cheap metal-and-plastic chairs jammed between them. It was hard enough to work your way through them with a tray of food. Add alcohol to the mix and it was cheap slapstick comedy with the aroma of cheap food overlaid.

Harold wormed his way through the chairs, heading for an unoccupied table toward the back. It was far away from the serving line, which gleamed in its stainless steel glory, currently empty of food. The place was fairly full for a midweek evening, so Harold had a lot of elbows to dodge and a lot of heads to avoid with his own elbows.

Base Command might have given up on keeping the commissary from becoming a bar in the evenings—difficult to enforce prohibition when few of the officers could distinguish a still from the normal maze of piping that hung from the ceiling of every room and passageway—but they were not about to provide it to anyone, so the tables that were occupied each had its own source of liquor, some in bottles, some in lab flasks, some in an open metal pot (for those to whom metal poisoning was not as worrisome as going dry for too long.)

Many people still wore the jumpsuits that were the standard uniform on the Base, maybe because they used their weight allowance for something other than clothes, but here and there people wearing fashions from home laughed and shouted and whispered to their tablemates. Mostly women, Harold noted, but a few guys wore jackets with padded shoulders or multi-colored robes or even breechcloths, for the maximum exposure of their masculine musculature (a costume that seemed to be very popular in the 3-Dollar-Bill corner).

He was not going to let any of them spoil this for him.

After all, he was risking his job and his bonus by doing this.

When he reached the table he had picked out, he moved around until his back was to the wall. He set his sack on the table, before picking the seat that seemed to have less dust and unidentified oily stuff on it than the others.

Settling himself down, he looked around.

The next table over held up Weird Wenoosh, the Iranian or Pakistani or Hindu or whatever she was, all frizzy hair and over-large brown eyes, mooning after someone or another all the time, but hardly ever speaking. As usual, she was facedown on the table, a tumbler of booze in one hand and her bottle almost three-quarters gone next to her. She could not possibly have drunk all of that, but she sure looked as if she had made a significant dent in a full bottle.

A couple of tables over, the 3-Dollar-Bill Club had pulled two tables together and were earnestly in low conversation, their heads leaned together toward the middle of the tables. Probably sorting out who was going to go with whom and stick what where. All guys. Harold shuddered.

Even the Base's Protestant chaplain belonged to the 3-Dollar-Bill Club. Inadvertently, Harold must have made eye contact. The chaplain, in his faux-leather breechcloth, waved at Harold, who halfheartedly waved back.

Harold had talked with the chaplain for several weeks before catching on to his proclivities.

The usual religious studies went on in their various corners, the Bible group in one corner glaring daggers at the Muslims on the other side of the hall, who glared back just as viciously. Both groups occasionally spared a glare for the drinkers, who outnumbered them ten to one, easy.

The Buddhists tried to stay out of the way of them all, sitting in their chairs and humming quietly to themselves. They did not drink much either. They did seem to like humming in public.

All of the various groups had approached him at one time or another, when he first arrived at the Base—even Wenoosh—and they had all lost interest eventually. Even Wenoosh. Thank God.

The reason he had come to the Base was to make his fortune and he was not going to be diverted from that. He would make enough money to win Naomi back.

Harold was an Arbitrator and, as such, part of his

package was that they paid him a percentage of every deal he cut, an incentive to maximize the deals. Those bonuses would only gild the lily, though, since the pay he received for the six-year trip out, his eight-year tour of duty, and four-year trip back to Earth was going to be astronomical in its own right, partly because there was nothing to spend any of that money on out here. His pay went directly into an account on Earth, earning interest. He would be able to buy an entire round of longevity enhancements and still be a rich man at the other end.

Young again and rich—and on Earth. Naomi would be back. He just knew it.

And yet, he was going to risk all of it, just for a few minutes with her.

The job was not even all that hard, since only four of the alien ships passed the Base each year (Earth Standard, not the 830-year orbit of DS133).

There were dozens of Arbitrators, backed up by some of the best linguists and cultural anthropologists who could be convinced to spend twenty years here on the edge of the Solar System.

The major downside was trying to figure out the aliens themselves.

Their first communications were incomprehensible. English words, but no one had a clue about syntax or semantics. The aliens taught themselves English from our TV and radio transmissions (predigital—you know, *I Love Lucy, Gilligan's Island, Magnum PI,* and the like.)

Quite a feat, actually.

One of the linguists explained it like this: watch some Kabuki theater and try to derive the Japanese language from it. Difficult for trained linguists, who were at least human; orders of magnitude more difficult for a different species.

More difficult still because these ships that were passing by carried more than one species of alien, each with its own idea how to speak English, its own cultural background, and completely alien biochemistry.

A different batch of aliens in each one.

In the twenty years of operation of Astor Base, the same alien race had not shown up on any two ships.

The staff on Astor Base had two months to try to make sense of what the aliens of a given ship were selling and make a deal, so that the shuttles the aliens peeled off their ships could slow enough to land at the Base and make the exchange, before they had to take off and catch back up with the ship passing by at .7c.

The alien ships themselves would never spend the energy to stop at a minor star system like Sol. They did not even always bother to make any sort of trade.

Of course, about the only thing Earth had that the aliens wanted was music. And the music players. Apparently, the players were part of the quaintness of the human music.

The Base warehouses were full of players and the latest music sticks, no more than ten years out of date, brought up on a low-energy trajectory. The rest were filled with all sorts of weird things from the aliens, waiting for transshipment back to Earth.

Harold reached into his sack and withdrew a tall, clear pint glass, setting it on the table in front of him. He reached in again and pulled out a gift that his sister had sent him, two shuttles back.

Clearwaters, it was called, distilled in Apple Valley, Minnesota. Michigan had been dry when Harold and his sister were growing up, so the big thing was to send someone to Minnesota to bring back as much Clearwaters as they could buy. Most counties in Minnesota had a limit on how much alcohol you could buy each day, and very few liquor stores in each county. At least you could buy it there.

Back in Michigan, someone would volunteer their house and everyone would get there before dark on a Friday (skipping school or bugging out of work early). Car keys went into a locked box that would not be opened until Sunday afternoon, and the Clearwaters were emptied into a big punchbowl, along with fruit juice or tropical punch or something. Clearwaters was 95% alcohol, so it went a long way toward giving the resulting slop a kick.

The first drink often tasted really foul, but by the second, the taste made no difference. Most people lost count by the third drink.

Harold had seen his first naked woman at a Clearwaters party. Sadly, it was his sister and that image stuck with him all that evening, until he had passed out. Fortunately, some of the other partyers dragged him back into the house, so he did not die in the snow.

After that, he had given up drinking.

But if he understood the alien's instructions, alcohol was needed for this experiment and the only alcohol he had was the bottle his sister had sent him. People might have asked questions if Harold had asked anyone for booze. He had been clear a number of times what he thought of people who drank.

And understanding what was going on was the real heart of the problem with trading with the aliens. Despite the best efforts of the scientists, they were often guessing what it was the aliens wanted to trade away.

The arithmetic of the trades were usually pretty easy to sort out—after all, mathematics is pretty universal at some level.

But what is "hulver notarial propitation on smooth dictate"? The aliens provided a direct word-for-word translation for things, but it was like reading a Chinese translation of a German novel in English: the words were familiar, but the syntax and semantics were completely off. Assuming they meant anything at all.

This last deal, everything seemed to work out fine. "Goop pleasure extremes" turned out to be a flaky brown substance that the test subjects said—after exhaustive lab and animal tests—tasted like a combination of chocolate, broccoli, and cleaning fluid. Anyone who choked a chunk down, though, was guaranteed a prime orgasm sometime in the next hour or so. Sinful, for sure, but Harold knew he had made a hit when a three-kilo sample he had brought into the office disappeared one afternoon, along with almost the entire female staff. He was not sure if the office women shared with the military or the technical types, but three kilos would not have gone very far if they had.

Most of the male test subjects had found the stuff a little too . . . messy.

But he had traded away five tons of music video players and rock videos for more than 65,000 metric tons of the stuff. It would take several shuttles to send it all back to Earth. Big bonus for that one, probably. Sin was making a comeback on Earth.

Assuming that the women on Astor Base did not use it all themselves. Security had discovered that nearly forty kilos had been chipped off of one block and moved it all to warehouses well away from the main part of the Base, then opened the access tunnels to DS133's vacuum. (Okay, it had an atmosphere, but it was all helium and only required a little bit of pressure to liquefy, it was that cold.)

And the alien had been overjoyed. At least, that was what Harold assumed the last message from the alien meant.

It was in a small pouch that looked metallic, with Harold's name printed on the outside. It felt strange, but the lab types said they had no idea how to tear it or cut it, yet it was as smooth and flexible as silk.

Harold had not turned over the cylinder the pouch contained, though, nor the note he found inside, written on the same metal-cloth.

"Equivalency complete quivering heaving grimace. Present. 2 drops heaven. Goop pleasure. Solution 4 in 10 ethanol. Quivering heaving grimace for" and a time equivalent to about fifteen minutes. "Most beloved exchange verbal. Psychotropic microbe telepathy. Not internalize."

This particular species of alien was apparently allergic to verbs, one of the linguists had said. Lila, the one with the awful disposition and the addiction to lavender. She left clouds of it behind her when she left a room.

But with two months' experience trying to communicate with this particular flavor of alien, Harold was sure the cylinder was some sort of life-form that was activated by alcohol and would allow you to talk to your "most beloved." The phrase "exchange verbal" had shown up many times in the context of speaking to one another, while he was trying to set up the trade.

Would this alien life-form work on humans? Harold thought it would.

The first thing with any new alien was to get the arithmetic decoded, then weights and measures. Descriptive language after that was usually the hard part, where a lot of guessing took place.

But pure knowledge was an exchange commodity, as well, one that was apparently used as some sort of currency among all the aliens of all the ships as well,

2 DROPS OF HEAVEN

since each ship of aliens seemed to have better knowledge and understanding of human biochemistry and physiology than the last ship did: our peculiar chemistry seemed to have hit the tops of the charts among the aliens in the ships.

Examplar: the "goop pleasure extreme" that the office girls were embezzling whenever possible. The aliens knew what it would do to human physiology before they offered it up for trade, without ever even having spoken to a human before.

So the alien probably knew what he/she/it was talking about.

If only Harold could be as sure that *he* understood.

Either it meant that Harold would be in telepathic contact with Naomi for fifteen minutes, or he would *think* he was in telepathic contact.

It was also possible that the microbes would eat his mind, then puke it back up when they got near Naomi. But then again, that did not sound like a "goop pleasure" on the order of the brown stuff, so it probably was nothing bad like that.

Either way, Harold fished the cylinder out of his pocket.

It was gray, with rounded ends, like a medicine capsule the size of his thumb. It was neither cold nor warm in his hand. In fact, he had dipped it in ice water and it had still felt neither warm nor cold when he fished it out.

From its size, he was relieved he did not have to swallow it. Or use it as a suppository.

The moment of truth.

If he turned it all over to Base Command now, they might reprimand him or even send him home, but they would have to acknowledge that he did not damage it in any way.

It might even be worth a small fortune back on Earth, if he managed to smuggle it home. A risky business, since Security assumed everyone would try to smuggle *something* home.

And—unless it ate his brain—if it dissolved in the Clearwaters, what evidence would remain?

Harold unscrewed the cap from the Clearwaters bottle and poured its contents into the glass. In the 0.5 Earth gravity, the fluid fell languidly into the glass, barely making a splash at the bottom, acting more like some sort of oil in the low gravity rather than the thin liquid of alcohol. Then again, water looked weird here, too.

The clear glass and the clear liquid almost looked like a cylinder of crystal, but Harold could still make out the edges of the glass inside, where it met the alcohol. Gravity did not affect index of refraction.

When the bottle was empty, Harold set it down and watched the meniscus ooze up the side of the inside of the glass, nearly a centimeter. Very hard to believe he drank the stuff once.

Unbidden, a memory of his naked sister popped into his mind and he choked as a bit of spit went down the wrong pipe.

His coughing woke Wenoosh, who raised her head

slightly, looked at him through her mop of hair, wobbled a bit, and fell back onto the table.

Harold looked around.

No one was looking.

He lifted his hand up, dropped the cylinder into the glass, and dropped his hand back to his lap quickly, hoping no one had seen.

The cylinder fell to the bottom of the glass and lay there.

The cylinder had drawn bubbles down with it as it dropped into the Clearwaters, bubbles which rose quickly to the top and vanished, though no bubbles stuck to the cylinder itself.

Otherwise, it was inert.

Harold leaned forward, staring at it.

Nothing.

A finger of doubt worked its way into his mind. Maybe it did not work with humans, after all.

He concentrated. Naomi. Naomi. Her gray eyes, her black hair, the little bump on the bridge of her nose. Naomi. Naomi.

In an instant, the cylinder was gone. It did not dissolve like a tablet or melt like an ice cube: one moment it was there and the next it was not.

A misty swirling started in the middle of the liquid, though, a faint hint of shape, then darker, slowing, solidifying, moment by moment, becoming smoke, then solid, tendrils at one moment and an uneven globe the next, uneven and then an edge.

Really, it was impossible to tell how it changed, because just as it seemed to start making an edge in one place it would stop and motion elsewhere in the glass caught his attention and when he looked back to the first place, there was nothing but swirling smoke and dark fluids.

Until Naomi's face popped into place, in the middle of the glass. Her long straight nose almost touched the near edge of the glass while the slowly swirling tips of her hair touched the sides.

But it was her. Right down to the . . . pimples?

"Harold?" the image said. Harold glanced around to see if anyone else heard, but no one was paying any attention to him.

"Naomi?" Harold whispered.

"Harold, where are you?" the image said, details crisp and clear now.

"I'm right here," Harold whispered. "Right in front of you."

"Harold?" Naomi's head said.

Then it popped out of existence, as someone brushed by Harold's shoulder, to be replaced by two men, one bent over while the other stood behind him, his pelvis . . . ewww.

Harold looked up to see one man leading another man by the hand toward the door of the commissary.

"Naomi," Harold whispered, trying to concentrate, to bring back her image.

And it did, this time the way he had last seen her, standing in her wedding dress getting married to a guy that was not Harold, her back toward him, her shoulder blades distinctly outlined beneath the fine lace that made up the back of her dress.

"No!" Harold shouted, jumping to his feet.

The image swirled in the glass and re-formed to a scene of the two people turning to each other, leaning into a clutch, and kissing.

It took Harold a moment to realize that it was very quiet in the commissary.

When he looked up, all he heard was the hum of the ventilators, while every face stared at him.

Except Wenoosh, who belched in her sleep.

Harold forced himself stiffly back into his chair, as people's faces turned away. He hoped the sudden strong smell of stale food was left over from dinner and not wafting over from Wenoosh.

Concentrating on the glass, he tried to recall Naomi's face again.

Swirls of smoke and cloudiness in the glass spun and whirled, but the only image he could get was . . . his naked sister again, standing on a table and whirling her bra over her head, while her bony butt gyrated to whatever music had been playing way back then.

He pushed himself away from the table and the glass cleared again.

He had been gypped. This was not at all what he would think of as his "most beloved" and seeing two guys . . . doing it . . . certainly was not what he thought of with the words "goop pleasure."

He only had minutes with this thing. He *had* to make it work.

He stared into the glass until the clouds and smoke appeared again. He drove everything from his mind but Naomi's face, concentrating on her dark eyes, the full lips, her dark brown hair.

Like a spinning wheel suddenly jerking to a stop, a face appeared in the glass again. Naomi, this time with hair cut short, a bulbous knob at the end of her nose, and dark green eyes.

But that was not her face. Her hair was black. Or maybe really dark brown. And her eyes were light colored, not dark.

Weren't they?

Was that the problem? Was he forgetting Naomi? After all, it had been nearly seven years since her wedding, two days before his LEO shuttle left for the deep-space shuttle. He had her pictures in his quarters, though he knew he had not looked at them for a while.

Not since the shuttle had arrived at the Base, in any case. He had taken the album and placed it in his personal drawer under his bunk. And he had all the digital images, portraits as well as vids. Of course, he had not watched those in a while, either.

That was it, his memory was fading.

To test it, he looked up at Wenoosh then at the glass, concentrating.

In an instant, Wenoosh's image appeared in the glass, crystal clear and solid-looking, facedown on the table as she was in real life.

Until her head raised up and blearily stared at him.

"Oh, Harold," the image said, slurring the words. "You do care for me after all."

Harold jerked his head toward Wenoosh's table, to see her head orbiting slowly over her tumbler, a drunken grin on her face.

He felt horror overwhelming him as she tried to get to her feet, but three quarters of the way into her bottle, she could not manage it and collapsed back onto the table, one eye showing through her hair.

In the glass, the image had disappeared when Harold took his eye off of it, but the motion there drew his attention, in time to see himself, standing in the glass as if at this very table, peering into the glass on the table, where a tiny figure seemed to be slightly bent over, staring at something . . .

He forced himself back into the chair, desperate to get something satisfying out of this thing before it burned itself out.

The image in the glass, however, did not sit down. Rather the image's clothes disappeared and Harold's tiny image started making motions with his hips as if . . .

Harold reached over to Wenoosh's table and smacked it with the palm of his hand. "Stop that!" he barked.

Wenoosh jumped a little, sitting most of the way up in the chair before her eyeballs rolled back in her head and she slid off to one side, to fall to the floor in a heap, silent except for a *whoof* of breath as she struck.

An breeze filled with the smell of stale food and somewhat used liquor wafted over Harold a few moments later.

All eyes were on Harold again. It even appeared as if a couple of people were getting curious about what he was doing, whispering to their neighbors as they stood up at their tables.

He was running out of time. He did not want to try to explain it away. If anyone got near the table, he would have to rush the glass to the serving line and pour the stuff down a drain. He could not afford to get caught with it: he could lose everything and be shipped back to Earth as poor as he was when he left.

The glass showed him walking down the street in front of his parents' old house (they lived in Mexico now, where it was warm) strutting in fine clothes for the young women that flocked out of the houses, mobbing him for even a little of his attention.

He stared at it.

Was this all that he really wanted? Money and stupid girls falling all over themselves for him? That wasn't all bad, of course, but he always thought he was supposed to want something special, not something so, so tawdry.

One of the men sauntering toward Harold was Security. Harold recognized his face from the forty-kilo "goop pleasure extreme" robbery.

Wasn't there anything more important than this in his life?

In the glass, his image reached up and took the

hand of the security man as he stepped up. The two images looked at each other with respect as they shook. The image then snapped into Harold, giving Wenoosh a hug and patting her on the back in a friendly manner as he stepped back. And then the same with the chaplain. And then with Lila, the nasty linguist that always made sarcastic comments. And others.

Then the image faded.

Try as he might, Harold could not get anything to appear in the glass again. His fifteen minutes were up, already.

And all he got was him hugging people and shaking their hands.

Was that his real "most beloved"? Was that what he really wanted or needed?

Was that all?

On the other hand, he was going to be pretty wealthy when he got home, no matter what. And he still had seven years to serve out on the Base.

The Security man reached Harold's table and peered into the glass for a moment before he picked up the empty bottle and read the label.

"You're not planning on drinking all of that, are you, Harold?"

Bill. That was his name. Like most Security personnel, his head was square, just like his jaw, and he swaggered when he walked.

"No, Bill," Harold said, standing up, praying that nothing would appear in the glass. "My sister sent it to me, probably as a joke, since she knows I don't drink." He smiled in what he hoped would be shyness rather than deviousness. "I figured on watching the alcohol crawl up the side of the glass and evaporate, watching the lights through it."

Bill looked entirely too suspicious for a moment, before he shrugged. "Okay, if you're that bored." Then he started moving away.

Harold thought that he could spend the next seven years without a friend, if he didn't do something. Naomi got him here, there being little more to do on the shuttle but stare at her pictures and daydream about how it would all be different when he got back to Earth.

But she was married. By the time he got back, her children would be having children.

Naomi was gone for good.

And he needed something to keep him going for the next decade.

Watching the tiny image of himself in the glass, the respect he saw in the other man's eyes—those did make him feel pretty good.

Maybe it was time to make a friend.

Maybe two.

"Uh, hey, Bill, could you help me get Wenoosh back to her quarters? She's pretty out of it."

The security man turned around and leaned over the table Harold had gestured at. Wenoosh was a shapeless lump on the floor.

208

"Yeah, I guess." He did not sound very enthusiastic, but he started around the table.

Harold hardly had to move at all, he was so close. He started to bend over to pick up Wenoosh, when he remembered the images in the glass.

He stood up and stuck his hand out to Bill.

"Uh, thanks for helping."

Bill stared at the hand for a moment, then took it.

"No problem, buddy."

For a moment, Harold did feel better. Maybe a few friends would not hurt at all.

He decided that maybe he got his fifteen minutes of "goop pleasure" after all, as he slid his hands under Wenoosh's limp shoulders.

Everybody Stops at Boston's

by Allan Rousselle

HERE'S YOUR SCOTCH. I promise you, it's replicated from the real thing—single malt, aged thirty-five years, and scanned unopened into a genuine Ericson back on Earth before the quarantine. You have never had a drink quite like it before, my friend, and you never will again. Not in this lifetime.

Now take a look around before you have your first taste. Smell the popcorn in the basket in front of you. That's real replicated butter. You don't even notice the recycled air of the station. Knock on this wooden counter—me and my boy took thousands of little replicated dark mahogany tiles, glued them together, and then sanded and shellacked the whole thing by hand. Four meters long by half a meter wide was a lot of work. A labor of love.

It's quiet here for now, just you and me and that poor fellow down at the other end of the bar, but it'll be busy as hell once the afternoon ferry from Io arrives. Funny thing about that guy, drinking like he won't see another planet-rise . . .

Yes, I'm the proprietor, and no, my name's not Boston. I hand painted that "Boston's Pub" permasign in the outside hall over a century ago when I first built this place. I had to name it *something*, and I wanted to commemorate the place of my birth somehow— yes, I'm actually from Earth. No, I wasn't one of the evacuees. I had left about a dozen or so years before the nano-plague hit.

Most people were desperate to stay Earthside during those years before that outbreak, but I wasn't the only fellow who felt the itch to cast off and find my fortunes elsewhere.

I left with two main advantages. The first was my background as a history major. You can laugh—most of the prospectors who've passed through this station en route to or from the Jovian mines have done as much. But while they keep coming and going, they all leave some of their money with me, just as you're doing now.

You see, the person who pays attention to history knows that some prospectors strike it rich, while the overwhelming majority don't. Yet those who supply the goods—air, tools, booze, hookers, food—well, they've always got a steady supply of customers who'll pay just a little bit more than retail. Hell, a lot more than retail.

The Jovian Trail is littered with engineers, mineralogists, astrophysicists, medical doctors, and the like.

There aren't so many of us social scientists. And yet, who does most of the heavy lifting? Those engineers. And who enjoys a more leisurely lifestyle by anticipating the needs of those heavy lifters? Me.

So that was one advantage. Understanding history. Understanding people, more like. The other advantage was more tangible. I owned—and still own—an Ericson, and had the connections to help me smuggle it off Earth.

Most people think of Ericsons as being these unusually precise replicators, but that's not it by far. Replicator technology is easy: all you need are the right kind of nanites and a box that can shield them while they do their work. At least half a dozen shops here at the station have faster nanites or larger cases than mine.

The advantage that mine has is the memory capacity. Disassembling and reassembling molecules is easy enough for the little worker nanites. But storing and retrieving the maps is another matter.

Think about it this way. There's something like three times ten to the twenty-second power atoms in one cubic centimeter of water. Pure water, that is. That number will go up or down depending upon the molecular composition of the impurities floating around in there. The amount of memory needed just to store a molecular map of, say, a shot of whiskey is outrageous. That bottle of scotch? Outrageous to the nth power.

But Ericson's compression algorithms and memory management techniques were light-years ahead of their time, which is why the Ericson machines are the only replicators that are, in any practical sense, user programmable.

Bring me a shot of your favorite beverage, and I can scan it into a ceramic memory brick and then reproduce a glass of it for you any time you drop by.

Not for free, of course, but you get the idea.

That's why there will never be a tavern on Copernicus Station that will stand up even one week against me. All taverns have replicators. But none have a library of drinks like mine. I go all the way back to Earth, remember, and my stock keeps growing.

Let me tell you something. I thought I'd seen and heard it all, making my way from Earth to Harriman Station to Mars and on out to here. I was on Mars when the Samphire elevator crashed. I was tending bar on the *Sagan* when Lambert discovered life on Europa. Truly, I thought I'd seen it all.

But it's quiet times like this that get to me, make me think of the weirdest thing I've ever seen. And the worst.

Do you believe that time travel is possible? Don't look so startled; of course, you do. Everybody does, even if they pretend they don't. But that guy down at the end of the bar? He says he's celebrating *because* of time travel. Says he's actually invented a time machine. And so he's drinking like there's no tomorrow.

One time I had a customer come in and order scotch—replicated from the very same bottle as yours—who had this look, this pall, that was disquieting as all hell. Death and solitude seemed to cling to this poor soul's space suit like moon dust. One drink led to another and then another and then, well . . . you know how alcohol can loosen the tongue.

This stranger claimed to be an assassin. A killer-for-hire of the literal sort. Had killed maybe a dozen or so people, usually because of some threat they had posed to some big corporate interests. People with unlimited credit and a lot to lose.

I've tended bar for more decades than I care to count, and I've heard a lot of stories. I have no doubts that some of my clientele have been killers. A few have even claimed as much to my face, and it's possible that one or two were telling some version of the truth. I'm inclined to believe as much.

But this was different. This person didn't have the I-dare-you eyes of a ruthless thug. This wasn't bragging or boasting, like our friend down at the end of the bar with the time machine. This was the cold, matter-of-fact confession of a professional killer.

"I've eliminated people who needed to be taken care of," the assassin told me, "but today is my last job."

At this point, as I'm sure you can imagine, I didn't want to ask for clarification. And Hubbard as my witness, I was pretty sure this wasn't the assassin's first time in my bar. Like, maybe there had already been a contract quietly carried out on my premises once before. I'm sure you can understand why I'd keep that to myself just then, too. The wise bartender knows when to show discretion.

But I didn't have to wait very long to find out what "today is my last job" meant. And as you can tell by me standing here right now, the last job in question wasn't me.

"This place looks pretty much the same as the last time I was here, except almost all of the pictures along that wall aren't there yet."

An odd thing to say, but I know you're already ahead of me. This single photo hanging above the cash register is my son. And yet, this person says that there used to be more photos above my cash register. You and I both know that I'm only going to add photos over time, not take them down. Likewise, any proprietors who might come after me.

But I'm a patient listener, and I let the assassin tell the story. Sure enough, the killer claimed to be from the future and was sent back in time to take care of— get this—the inventor of the time machine. Not only that, but the assassination had to take place before the first time jump took place. In essence, the job was to go back in time to prevent the possibility of going back in time. And the presumed inventor of time travel was sitting in my bar on that particular day, at that table over there by the wall, even as we spoke.

As I said, I studied history, not physics or engineering, and I'm not quite sure how or whether a causal loop can be created in order to prevent itself. It just doesn't make sense to me.

But a good listener knows when to ask questions, so I asked this killer from the future, "What happens to you if you succeed? Do you disappear? Do you stay stuck here?" And the killer downed what was left in the glass and asked for more scotch.

"We'll know pretty soon."

It was contact poison, some kind of eight-hour deal that had't even been invented yet and for which there wasn't—or isn't—a cure. The assassin favored contact poison, and had already casually bumped into the target as they were entering my establishment, and then ditched the poisoned glove even before sitting down at the bar.

The damage was already done; an unstoppable chain of events had already been set into motion. It might be four hours before the first symptoms would appear; the remaining hours would be excruciating. But the point, I was told, wasn't the pain; the point was that the target died. That man sitting at that table was already dead. He just didn't know it yet.

I don't mind saying that it's rather disquieting to be talking matter-of-factly to a killer who has just murdered someone in plain sight, while nobody noticed. Not even the victim.

"If what you say is true, then it's all a done deal. The inventor is guaranteed to die before testing his time travel machine, which means he doesn't invent or discover time travel, which means your employer will have no need nor means to send you back here, which means you're not here."

"And yet," said the assassin, "here I am."

The killer bought a round for the inventor and his

friends, I guess the way an executioner might order a last meal for his intended victim.

Sure enough, the inventor started to clutch his stomach and he looked a little pale, and then he and his buddies got up and left soon thereafter.

The assassin, who didn't look so good either, stood up and started to pay for the last drink.

"Forget about that last one," I said. "It's on me. Just don't come back." I got a grim smile in return, and the killer walked out.

Later that day, my customer did indeed die, and the station cops never could figure out what it was that killed him. My other customer, who claimed to be from the future, never got any attention that I heard about after walking out of my establishment.

But that's not the end of the story.

Here, let me pour you another. This one's on me. And don't even dare to think about offering to buy a round for our friend at the end of the bar. My sense of humor has dried up on that particular topic.

Now, then. I told you how I had been a student of history. Anyone who takes a look at history recognizes that the big inventions and discoveries happened with multiple people in multiple locations, all at about the same time. Certain ideas just seem to pop up out of nowhere and suddenly they're everywhere. The steam engine, for example. Interchangeable parts for firearms. The internal combustion engine. Harnessing electricity. Audio recording. Video recording. Thought recording.

But while several different folks might come up with

217

similar ideas at the same time, they nonetheless had to start within similar cultural milieus . . . Now there's a word for social scientists like myself. "Milieu." No astrophysicist ever had use for a word like that.

My point is, the engines that drove the industrial revolution came from the minds of Europeans and Americans at around the same time; they did not come from Eskimos or Bushmen of that era. Likewise, the space race, the information age, and the nano age were all propelled by like-minded inventors from different but comparable societies.

So it did not completely surprise me the second time a fellow came into my bar and, after a drink or two, told me that he had discovered the principles of moving backward and forward through time. Nor was I shocked the third time it happened. Nor all the times after that. All separated by several years, of course, but close enough as historical ages go. There's something about Copernicus Station and its unique location near the asteroid belt, I think, that combines with this particular period of history to produce a breakthrough in time travel.

So I wasn't expecting it, but I wasn't surprised by it. What *did* surprise me was that before I encountered another inventor of a time machine, I saw that assassin come walking in again. The very same one as before. I forgot to breathe at first. Looked younger. Same haunted eyes. Same aura of death and solitude. Same sense of purpose. But definitely younger.

The assassin did not recognize me, however. I

forced myself to breathe; to move; to tend my customers. While delivering a round of pilsners to three young bucks at the table by the entrance, I learned that one in particular was celebrating his recent invention. He was going to travel through time, he said, and things were going to be different from here on out.

Again, that inability to breathe. My mouth went as dry as Europa ice. I managed to nod my congratulations, and then darted back behind my refuge. Four meters by one half meter of well-tended wood.

The assassin sat at the bar and, after a few drinks, eventually told me about being a killer, about how this was the last job. About coming back in time to kill the very person who made it possible to come back through time.

Was there anything I could do to stop it? No, of course not. The job was already done. Contact poison. "Have you ever been on a job like this before?" I asked.

No, again, of course not.

What will happen to the killer after the inventor dies?

"We'll know pretty soon."

Only, soon after the inventor walks out, the killer walks out, never to be heard from again.

The first time this had happened, it shook me in ways I can't possibly describe. Emotionally, more than anything else. Screwed me up for years. But after it happened a second time, I lost a lot of sleep doing a lot of thinking, more than anything else.

Mostly, I asked myself those imponderable questions. Like, how was it that you could have different guys invent their respective time machines, but it was always the same guy who got sent back to stop him? Who was it that hired this assassin? And how could they possibly propose to compensate the assassin once the job was done?

This last one bothered me for a long time until I realized that I had been thinking along the wrong lines.

If you want to send somebody back in time to change something, then you would never have to pay for the favor. Either the change took place, in which case the thing that motivated you to send back your hired gun never happened in the first place, so it would never occur to you to follow through on any payment plans to rectify something that never happened. *Or* the change *didn't* take place, so you wouldn't have to pay, because the job wasn't completed.

So if the hired gun could never be paid for a job well done, the only other possibility, it seemed to me, was that the killer was escaping something terrible in the future by taking this job. Even the uncertainty of what would happen to the assassin after a successful hit must have been preferable to the certainty of what would happen in the killer's "current" timeline by staying in the future.

At least, that was all I could think of.

I came to believe that this terrible fate, whatever it

must be, combined with the assassin's capabilities in that particular line of work, made for an inevitable choice of who must be picked to carry out the job. The timing of arriving at that inevitable conclusion might vary, but the conclusion itself was foregone.

Of course, the only way to test this hypothesis would be to see what happened if another time machine inventor happened to announce himself or herself to me at my establishment. And how many time machine inventors would have to show up at my doorstep to comprise a statistically significant sample size?

I'm not a scientist, as I've said, but it seems to me that having two inventors of a time machine is already pretty damned statistically significant.

That said, I wasn't really shocked the third time the assassin showed up. Followed by a third time machine inventor, who would eventually have to leave my pub with stomach pains.

The third assassin was the same person, only this time not as young as the second, but maybe still a bit younger than the first. The inventor, on the other hand, was completely different from her two predecessors. But of course that made sense. Her two predecessors had already predeceased her.

But getting back to the returning assassin who had no memory of ever having been here: after a little bit of lubrication courtesy of Scotland's finest, the topic of being a killer and being on the last job came up, plus the unavoidable topic of the intended target and the method being employed, etc.

"Why did you take this job? You can't possibly stand to receive a reward, so what penalty are you escaping?" I didn't get an answer, but I did get a grimace that convinced me I was on the right track.

I learned a little bit more about the assassin's history. About getting into the field, about becoming a contact poison expert. I'd already learned a little bit from the first time around, but this time the conversation had more depth because, quite frankly, I had a better sense of what kinds of questions to ask.

I found out an answer to another question: why my tavern?

"This is the only pub on Copernicus. Even for people who don't drink, everyone at the station will eventually end up here. History doesn't record the daily activities of an inventor, even one as important as this one, but we knew where the first jump would begin. Copernicus. It's easier for me to stake out a pub in a major spoke of the station rather than trying to sneak around private quarters. QED."

I may be merely a bartending history buff, but I know enough geek-speak to know that QED is short for a Latin phrase that means: "I'm one methodical sonofabitch."

If I were a killer, I don't know if I'd have come to the same conclusion as my assassin friend about the best place for a stakeout, but the reasons for making the choice aren't important. Maybe there's some piece of information that I'm not privy to. What's important is that, once this same person is given this particular job, this person's training and method of operation ultimately and necessarily lead to the same choices every time. Stake out my pub, and zap the target while entering. Ditch the murder weapon, and QED.

So victim number three eventually develops stomach cramps and limps out of Boston's Pub, next to be seen in the obituary section. The killer's not looking so hot either, and leaves not too long after.

Speaking of which, there goes our friend the inventor who's been enjoying his celebratory drink—thanks for dropping by!

Between you and me, I think he's not feeling well.

Okay, I'm sorry. I didn't mean to be cavalier like that. I guess I've become a little bit jaded over these many decades. Humor is a coping mechanism, right? Even if it is gallows humor.

So, as you've figured out by now, that third time wasn't the last time I met the assassin, and it certainly wasn't the last time I had an aspiring time traveler sit at one of my tables. In fact, I figure that scenario has played itself out over a dozen times now.

I guess time travel very much wants to be discovered. And yet, there can be no shortage of people who stand to lose something important to them if time travel is allowed to exist. People with means. People who can find just the right assassin with just the right motivation for the job, whatever that motivation might be.

So if inventing time travel is inevitable, it would appear that it also contains the seeds of its own prevention. Any society capable of producing time travel is also capable of going back in time to prevent it from happening. Nature's self-correcting mechanism for keeping time moving forward, I suppose.

But what happens to the person sent back in time to prevent time travel from being possible?

Before you go, I want you to know that I have at least half an answer, my friend. And I can tell from your shallow breathing and your white-knuckle grip on the bar that you'll be leaving quite soon.

You see that photo hanging on the wall behind me? That's my son. He was the first person that I am aware of to have discovered the principles of traveling back and forth through time. He's the one who told me about how Copernicus' unique orbit made that discovery possible.

I don't think the first assassin who came through here realized that Boston's Pub was not named for the proprietor, nor that the proprietor was his intended victim's father.

Nor do I think the assassin imagined that a simple bartender would, during those few hours of our acquaintance, locate the poisoned glove with the last remaining traces of a very toxic contact poison on it and very carefully bring it into my back room where my Ericson resides.

Did I mention that the Ericson is unique in that it is the only replicator that is, in any practical sense, user programmable? Bring me a shot of your favorite whiskey, and I'll be glad to produce a glassful soon afterward. Not for free, of course, but you get the idea.

You get the idea.

I recognized you as soon as you came in, even though you didn't recognize me. And I knew what that meant for my only other customer here this afternoon. I feel bad for him, I really do.

But as to what happens to you now that *his* fate is sealed, I want you to know that at least part of the answer is certain. The assassin who has traveled through here so many times without ever being the wiser has never been heard from again after leaving. Neither dead nor alive. But even though no inexplicable corpse of someone from a near-future generation has ever been found, I assure you that the assassin could never be found alive either.

Killing you won't bring my son back. It certainly hasn't so far. But as long as you keep giving me the opportunity, I see no reason to stop.

And I'll keep telling you this story until you figure out how it ends. You'll have to stop me next time, of course, if you've heard it before.

Spot-Man's Chest
by Daniel M. Hoyt

"THEY'RE GONE, SIR," crackled a reedy voice in Sam's earset as he sprinted toward the bridge of his personal space transport, the *Jonathan*. "The pirates just . . . disappeared."

"On my way," X. Samarkus Mendelson barked between grunts, his lungs bursting, acid bubbling up his throat.

I'm getting too old for this, Sam thought as he neared the bridge door, pausing only a second to catch his breath as the door whooshed open before bursting through. *But I need to know where my cargo's gone.*

"What happened, Blip?" Sam shouted, and leaned against the wall as the door snicked shut behind him. The bridge was plush, but spare for a personal transport—roughly a square, with only three permanent stations: communication, astrogation and technical, each with its own private specialized displays, more like an office than a bridge. Overstuffed, supple leather chairs graced each station, with a couple of extra floaters, but no captain's station—no *need* for a captain on such a small vessel. Despite the size, most of the crew of sixteen had managed to crowd in for the pirate pursuit, as if it were a play, staged purely for their entertainment.

The *Jonathan*'s astrogator, Tren Wheyton—better known to owner and crew alike as "Blip"—looked up from his display and shook his head. "They were *there*. And then they weren't. Just like that."

Sam bulled his way over to Blip's display while Blip spoke, scowling and ignoring the buzz of whispers surrounding them as the crewmen jumped aside. Sam knew his extraordinary presence on the bridge was, to say the least, unsettling, even more so than the recent excitement caused by the pirates. One of the richest men in Rah system, Sam rarely ventured out on the spur of the moment like this, much less without informing the crew of their destination up front.

Once underway, the minimal crew had been instructed to discreetly follow one of Sam's own transport ships—the pride of Swift Transport's fleet, the *Achilles*. They'd been noticeably puzzled, but offered no complaints. Without skipping a beat, instruments flickered to life and coffee flowed freely as the crew settled into their tasks.

Sam lingered briefly, savoring the sweet aromas of vanilla, hazelnut, and chocolate mingling with the sharp tang of the coffee. It was only there for a few moments before the air recirculation system dissipated it, but Sam couldn't resist waiting. *Reminds me of breakfasts with Blip and my grandfather, back on Rah III, late in the morning, when all the servants were too busy to dote on them. Relax. Talk. No worries. You really believed that everything would be fine.*

Afterward, Sam had returned to his cabin to wait.

It hadn't been long before the *Achilles* had been attacked, practically right in front of them, sensorwise, and Sam had hoofed it back to the bridge.

Blip pointed at a blinking bull's-eye on the display as Sam looked on, standing near him. "That's where they were when they disappeared. We set the same course, too, but I don't think there's anything there. Should be in range in a few minutes to scan. Then we'll see."

"Why don't you think there's anything? There's something on your screen, isn't there?"

"Yeah, but . . . At first I thought the blip was a station, but now I'm pretty sure it's just an artifact, a ghost. Nothing on the other sensors, nothing on the star charts matching it, and it's not registering on the *Achilles'* system." Blip smacked the side of the display, a technical maneuver respected throughout known civilization, and looked up at Sam. "It's this crappy astro system you got on Cirma, Spot-Man." Blip's mouth crinkled in disapproval, and he turned away from Sam. "SurePost 6000, my ass," he muttered. "Should've been called the Sure*Ghost*!"

Sam bristled at his childhood friend's inappropriate—

and needlessly informal—reproach, but choked back an angry response. He felt claustrophobic with all these crewmen around. Sam glanced around wildly and shouted, "Bridge crew only; the rest of you get out!" Turning to Blip, he said evenly, "I had no choice. We've been over this several times, Blip. The old astro sizzled in a freak electrical storm on Cirma. I had to replace it with *something*, or we'd still be stuck on that rock."

Sam leaned close to Blip's ear and whispered, "And don't call me that on the bridge."

Spot had been a groaner when they first met as preteens—"X. Samarkus the Spot, eh?" was the first thing twelve-year-old Tren ever said to Sam—and it was still a groaner a quarter decade later. It had taken Sam nine patient years before Tren finally settled on a career before Sam could return the favor and saddle Tren with the moniker "Blip." And Blip stuck.

But from anyone else, the mere mention of "Spot-Man" would end a career at Swift Transport.

"Could've at least let me replace it when you got back," Blip mumbled. "This piece of crap—"

"I think that's enough, don't you, *Astrogator* Wheyton?"

Blip bit his lip and bared his teeth. "Yes, *sir*. Sorry, *sir*."

You should be, Blip. I let you get away with a lot, because we go way back, but I'd appreciate it if you didn't openly sass me in front of the crew. Remember

*that embarrassing incident at graduation with the auto-
nav flycar, duct tape, and you and your mother's under-
wear? It could happen again, buddy.*

To be fair, the Cirma techs had sneered a little too
openly for Sam's taste. And the SurePost had been
mightily expensive for him to believe it was the *only*
astro available—but the price gouging didn't bother
him as much as the SurePost's rock-bottom reputation.
Blip had warned Sam about it on Cirma, but they'd
needed to get back to Rah III as soon as possible, so
there really hadn't been a *choice,* had there? There
had been a dozen pirate attacks on the Swift fleet, and
Sam *needed* to get home and take care of it while he
still had a business to save. With at least one transport
losing its cargo each day, Swift was hemorrhaging cap-
ital at an alarming rate.

"Tren," Sam said gently, barely above a whisper.
"I *know* we got taken. I *know* everyone replaces the
SurePost as soon as they can. I *know* I can afford a
top-flight astro. But there just wasn't *time* after we got
back. After this trip, I promise you can fix it. Let's
just get through this crisis first, okay?"

Blip softened. "I'll hold you to it." He pointed at
the display. "Almost in range now." Blip sat back in
his chair and waited.

An incoming message buzzed in their ears. "Sure-
Post 6835-Alpha-12-Whiskey-354. Dock 18 okay?"

Sam glanced quizzically at his astrogator. Blip
shrugged and reached for his earset to respond, but

Sam batted Blip's hand away. He shook his head slowly. He turned behind him to a crewman at an analysis station.

"Where's it coming from?"

The crewman ticked a few keys and fiddled with some knobs. He looked up, surprised. "The ghost, sir."

Sam turned back to Blip, who responded with one raised eyebrow.

"Dock 18 good? Hello?"

Sam quickly reached up to enable his own earset. "Eighteen's good. Instructions?"

"The usual."

The characteristic inside-out pop of a comm channel being dropped echoed in Sam's earset. "Skitch!" Sam swore aloud. "What does *that* mean?" Sam tore his earset off and slammed it on the edge of Blip's display. It bounced away harmlessly and skittered away under a chair.

"Sir?" a nervous voice behind him said.

Sam whirled to the crewman at the analysis station that had tracked the comm signal. Now red-faced, his hands shaking awkwardly, the crewman shrank into his chair.

The *Jonathan* lurched sideways suddenly, spilling Sam hard to the floor.

"What the skitch was that?" Sam glared around the bridge.

The terrified analyst swallowed loudly, catching

231

Sam's attention. "They're bringing us in. There's some kind of remote control signal coming through, and I can't block it. But, sir, there's another comm."

Sam fished under the chair for his fallen earset and crammed it on while scrambling to his feet. He motioned to Blip to tune in the same comm.

"Sorry, Salty," a coarse voice growled in Sam's earset, "but fair's fair. I got the chest first. Buy you a rum in the wet mess?"

Sam scowled. "Sure." He hesitated a couple seconds. "How do I find you?"

A laugh like a grater on slate boomed in Sam's ear. "I'll find you, Salty. No-scars stick out." The inside-out pop stopped another booming slate-grater mid-guffaw.

Sam jerked a thumb at the bridge door. "Come on, Blip, we need to talk." The door whooshed open and he stepped through just ahead of Blip.

"Ideas?" Sam asked, a few nearly-sprinting steps away from the bridge.

"I'm pretty sure it's that SurePo—"

Sam rounded on Blip midstep. "Give it a rest!"

"No, wait, Spot-Man, hear me out. I'm serious."

Reaching his cabin, Sam stopped, thumbed the gen-lock and ran inside, Blip close on his heels.

The door snicked shut and auto-locked behind them. Sam plopped down on his goose-down duvet, flicked on the vanilla air scenter to counteract the stale air, and took a deep breath. "Okay. Convince me."

"That last message—I think it was from the pirate

that attacked the *Achilles*. My pirate lingo isn't first-hand, mind you, but I'm pretty sure he thought you were going after it, too. He got there first and headed straight for . . . wherever we're docking. There's *something* here, obviously, and I think it only shows on the SurePost astros."

"Why would you think that?"

"They addressed us by the astro's model and serial number. And they remoted us in. I don't think they can do that with just *any* astro."

Sam considered this. "Maybe. But how could the guy in the second comm recognize us in the bar?"

"That's what convinced me, Spot-Man. The *only* way he could know that you're a *new* pirate—No-scars, he said; it means a newbie who hasn't seen battle yet—is if they're tracking your pirate 'career' somehow. Which would imply they know you've never come here before—which you couldn't have done before the SurePost was installed, 'cause you wouldn't have been able to *see* the station before!"

Sam nodded. "Yeah. I can buy that. Which probably makes this invisible station here a pretty insular community." Skitch! "And we're about to walk right into it! Not to mention that they probably think we're pirates, too."

"I think the SurePost is more sophisticated than the general public knows," Blip said thoughtfully. "The highway-robbery price and poor reputation might be an intentional cover."

Blip's face darkened. "There's one more thing,

Spot-Man. Pirates *never* give away things—like docking at this station—for free."

A waiting guard—or maybe a gorilla, considering the tangled mess of hair sprouting from every inch of his skin—grunted at Sam and Blip as they disembarked. Their dock opened directly to a private hallway, bare and clean, with the faint aroma of strawberries. Someone went to great expense to make the environment pleasant, but not homey. The place looked brand-new.

Except for the gorilla. *He* looked . . . experienced. Two heads taller than either Sam or Blip, dressed in what could kindly be called Rah system flag remnants dyed to Day-Glo gaudiness, his feet planted firmly and hands folded across his chest in the universal don't-mess-with-me guard pose, the gorilla tossed his head to his left. "Wet mess's that way."

The gorilla eyed them cautiously until they passed.

Behind Sam, he thought he heard the gorilla mumble, "No-scar scum," and spit at them. "Now where's my *real* clothes?"

Blip turned to Sam, grinned, and flicked his glance back at the guard. "That was so we'd *know* this is a pirate station." He chuckled. "Probably wears a dress uniform normally."

Ahead of them a few steps, a hidden door slid sideways. Raucous laughter and breaking glass shattered the quiet of the hallway. A warm breeze breathed in Sam's face, carrying with it the whiff of too many sweating bodies in close contact and the sting of hard liquor vapors. A broken wooden chair leg sailed past Sam's ear, clattering down the hall behind them.

Sam half expected the din to stop suddenly as he and Blip entered, but their entrance went unnoticed. Fights broke out and broke up randomly, as dozens of drunken men and women dressed in mishmashes of brightly-colored silk argued in shouts and brawled openly. In the corner, a poker table flew upward with some help from an angry player, scattering chits and splashing beer onto the next table. Bits of pungent foam swatted Sam's face as he passed. The second poker table went flying, too, and the participants of both games faced off. Throughout all of this, a beefy, red-headed bartender in an orange smock casually wiped down the counter, ignoring the wanton destruction all around him. His expressionless, plum-pudding face remained calm, no hint of stray thoughts marring his blank eyes.

I've seen this scene at an amusement park somewhere. Sam chuckled.

"No-scar!" came a booming voice behind Sam, following quickly by a crushing slap on Sam's back that knocked the wind from him. The pirate laughed—piercing over the comm channel, eardrum bursting here—and bellowed, "Rum for No-scar!"

The fighting paused as laughter erupted throughout the wet mess, then resumed no less vigorously than before.

As Sam struggled for breath, a shovel of a hand

clamped his upper arm and steered him to the only empty booth, plopping him down unceremoniously in the middle of a beer puddle covering one bench. Blip's escort similarly seated him next to Sam, roughly shoving Sam against the wall.

An obese, yet muscular man squeezed into the bench opposite them and slapped a ham-sized hand on the table hard enough to make it jump. Bald and freshly shaved, stray drops of sweat beading on his forehead, he looked more like a circus strongman than a pirate. To be fair, he *smelled* like a pirate—or at least a not-so-recently-washed pirate. His jowls bouncing as he spoke, he extended a sweaty maw and said, "Slocum Hardy, friend. Call me Slipknot."

Without hesitation, Sam grabbed Slipknot's hand and pumped it hard. *Okay, now. This I understand. Just like a meet-and-greet, but with less soap.* Sam assumed his CEO face. "Sam. Sam . . ." He glanced at Blip, who looked dazed and terrified. "Spotter. Friends call me the Spot-Man." Beneath the table, he kicked Blip in the ankle.

A stack of poker chits spattered over their table and bounced off the wall. A thin man with a beard dyed green launched himself at the chips on the table, while a couple of other pirates scooped up the chits that had fallen to the floor.

Slipknot threw back his head and guffawed.

Sam cringed, his eardrums throbbed from the outburst, but he recovered quickly. "So, Slipknot, what was the cargo?" He knew, of course, since it was from his own ship, but he needed to make sure Slipknot was the right pirate. It wouldn't do to mark the wrong man. Sam wasn't sure what he would be able to do about it when he got back, but he needed to find out everything he could about this pirate before then.

Just then, the bartender leaned over the table between them and wiped it. Slipknot rolled his eyes and waited until the table was cleaned and the bartender sauntered away without a word.

"The chest? Medical supplies, mostly. Some of it's junk, but some'll fetch a pretty coin on the black market. A good day's work." He eyed Sam suspiciously. "You're not thinking of trying to pirate *me*, are you, Salty?" He laughed uproariously and slapped the table repeatedly.

A pirate in the booth behind Sam leaned his head back and breathed in Sam's ear, "Luck to you, if you try that. They call him Slipknot 'cause they catch him and he slips away, every time. More likely you'll lose your *own* chest."

A shark, then. Met plenty of them in my career.

A trio of whiskey glasses nearly brimming with dark, golden liquid slid across the table. Sam watched the bartender's receding bulk, casually pushing through a cluster of pirates slashing at each other with broken bottles and screaming obscenities. He stopped briefly for one particularly buxom pirate girl, whom he grabbed from behind, whirled around and sloppily tongued before going on his way, all without a single word.

Slipknot grabbed the nearest glass and drained it, then slammed the glass down.

The rum stung his nose and burned his throat, but Sam sipped his and tried not to let his mouth twist into a grimace. *Skitch! Where's a good glass of port wine when you need it?*

Sam smirked and shook his head. "Wasn't even thinking of going after *your* chest. Friend. I was just curious what I lost out on."

Slipknot leaned over the table, surprising Sam with his dexterity. Slipknot's face darkened. "Good thing." Sam sensed that this pirate was even more dangerous than the helpful voice in his ear implied. He had the distinct impression his cargo was the *least* he'd stand to lose if he crossed Slipknot.

Sam noticed Blip still hadn't taken a drink, took another sip of his rum, and kicked Blip's ankle. "Good rum, Blip," Sam said, waving the glass. "Drink up while you can."

Blip looked at Sam with a pained expression, and touched his lips to the pungent rum without drinking it. To his credit, Blip managed to keep a straight face.

That's settled, then. Port when we get back to the ship. You deserve it, old buddy.

The pirate leaned back and smiled broadly, the menace gone as quickly as it had appeared. "Forget the chest. It's mine now. Worry about the next one."

The din in the bar crescendoed just as a rum-filled bottle sailed between them and shattered against the wall next to Sam. Instinctively throwing his arms up to protect his face, Sam's forearms caught a few shards as the exploding bottle's contents soaked his shirt.

Slipknot wrenched the table away from the wall and threw it aside. Standing, he bellowed angrily in the direction of the bottle's thrower, "Karl!" Incredibly, the wet mess went silent immediately. A chair, already in motion, broke against the wall with a resounding crack.

A quiet voice from the doorway announced itself with a discreet cough. "Yes, quite. It's all fun and games when someone new comes aboard, isn't it? But your aim, Karl, needs improvement." A tall, thin man dressed in a dark red business suit stood in the doorway, flanked by two beefy musclemen in black. Long white hair flowed down his back.

Clearly the boss around here. This is where the deal starts. Whatever it is.

The boss man turned to Sam. "Welcome to my station, Mr. Spotter. I am Mr. Klost."

Blip stifled a surprised "Oh," then tried to disguise it by clearing his throat. Sam ignored him.

"This . . ." Klost waved a hand vaguely around. ". . . is for your benefit. It's customary to make Noscars feel . . . comfortable and accepted. All the pirate tropes, just this once. It's our version of a surprise costume party. *You*, of course, will assume the damages." He smiled. "As is our custom."

"Of course." *An initiation fee, then. Fine. Pay up and get the skitch out of here.* Unspecified dread washed over him Sam, but he pushed the feeling away.

Instead, he stood and displayed his bleeding forearms. "I need to get back to my ship and clean up."

Slipknot's arm shot out to block Sam.

Klost nodded his head to the right and the muscleman on that side vanished, his thudding footsteps receding down the hall. "We'll take care of that. We need to discuss your docking fee." He motioned to another part of the wet mess, where a just-cleaned, empty end booth waited.

Several pirates drifted toward the door. Others starting righting fallen chairs and tossing broken pieces to one side of the bar, coordinating the cleanup effort with clipped gestures and whispers. A short blond man grabbed a broom from behind the bar and started sweeping up one of the messes. The bartender continued to wipe the counter.

Blip cleared his throat. "Let me do the talking," he said in a low voice as they were shoved toward the clean booth, dodging several brightly-clad pirates cleaning up messes. Blip slid in the booth first, on the side with its back open to the rest of the wet mess. Sam followed, holding his wounded arms up. Klost sat facing them, as Slipknot had.

Blip held out his hand. "Sparks Klost, I presume. It's an honor."

Klost grinned. "Yes, I am Sparks, Mister . . ."

"Wheyton. Call me Blip. Been reading about you, sir, since your SurePost 1000. Very impressive astro. And this station setup." Blip glanced around. "Amazing."

Klost actually blushed. "I'm always pleased to meet a fan. There is more to you, I think, than you appear. Your eyes betray an intelligence most of these simpletons lack."

"Thanks. I'm an astrogator, too. Tinkered around with some astro systems myself from time to time. Nothing like yours, of course, but I can appreciate the technology needed to cloak a station this size from sensors and rival astro systems."

A thin man with thinning black hair and a thin black mustache pulled up a chair next to Sam, muttered a greeting, grabbed Sam's nearest arm, and meticulously picked bits of glass from Sam's forearm. Sam ignored the prickling.

Klost swept a stray hair from his face and shifted in his seat. "Thirty-*eight* stations now, with this one. Your installer probably told you thirty-seven, yes? But we just put this one in operation this week—that's why I'm out here personally. You're lucky to have caught me here."

"Yeah, thirty-seven," Sam said, gritting his teeth as the medic slathered an antiseptic on his arm, then smeared the bleeding spots with a fruity paste that instantly disappeared into an invisible bandage. "We weren't expecting a station here. Or Slipknot." He half grinned.

Klost laughed. "Hard to avoid that skitcher. One of my best customers." Klost's smile faded. "Now about your docking fee."

"How much?" Sam asked quickly—too quickly.

Blip stomped on his foot, but Sam already realized his mistake. *Never appear too eager in negotiations; they think you're up to something.* Sam held his breath and waited silently as the medic started on his other forearm.

Chewing his lower lip, Klost narrowed his eyes. His eyes glazed, as though he were lost in deliberation.

Dread welled up in the pit of Sam's stomach. *Think like a pirate. Be like a pirate. Be. A. Pirate.*

Klost inclined his hand slightly. Two musclemen grunted and closed in behind Sam and Blip. "Have we made a mistake here, gentlemen? You were heading straight for that transport, as was Slipknot, then you set a course directly for the station. We assumed you were one of us. Yes?"

"Of course," Sam said automatically. *Never dispel a favorable impression, even if it's based on a lie. Important rule of business networking.* Also, Sam had a sinking feeling about the fate of nonpirates who happen upon the station.

"Don't worry, we're with you," Blip said. He nodded toward Sam. "Spot-Man didn't deal with the installer; I did. He mentioned something about docking fees, of course, but then his wife called—a real nagger, I can tell you, from what I saw on the viz-comm—and laid into him about missing his kid's school play or something. I felt so bad for him I just told him I already knew about the fee structure and got the skitch out of there before she started in on *me* just for being there!"

Klost glared at Blip. "Who is this installer? I'll have him . . . retrained."

Blip waved his hands in front of him. "No, no, that's not necessary. Really, it was my fault. The poor guy's got enough problems with wifey, don't you think? I'm sure it was a one-time thing."

Klost said nothing.

The medic finished, mumbled a good-bye, and left. Sam watched him leave. The bartender still wiped the counter. Maybe he *always* did.

Sam's arms throbbed, and he could feel a muscleman's hot breath on his neck. *Give up the installer. They probably won't check until Blip and I are long gone.* "It was on Ci—"

Klost held up a hand. The musclemen behind Sam and Blip eased back. Klost's dark countenance lighted considerably. "You're right. He's been punished enough with a companion like that. But I shall make sure it doesn't happen again. Anywhere." Klost touched his ear—Sam couldn't see any earset, but imagined Klost had some kind of hidden ear comm—and barely vocalized one word, "Reorientation."

Dropping his hand, Klost sat back and crossed his thin arms over his thinner chest. "Ten percent of your chest is standard. But you lost the chest to Slipknot, didn't you? And I daresay your ship's hold is somewhat small for taking on the cargo from a freighter that size, anyway." Klost's eyes narrowed. "So, the question is, what exactly were you after here? Maybe just a small *part* of the chest? Yes?"

Sam's heart beat in his chest, and his throat constricted. *Got to quell his suspicions fast.* "You're right," he said confidently. "It wasn't random. We followed that specific freighter, waiting for a good opportunity. I've got a . . . spy . . . in Swift." He racked his memory, trying to figure out what in his transport's cargo would be small enough to fit in the *Jonathan*, yet valuable enough on the black market to be worth selling. *Drugs? No. Too easy to obtain legally. Medicines? Maybe, but only if you've got an epidemic somewhere. What, then?*

"And *what* were you looking for, then?"

The low buzz in the bar abated for a moment as the pirates nearby cartoonishly leaned in, straining to hear the answer. Klost glared at them, and they left quickly.

"Glonion," Blip said in a low voice, before Sam could answer.

"Ah," Klost said. "I see. You are not just pirates, you are . . . runner suppliers."

Glonion. Of course! Watered-down nitroglycerine, used as a neurotic. Full strength, it's an explosive. Good job, Blip!

"Yes," Blip said quickly. "We're working on a way of . . . reconstituting the solution full strength at combust time, so it can be transported and stored while stable, then restored on the fly for an explosive engine boost."

Klost smirked and licked his lips. "And the kids modding their ship engines will pay anything for more

244

thrust, won't they? I'd guess you're seeing a twenty, thirty percent boost?"

"Thirty-seven," Blip said proudly.

"Nice."

"If it doesn't explode," Sam added.

Klost laughed and waved a hand. "Still got stability problems, yes? No matter. Kids don't care. At that age, they're reckless; they think they're invincible." He inclined his head slightly. "Brilliant, gentleman. Absolutely brilliant. Does Slipknot know what he has?"

Blip shook his head and raised a finger to his lips. "Should he?"

Klost laughed again. "No need. Just make sure *you* get to the next shipment first." He leaned forward. "I want a piece. I can give you a distribution channel. Secure, unencumbered by space authorities who might take a dim view of this endeavor." He sat back. "But there's still your docking fee."

"Port wine," Sam said, almost without thinking. *Skitch! What was he thinking? He was counting on a good bottle of port when this was all over.* On the other hand, they *were* pirates, right? Didn't pirates on the high seas once go after port wine cargos? "A hundred bottles, grower's reserve, straight from Rah III's best."

A low whistle from Klost accompanied his extended hand. "Two hundred, and I'll take care of the cleanup here, yes?"

Sam glanced at Blip. Blip shook his head slightly.

"I don't think we have that much aboard. Leave me

245

a bottle of my choosing and you get the rest?" Sam, glad to be back on the familiar ground of business deals, offered his hand, too, but didn't take Klost's.

Klost shoved his hand into Sam's and pumped it. Sam found his grip dry and surprisingly strong.

"Deal, Spot-Man."

Handshake still pumping, Sam turned to Blip. "Take care of it, will you, Blip? Sparks and I still need to work out the glonion deal."

A couple of hours later, Sam leaned back from the poker table in the wet mess, and rifled the cards in his hand. Smelling more of pine antiseptic now than beer, the wet mess seemed more like a hospital waiting room than a bar. Dozens of people still crowded around, but they spoke in whispers rather than shouts. Every now and then, a laugh would ring out, then quickly die off to embarrassed silence. The multicolored silks were gone, replaced by business suits and other normal, more comfortable clothes. In fact, the wet mess could have been any sedate hotel bar, filled with business travelers.

Even with a beefy, redheaded bartender, silently wiping down the already-clean table.

Sam's poker game was lowkey, too, with four quiet pirates in billowing shirts opposing him, and a modest stack of chits in front of him.

"Your call, Spot-Man," one of them, Greenbeard, reminded.

"I'll see Toeless' fifty," Sam said, flipping some chits

into the pile in the middle. "And raise a hundred." He riffled a chit stack in front of him, picking off the number he needed, and tossed it into the pile.

Greenbeard threw down his cards with a sigh. Chesty, the only one at the table who *needed* a billowing shirt, took a deep breath—which made her already straining shirt threaten to burst open—then slowly slid a stack of chits to the pile. Toeless folded without a word. Goldilocks smiled wildly—displaying a row of perfect, white teeth—and threw back his head to shake his brown hair. "Too rich for me," he said and laid down his cards.

"Call," Chesty said in sultry tones, staring demurely at Sam, licked full and sensous, pouting lips—Sam understood why the bartender felt the need to kiss her; he wanted to himself—and exposed her cards one by one, as if she were stripping. Two pair, aces and nines.

Sam smiled. "Three twos," he said and dropped his cards faceup. *It's all about bluffing—a lesson I've learned well in business.*

Chesty looked betrayed, Goldilocks blew a raspberry and cursed himself for folding, Greenbeard just grunted and shook his head, and Toeless vowed revenge on the next deal.

Sam glimpsed Blip coming into the wet mess. A blonde girl pirate whistled at him and waved him to her table. Blip smiled and veered to her table, whispered something in her ear—which earned him a quick butt squeeze from the girl—then moved on to an empty table.

"Sorry, salts, got to go now." Sam scooped up his winnings and headed for the table Blip appropriated.

"Getting the SurePosts installed in our fleet as we speak," Blip said in a low voice as Sam sat down. "Turns out you can cloak your own ship, as well. We'll be taking advantage of that." Blip winked and smiled wickedly.

"We'll still want to send out some transports for the pirates to find, though," Sam whispered. "Or they'll figure out who we *really* are."

Blip nodded. "Meantime, we need to get back home. We lost this chest; let's not lose another."

"Yeah. And it looks like we're going into the illegal engine-modding business, and Sparks'll be expecting to see a prototype soon."

Sam swaggered out of the wet mess, whistling. *It's a pirate's life for me, for me.*

God Uses A Dishrag

by Peter Orullian

THE GUY ACTUALLY WORE a fedora. No one did that anymore. Oh, a few throwbacks tried putting them on early in the twenty-fist century, but they possessed none of the class of a Sinatra or Crosby. And in the year of our Lord 2248, the marvel was that a fedora existed at all. Of course, I see all kinds come into my bar. But something about the way that hat sliced through the haze of smoke and caught table-glow on its brim got my attention. This guy was unique, all right. Familiar, even. But was it enough to make him the Son of God?

He took a seat at a far booth, a quiet corner. Good. Even though I hoped he proved more social in the long run, I wanted our first conversation to be private. I adopted the persona of a server, complete with apron (another throwback I thought he might appreciate) and navigated through the late-night crowd toward him.

"Get you something?" I asked.

"Beer."

How delightful; hardly anyone brewed beer anymore. "I don't think you came here to drink," I said. "May I sit down?"

The man buried his face in his hands as if my impertinence were the last straw in a long day of disappointments. I took that as an invitation and sat opposite him.

"I think I know what will help you."

His face still in his hands, the guy chuckled tiredly into his palms and said, "Really."

"You need to serve someone else. It eases one's own burdens. Intoxication isn't even smart escapism."

He finally glanced up at me, and I got my first good look at my successor. Dark brown eyes deep sunken under a strong but gentle brow. Creases in every corner of his face, telling stories of intense worry and gladness. And a shag of black, uncombed hair that seemed more natural than messy. Thirty-five standard solar years in that face—plenty wise enough to see the value of what I was prepared to offer him.

"You think I'm trying to escape to someplace?"

"With that hat . . . yes." I folded my hands on the table between us. "Do you know where you are?"

"I know where I'm not. I'm *not* in a bar that serves beer. And I'm *not* in the mood for meaningful conversation with a stranger." He sighed. "I'm here to celebrate two years without a job, and I don't want company."

I smiled. Could I pick 'em, or what?

"What do you do? Maybe I can help?" And I meant it.

For the first time, I saw earnestness touch the creases in his face. It's a familiar look, close cousin to desperation; I call it the "bar face."

"I'm John Cahan," he replied, and offered his hand.

If I'd had a corporeal body, I think I would have shat myself. No one shook hands anymore. The simple, genuine gesture had become archaic long ago. That, and I knew the name. I decided the fedora had been a sign.

"Call me Ubi," I replied and took his hand.

"Ubi? That a nickname?"

"Indeed it is. Now, about your occupation."

"I was an Intelligence Engineer. Spent eleven years with the Civil Corp working on planet-side infrastructure: housing, transportation, like that."

"Two years without work," I mused aloud. "About the time the Feds licensed the intelligence software to the private sector—"

"That's right."

"—and about the time this establishment came into being." I gestured grandly at the bar. "Seven Gables we call it because when we launched we had jump access to seven worlds."

John's brows went up. "You've got jump access here in the bar?"

"Better than that, my friend. The bar itself is laid out to service unique off-world spaces . . . and drinks. It's as easy as walking from one room to another."

"I can visit seven other worlds without visa credentials?" He sat back, interest lighting his face.

"Seven worlds when we started serving drinks two years ago. Over a hundred worlds now. We get around visa cred by allowing only indigenous customers to exit the bar." I pointed across the room at a diminutive, hairless fellow drinking alone. "That little guy is Auralian. He comes here for French Chablis. He's welcome anytime, but he has to go right back where he came from or to another world-room to drink. He can't exit the bar from here, only from his home world. Make sense?"

"Hell of a system. Nice use of the technology, too," John complimented. Then his eyes started to grow distant again as though consumed with his own concerns. It was time to get at it.

"Do you want a job?"

Puzzlement folded John's brow. "Here?"

"Well, here . . . and on a hundred other worlds."

"Doing what?"

I sat back, appraising him, taking a moment to be sure I really wanted to do this. Was this guy in the fedora the right one to take the reins? Did I care? The burden of it weighed on me: all the people, all the problems. For the most part, happy people don't come to the Seven Gables. Every damned one of them had a story . . . and a need.

Yeah, I wanted out. Fedora was it.

"My job," I answered.

"Serving drinks?" John's puzzlement twisted into amusement. "I don't think so."

"Beneath you?" I shot back.

"It's not that—"

"Take a walk with me." I stood, but John remained seated. "Please," I asked.

He looked up from beneath the brim of his hat, searching my face for guile. He found none, and followed.

Ubi led John from his secluded booth past a few tables. The guy struck John as a little presumptuous, but somehow, he trusted him—there was something familiar about the man. Waiting tables didn't hold much interest for John, but he guessed Ubi planned to try and sell him on it by taking him around to some of the great off-world establishments to which the bar had jump access. Worth the price of admission, John thought.

They hooked left toward a wide doorway over which an unlit sign read: Palasia. He'd heard of the world; it had been in the news a lot lately. The Catholic Lobby had tried to block Palasia's inclusion in authorized trade routes. John couldn't remember why.

Looking into the room that existed just a few steps away on a different planet, he decided he knew.

Stepping into the room, he'd expected to feel some change as a result of the jump across space. But he transitioned seamlessly, feeling only a slight change in gravity.

Low-slung chairs sat grouped around projection tables where holographic women did a thousand lewd things as they removed their clothing. Music pulsed in the dim chamber as though setting a rhythm to have sex by. No talk, or low talk. Men and women here were preoccupied with other things. A sour smell tinged the air, like burned oranges, leaving John lightheaded and . . . acquiescent. He wondered if he were breathing a Palasian equivalent of secondhand opium.

Ubi led him deeper into the Palasian room, and somewhere along the way, the women became real, the holograms left behind. Clothing at first grew more extravagant—silks, gilded velvet, vests embroidered with rich shades of crimson and jade—then the colors changed as clothes lay piled on the floor exposing flesh tones.

Palasians didn't appear biologically much different from humans. They were generally shorter and almost universally light in complexion. Translucent eyes made it clear you were talking to a Palasian, as did the fact that they were lean to a person. The only fat people in the Palasian room were off-worlders.

A race evolved for sex, John considered.

At the far end of the room, Ubi gestured to a seat at an empty table set before a sunken stage. John sat, still craning his neck at the sight of men and women doing things in public that would have earned them a fine in the next room.

"Surprise you?" Ubi asked.

"Yeah, a little," John replied. "I get that it's a different world with different customs and laws, but if you don't know that coming in . . ."

Ubi smiled. "Does it make the job more appealing?"

"Because I could watch alien sex habits while serving a drink? Not really. You'll have to do better than that."

Ubi's smiled widened, and he turned his attention to the stage, where dim red lights illuminated a very private stage—one hidden to all but Ubi and John.

A few moments later, two Palasian males dragged a woman onto the stage and shoved her to the floor. A spark of anger lit in John's chest and he turned to see Ubi's response.

The waiter sat unmoved, looking at the girl.

With the music pulsing around them and the smell of burned oranges in his nose, John watched as the two men circled behind the girl and two more Palasian males emerged from a rear curtain onto the stage.

John's gut churned at the thought of what was about to happen.

The men regarded the girl for a few moments, blank, uncaring expressions staring down at her, illuminated by the red baleful lights.

Between two of the men, John could see the girl and thought her face battled horror and the same acquiescence that had gotten inside him.

It wasn't until the men began to circle in on the girl that John realized she wore no clothes.

"What the hell is this?" John said, pointing.

"It's Palasia, one of our more frequented affiliates." Ubi's face showed a kind of resigned regret at the scene before them, but he sat still as the private show rolled on.

"But it's your bar, right? Don't you have some provisional authority here?" John twitched in his chair.

Ubi looked away at a window against the wall to his right. Beyond it, the night lay interrupted by vertical columns of light in an alien skyline. "It's a condition of inclusion that the room be governed by the host-world's law."

John looked back at the sunken stage and saw terror clear in the young woman's eyes. She began to scramble to avoid the clutching hands of the men, who tightened their circle, their faces now taut with expectation and savage delight.

"Then turn this damn room off," John yelled over the din of the music. "All you're doing is creating a venue for this bullshit." John's voice quavered in sympathy for the young woman.

This touched a nerve he didn't want exposed.

Ubi said nothing.

John rubbed his eyes, which were stinging now from the heavy smoke. Did they release this opiate to encourage customers to partake?

The rapists had teased at the girl long enough. With an uncanny synergy, they lunged in on her and pinned her arms and legs down. Well-sculpted muscles danced in the light, a horrific ballet of flesh as four males prepared to take something that didn't belong to them.

"God damn it!" John pounded an open palm on the table beside him, sending shards of pain up his forearm.

The men either didn't hear him, or ignored his indignation.

Tears came to the girl's eyes as she screamed and thrashed to preserve something others were content to watch have taken from her.

Leers grew in the faces of her attackers, excitement, shit-eating grins that John had seen aplenty in the world a room away.

He didn't so much stand as launch himself from his chair. He threw the full force of his weight into the Palasian who'd deemed himself first to violate the girl. They went over into the curtains behind the stage, and John lost his fedora. As they tumbled, he caught a look at Ubi's face. John had hoped, maybe expected, the waiter would throw in with him to stop this thing.

The Seven Gables employee hadn't left his seat.

A heavy fist buried itself in John's chest, driving out all his air. The Palasian then hauled John to his feet and put ironlike fingers around his throat. Behind the beast, the other three closed their circle, preparing to continue their "show."

The nonchalance of it brought new fire to John's disgust. With all his strength, he drove one knee up into the exposed genitals of the guy holding him. A look of surprise spread on the Palasian's face, as if John had transgressed some strict taboo on this freakin' planet.

But it worked.

The Palasian's grip loosened, encouraging John to strike again. This time, he took hold of the guy's shoulders for leverage and put his hips behind his strike. The Palasian collapsed to the floor.

John whirled at the sound of the girl's screams and saw one of the remaining three kneeling, preparing himself for access to the girl's womanhood. His head bounced to the beat of the music infusing the room. The others swayed to the sounds, too. Happily, the rapists were too caught up in their doings to be bothered with John.

So this time, John calculated his attack. Taking two running strides, he kicked the sonofabitch from behind, catching him where he lived. Number two slumped forward onto the girl, moaning. She shoved him aside.

The remaining two shared a look of bewilderment and walked off the stage, disappearing behind the curtains.

John chuffed from exertion. He extended a hand to the girl, intending to help her up. She shrunk from him, easing herself toward the same curtains the men had just used to exit.

"I'm not going to hurt you," he said, sparing a look at the two Palasians clutching their goods.

She shook her head. Did she distrust him? Did she not understand English?

"Come, John, we should go." It was Ubi, standing now, disappointment clear upon his face.

John let a bitter smile touch one corner of his mouth. "What the hell is going on?"

Ubi pushed in his chair, pivoted on one foot, and started back through the bar. John gathered his hat and went after the waiter. When he caught up to him, John reached out to pull the man around face-to-face.

John's hand landed heavily on the waiter's shoulder . . . and Ubi flickered.

"Oh, my God, you're Artificial Intelligence." John looked at his hand and chuckled.

"I'm a good deal more than that, sonny. And you just stopped the conception of this world's next great senator."

John scrubbed his face. "Wait a minute. Are you telling me that was consensual?"

"No such thing," Ubi answered. "But Seven Gables is not a place to make assumptions based on what you see."

"What did you expect me to do back there?" John leaned in close, challenging the waiter.

Ubi didn't reply.

"Never mind. Good-bye." John started to leave.

"I can help you forget your own worries," Ubi said, stopping John. "I'm not just some sophisticated AI who keeps accounts and serves drinks. You need a job. You need to feel *wanted*. That's why people come to a bar. Even one as elaborate as Seven Gables."

"What makes you think I would want a job in a pit like this?"

"Trust me, John. You just need more information."

John paused and looked around him at the various sexual appetites being sated in this corner of the universe. He wasn't about to bite on the whole "need" line Ubi was selling. He needed a job, to be sure, but when it came down to it, he meant to stick around a while longer for only one reason: Ubi was one hell of an AI—it was a matter of professional curiosity. At least, that's what he told himself. After all, in his former life, he'd been an intelligence engineer building dumbed-down versions of Ubi for the state.

"Where next?" John asked.

I can't say I was surprised when John tackled the Palasian consummator. He couldn't have known what was happening. I'd set him up, sure. But having this job meant understanding a greater good. Sometimes God says no, right? To stand at the head of the Seven Gables, one has to take the long view.

That's why I was so damned tired. Why I needed out. And on some level, John's reaction showed a decency that confirmed my original assessment that he was the right guy to take the reins. He'd grow tired, too, in time. But that was his problem.

Still, I needed to know he could show temperance. Even good bartenders possess the skill. And what I intended to offer him far exceeded slopping drinks.

"Why did you jump to that girl's defense?" I asked as I led John from Palasia and deeper into the bar.

"She didn't look like she was having any fun?" John smiled to himself.

"Really. Are you an expert on the customs of Palasia? Or anyplace besides your own world for that matter?" I needed John to start accepting that he couldn't save everyone. Very important for this job.

He ignored my question completely. "You're not biological, but you seem to have mass."

"A design of energy," I answered. "And really, all mass is, is energy."

John nodded. I could virtually see his mind racing behind his eyes. "So the bar is 'intelligent'?"

"Why, thank you," I answered, bowing as we went.

John smiled more genuinely. "I'm guessing that was some kind of test. Either that, or you take me for a letch."

"We're all letches, John. Even me. It's just a matter of *appetite*."

John nodded, and seemed to get that I didn't plan to admit I was testing him.

"Where are we going now?" John asked.

"To gamble," I replied.

We climbed four short stairs and pushed through a set of double doors into the Cumulous Casino.

John hated to gamble. His dislike for the pastime probably stemmed from his statistical work and pattern theory when he'd been studying for an engineering career. But that very coursework had made of him an exceptional gambler, or more accurately, an exceptional identifier of cheaters, which sometimes meant the same thing.

As they entered the casino, John found his preconceptions challenged and defeated.

The expansive room lay bathed in bright but soothing light that fell from great skylights. In this world it was clearly daytime. Completely absent were the garish lights, the bells and chimes. Instead of ashtrays, plants and small trees (real ones) stood here and there.

As they surveyed the many games underway, John was struck that it appeared like nothing so much as a civil midmorning tea. He couldn't call out one working girl or desperate laborer throwing away his check on payday. Rather, people either strolled or sat calmly as though the axis of the place weren't money, but polite interchange in modest, neatly pressed clothes.

"You're kidding me, right?" John said without thinking.

"Refined, isn't it?" Ubi led on to the right where the games ran to interesting variations of chess and other strategy entertainments.

Passing several tables, John distilled the difference between this place and Palasia: Here, the men and women crossed their legs when they sat to table.

Deeper into the room, John marveled at the white stucco walls, which scaled a hundred feet to great, clear domes. Underfoot, he noted that his shoes didn't grind on the red, marble tile.

"Someone spends a lot of time sweeping," he muttered.

"What's that?" Ubi asked over his shoulder.

"Nothing. Anyway, this is a waste. I'm not much of a gambler, and I don't have any money. I'm out of work, remember? That's why you're trying to pawn your job off on me."

"I'll stake you," Ubi answered.

John expected as much and laughed. "What's the buy in?"

"Just play your best."

Ubi drew up at a short distance from a table where two men sat engaged in a game of cards. He bowed and approached a man in an oversized white robe. The garment looked comfortable, perfect for the stress of—

"Poker," Ubi said, turning to John. "You're in." On the table before an empty seat, he placed twelve small white figures that resembled chess pawns. "The difference here, John, is that there's no ante, and each raise is limited to one."

"One what?"

Ubi placed his index finger on one of the pawns.

"Standard deck?" John asked.

"Yes. Have a seat and wait for the next deal."

John shook his head and planted himself. At the highest level, he knew real players played people, not cards. That was out the window with these two.

"Who am I playing?" he asked.

"Cumulous Casino belongs to the world of Rowls.

These distinguished competitors are Rowlian." Ubi bowed again to each of the others at the table.

John appraised his competition. The two aliens (who he guessed were male) each wore a similar robe, sashed at the waist and chest. Superfluous buttons, also white, had been sewn in simple lines at the hems and cuffs. Burnished skin spoke of much time in their system's sun. And long hair woven in an intricate queue lay draped across their shoulders like a snake. A third Rowlian (with a much shorter braid) dealt and gathered cards, setting them in piles at the edge of the table.

John gathered his cards on the next hand and began to do the math and probabilities as the table cards turned up.

Really, it all seemed rather banal. Why did Ubi want him playing poker with a couple of aliens in an antiseptic casino that looked like it fell out of a cloud?

Several hands later, he thought he knew.

Despite the superior play of the Rowlian on John's right, the guy had been losing.

The player on John's left was cheating.

The shark had a superb gift in manipulation of the cards and had clearly inserted winners to bolster his hand when he needed something to take a pot. John hadn't seen it, but he'd swear to it based on the probabilities he'd calculated over a few dozen games.

There was something else.

When he'd been introduced, John thought the two strangers appeared virtually identical. A couple of hours of poker made them as distinct as any two humans John had ever met. It wasn't their clothes or hair, but something in their faces, in their eyes.

The Rowlian to John's right (who hadn't shared a word the entire morning) never flinched, never showed any animation over a win or his many losses. His manner was easy and aloof.

By contrast, the fellow on his left (the man cheating his ass off) showed a quiet desperation to win. Once or twice, a note of glee escaped his lipless mouth over a particularly large pot. Yet, for these spates of emotion, he never struck John as a gambling addict or even a poker player with bad manners.

Perhaps his nerves bothered him; he *was* cheating after all.

And that pissed John off.

It may not have been his stake that got him in the game. But the player on his right continued to give up his cache and did so without a word of remorse or bitterness. Meanwhile, the increasingly sweaty player on John's left gathered in pawns like a miser, smiling over each figurine.

If anything bothered him more than bad intelligence work, it was the frustration of loss when others didn't play by the rules. In a significant respect, it was the human element, the one thing that could never be coded for by an intelligence engineer.

And the one thing John was often grateful he'd never been able to replicate.

Part of him wanted to slap the pawns out of the

swindler's clutches and call him out for what he was right here in front of Ubi and everybody.

No tact there.

He didn't mean to earn the waiter's job, but he didn't want to make a mistake here like he apparently had in Palasia.

"Sir," John said, shifting in his seat to address the cheating Rowlian.

"John," Ubi said softly behind him.

John held up a finger without looking back again at his guide. "Hold on, I've got this under control."

The Rowlian narrowed his eyes and pulled his arms tighter around his bounty.

"My friend, while I'm new to your world, and unfamiliar with your customs, poker is poker. And I can't sit here and watch you steal the rightful winnings of this gentleman." He gestured to the other Rowlian without lifting his gaze from the first.

A series of ticks and vowels escaped the dealer's mouth as he interpreted what John said.

"He says," the dealer returned, "he has done nothing wrong, and he withdraws from further play."

John focused on the dealer. "Then he won't mind if we check him for cards, will he?"

When the dealer spoke back to the cheater, a look of anger passed quickly over the tanned skin, but soon turned to despair.

Some poker face.

It took only a few moments for the dealer to stand, draw back the other's long robe sleeves, and reveal the instruments of the Rowlian's deceit. To his credit, he stood still, accepting that he'd been caught red-handed.

What happened next would live with John for the rest of his life.

I wanted to warn him. In some ways because I needed him to replace me, but more importantly because I didn't think I could stand it if John ratted the poor father out.

I may have been wrong to hold my tongue. But in the end, I knew John really needed to have this lesson driven home.

The outed Rowlian broke down, the grief as human as anything I've ever seen or felt. Through his sobs, he clucked and cawed, slumping back to his seat.

I spared a glance at the upper caste Rowlian as he accepted the lion's share of the table pawns, not once thanking John. Impassive, the sonofabitch gathered the markers and left the table.

"Ubi, you better tell me what the hell just happened? I'm getting tired of all the shadow and.mirrors bullshit."

"Not now, John," I said.

"Now!" he yelled back. The echo of it lifted up the sheer walls and resounded against the domed skylights. Gamblers paused to look over at the humans, then returned to their civil games.

I sat across from the still weeping Rowlian and gave John a regretful look.

"The stakes were this man's children."

Pallor lifted in John's face. "The hell you say."

Any other time, I'd have gladdened at the use of the old adage. Not today, not now.

I really needed to get out of this damned job.

"The ways here in the clouds are unconventional. The upper castes have certain claims on procreation. The poor have the opportunity to win the lives of their offspring back through card sports like you just played. It's . . ."

"Oh, my God." John turned to the Rowlian. "I'm sorry. I didn't know." He then stood and cast his gaze around, looking, I'm sure, for the other player—perhaps thinking to strike some bargain.

"Leave it," I said. "There's nothing to be done now."

I do think something broke inside John at that point. I believe I was a heartless sonofabitch to do it. A lot of greed in that choice. But you have to take the long view. And John had some good years in my seat if he could internalize this one point.

"But what about—"

I cut him off. "I could spend a week explaining all the details of Rowlian culture and you'd still be pissed off and self-loathing over what just happened. Come on."

I stood and headed for the door. I heard John's chair legs scrape across tile as he pushed back from the table. "I'm sorry," he repeated, and came along.

* * *

"What's the trick this time?" John asked.

Ubi stood silent, looking at the woman seated at the open-air patio that looked out over a violet ocean and russet sunset.

John exhaled loudly. "Why am I even still here? Hell, I just wanted a beer."

"You're here because you need to feel wanted. I told you that." Ubi pinched his eyes in a very human gesture.

John opened his mouth to refute that, but said nothing. Then, "Why's she here?" and he nodded at the woman seated alone and staring into the distance.

"Go talk to her," Ubi said. "No deceptions this time. Just talk."

"Is this what a waiter at the Seven Gables does?" John let a mirthless guffaw.

Ubi nodded. "More than a little."

John had to hand it to Ubi; the AI really had the human thing down. But John didn't know if he had it in himself to do one more thing. He didn't understand alien cultures: condoned rape, gambling one's own children.

But after what had happened already, he secretly wanted to know what came next. How much lower did this ride go? He tugged his fedora on tighter and went to the seaside table.

"May I sit with you?" he asked.

The woman looked up and smiled wanly. "I'm not here to make anyone's acquaintance," she replied.

"Me neither. I just need a place to rest my feet and eyes." He motioned to the beach, where foamy waves crashed up on wet sand.

She hunched her shoulders.

John sat. "You can kind of lose yourself in the view, can't you?"

"That your best line?" the woman remarked.

The corner of John's mouth tugged into a lopsided grin. "It's not a line, really. I'm just an out-of-work engineer who came for a beer. I met an artificial bartender who's been showing me the seamier side of the galaxy room by room. He brought me here, pointed you out, here I am. And frankly, the risks of procreation from incidental sex seem too great right now for me to even care you're a human female."

A genuine smile spread on her chapped lips. "I'm Helen," she said. "And you're . . ."

"John."

They sat in silence for a long while. Then he asked, "Why are you sitting here alone, staring out to sea."

Without missing a beat, she said, "Why not? I love the view. There's not a better sunset than on Delin."

John looked again at the rich color of the water and sun, strata of clouds lilting like ribbons against a lapis-lazuli sky. There weren't any beach-goers, perhaps it was forbidden—keeping a pristine view for the drinkers to gaze upon.

Except there weren't any other drinkers in this room.

The jump had been as seamless as the rest, the difference: the open air, and single occupant.

"I guess I agree," John said.

"Helps you believe in providence just a little, doesn't it?" She sipped at her peach cocktail.

John turned to look at Ubi, who stood far back near the door. The bartender/waiter/servant stood by and gave no inclination about what John was to do.

Then Helen put a hand over John's. "You can make up for the past, don't you think? I mean, if you really make good on new promises."

And when she turned to face him, to have his answer, John's own reality began to crumble. He didn't tear his hand away, though that's what he felt like doing. He didn't lash out, though part of him insisted that he do so. And he didn't speak recriminations.

Not one.

Not to a mother who'd abandoned him a lifetime ago.

Helen cocked her head, as though something in John looked familiar, but she finished by simply tugging at the brim of his fedora. "Nice hat," she said. "Reminds me of a man I once knew."

Then she stood up, gave a long, last look at the ocean and walked out past Ubi.

As I led John back to the room where we'd first met, I wondered if I'd done it right. Would he be ready to step into my shoes? I might have gone too far. But John had made his own choices, however manipulated they might have been.

The bar in the main room had been built of real mahogany. Another throwback. I guess I was partial to throwbacks, as it happens. In any event, we could only finish our tour in one place.

I ushered John in behind the bar and through a door. This was home.

The data servers and network had its hub here, powered independent of the planet infrastructure that John had helped build. I turned to get a look at John's face and found pretty much what I expected: astonishment and chagrin.

"Like it?"

"Impressive. I might have guessed you were one of those who licensed the intelligence software." John ran a finger along one sleek panel.

"A clever man might call that software my father." I laughed earnestly and hoped John would join me.

He chuckled. "Does Ubi mean what I think it means?"

"Ubiquitous," I supplied. "What you don't know, John, is that something miraculous happened when the Seven Gables powered up their jump points that first day."

"Do tell." John crossed his arms over his chest.

"The combination of the jump technology and the end-node transfer from those original seven worlds, and the intelligence software we licensed from the state . . . well, it created me."

"I hate to burst your bubble, Ubi, but I think I created you."

"You don't understand, John. I'm not artificial. I'm sentient."

John's face slackened. "You mean you *think* you're sentient."

"Look, I've had this debate a thousand times. Often with myself. The fact is, I feel pain: sadness, loss, despair. Get it? That one thing you couldn't account for in your programming."

John stared. "So you took me on a tour of my own . . ."

Epiphany flared in John's mind. A rape he wished had never happened; the loss of a child through a parent's own poor choices; the hope of redemption, reconciliation with a mother . . . the shadows of his past.

He gripped the hat atop his head and shut his eyes against the revelations.

"And now it's my turn to rest," Ubi said, weariness heavy in his voice. "I'm God here, John. In every real sense. You helped create that, but now I deserve to step down and you to step in. You can be the ghost in the machine now. I can help you transfer your mind into the network so that you can manage the affairs of Seven Gables.

"I've helped you see the need to respect the choices of others, to intercede with temperance. They're good people, they just need help—"

"You sonofabitch!" John screamed. "All I wanted was a damn beer!"

"I didn't ask for this either," Ubi shot back.

John looked around and spotted the emergency server shutdown toggle. Before Ubi could blink, he lunged, slammed his fist on the switch, and whirled to see what would happen.

Ubi hadn't moved. "I kind of thought you might do that. It's murder, John. I'm as alive as you are." He paused, a wan smile touching his lips. "But I'll tell you the truth. Death is no bad friend. I leave it to you now."

Ubi flickered, disappeared. Hundreds of lights blinked off, showing the jump access terminated all across the Seven Gables network.

Beyond the door, it was just a bar now. With a lot of people who needed a drink . . . wanted to belong.

John stepped out from the network room and picked up a wet rag used to wipe down the bar. Seated across the mahogany was an old man with deep folds of skin cascading down from his brow. The fellow looked unhappy, alone.

You can make up for the past, don't you think? I mean, if you really make good on new promises.

Perhaps he'd serve after all. John hefted the rag. "What can I get you?"

The Hyperbole Engine
by Michael Hiebert

THREE DAYS AGO THE dust finally settled enough for me to leave the Proog System without too many questions being asked. I tell you, waiting those weeks out was one of the hardest things I've ever done. Now, I'm maybe a fifth of the way home in some uncharted millipod in the Jahan sector, just looking for somewhere to lay low for a while. Somewhere I can get a drink, relax, and not be bothered.

Sectors like this, it's not hard to stumble onto what I'm looking for. The important thing is to find a place that caters mainly to bipedals, humanoids or, at the very least, carbon-based life-forms. Gotta watch what you ingest at some of those other fine establishments, you know what I mean? And for God's sake don't get too drunk, or you never know what the hell you'll wake up to the next morning. Takes that whole "coyote ugly" thing to a brand spankin' new level.

From the outside, this place looked perfect; quiet,

dark and most of the clientele (which is far too fancy a word, really) seemed to be keeping to themselves. You could feel the subtle criminal element creeping through the shadows; just enough to offer me the privacy I was looking for.

Except now that I'm in here, I'm having second thoughts. Especially since these three people just walked up to my table.

Two guys and a girl. One guy is a talker. If you ever watch them old Earth movies, he's Steve Buscemi. He's Joe Pesci. He's Kkaåyg Üt!kaå, only without the third eye. And the other guy, he's the muscle. You can always tell. Thankfully, this guy's not literally a muscle, not like that one I ran into in that dive on the outer rim of the Hemi a few years back. That was just . . . odd. But here, just like there, the talkers don't dare go anyplace without the muscle—they'd be ripped to shreds, and the muscle knows better than to say too many words; the muscle knows he's not very smart.

But the talker never does. He's fooled into believing his own shit stories, and that's his weakness. Everyone has a weakness.

The woman with them is Alladarian.

Welcome to my weakness.

Alladarians are gypsies. Fortune-tellers with blue skin and double eyelids. I've heard they make incredible life partners in the right relationship, if you can get one to settle down. Slightly empathic, they are born nurturers and mothers. They like to deal in stories. Before realizing their companionship was so valuable, they used to buy and sell traveler's tales. But now, they can often be found in bars like this one, spreading goodwill for a price. Too often, Alladarians are written off as simple whores, but this is their strength. They have far, far more power than they'll ever let on. I'm pretty sure if you add her IQ and mine together we probably outranked the rest of this place combined.

"What can I do for you?" I ask as they sit down.

"Don't remember seeing you around these parts before. My—" he glances quickly to Muscles, "—associate and I make it a point to introduce ourselves to all new prospective—clients who come in here." His voice suits him; staccato and high with an edge to it that might be nervousness or might be mania. You can't tell, and he, no doubt, uses that to his advantage.

I sit back in my chair. "And you are?" I ask.

"Name's Tycho. This here's Gwort. Why don't you tell us where you're coming from, Spacer? Where you're headed. What you might be needing in between." I get the idea. He's a dealer. They're everywhere. In places like these, they aren't even subtle about it. They deal in synthoids, weapons, anything that might fall into the realm of a black market transaction. I'm sure the Alladarian will be put on the table for negotiation if I let on that I'm interested.

By his edginess, I also suspect Tycho's already taken

some amphetamine-based synthoids himself this evening, which means I have to be careful. You never know when guys like him might actually snap.

"And who are you?" I ask the Alladarian.

She blushes. Alladarians have bioluminescent skin the color of cobalt that deepens when they blush. It's the second most beautiful thing about them. The first is their eyes, which she diverts to the tabletop as she blushes. "Sonja," she says. Only she pronounces the J like a J, not a Y. Like all Alladarians, she speaks in song, her mouthed voice chorused with musical timbres resonating through the fluted holes in her throat. But I'm no fool—this blushing and diverting of eyes trick is rehearsed, something she's done many, many times to persuade guys like me to hand over galactic credits to girls like her.

A fool and his money are soon partying. I must say, it almost works. Unlike most guys that come in this place, though, it's not her sensuality that chisels away at me, not the pure erotic beauty of her breasts (I've heard the breasts of Alladarians described as two magnificent giant scoops of bubblegum ice cream) or the way her deep red hair tumbles down beside her freckled neck, or even the long-lashed blinking of the double eyelids.

It's those eyes. Deep, glorious, speckled oceans of infinite sadness. They've watched so many stories being told you get the feeling they know Life and the Universe's dark secrets. But if there's one thing

Alladarians are good at, it's keeping secrets. And that's what captivates me the most about her—that she's some sort of enigmatic puzzle waiting to be unlocked.

"So you're ISF, right?" Tycho asks. "I can spot you guys a mile away. Yeah, yeah, I can tell what you're thinking. How'd I know, right? I got a nose for these sorta things. Don't worry, I won't blow your cover. Where you coming from?"

He's got red Phohonese characters tattooed on his eyes; a different one on each pupil. I never did learn to read that stuff, but I can guess what they mean. Probably something like Death and Destruction. Or maybe he went for the more classic Love and Hate. Actually, there's a good chance *he* doesn't even know how to read them and just trusted the tattoo artist when he told him they stood for Honor and Victory when, in actuality, he's a walking advertisement for Pengo's Fried Chicken.

Where you coming from? I run my tongue over the front of my teeth, deciding whether or not I should acknowledge his comment. Fact is, he's almost right on the money, but it's a guess. He knows it and I know it, too. Best to just let the comment slide. When in doubt, it's always safer to just hold back information than it is to try and cover with false information.

"Coming back from the Proog System," I say. And it's the truth. This is another tactic I've learned; whenever possible, tell the truth. Always easier to keep up a cover buried in truth. Besides, left by themselves out in the wild, stories have a habit of acquiring whole loads of compost on top of them.

"Proog," he says, then to his friend, all confident: "The Hyperbole Engine." He turns back to me. "That's why you were there, right? Trying to find out what the hell happened to it?"

I lean back in my chair, put my hands in my jacket pockets, and shrug. "From what I've heard, there's no such thing as the Hyperbole Engine." It's the truth. I've heard it doesn't exist. I've heard it does exist. I've heard it only exists in another dimension. I've even heard it's the size of a small planet. I've heard it's guarded in the center of a statically charged perma-nova by seven squealing fanged monkeys with wings. I've heard it all, stories about the Hyperbole Engine are so infamous most of them cross the line into ridic-ulousness. After all, that's why it's called the Hyper-bole Engine.

"It exists," Tycho says, pointing at me. "Trust me. I know. I know people've seen it. And I know recently it's gone missing. Stolen. You were dispatched to try and get it back, weren't you? Come on, you can tell us. We're good guys." He nudges Muscles beside him, who just nods dumbly.

I shake my head, fingering the thing in my pocket. "Nope, my friend. I'm afraid you're wrong." And he is. Again, better not to lie. Neither of them know for sure if the Hyperbole Engine exists or not—shit, only maybe a dozen people in the galaxy know for sure.

"Oh, come on, you've got Agency written all over you."

"What's the Hyperbole Engine?" the Alladarian asks, batting her lashes. It's almost laughable, her pretending not to have ever heard of it. Everyone's heard of it. It's as legendary as the Tangolian Quasar Serpent. And if there's one thing Alladarians are, it's smart. Smart enough to know when it's in their favor to look ignorant. I'm really starting to dig this Alladarian; too bad she's with the sideshow freaks.

Of course, Tycho believes her. That's the kind of guy he is—a talker, and she just gave him a reason to talk. I look at her in wonderment. How easily she manipulated him; how unequivocally she leveraged her power and didn't even have to move a muscle.

He freaks out. *"What's the Hyperbole Engine? What's* the *Hyperbole* Engine?!"* He takes a long pull on whatever the hell is in his bottle and starts into an explanation.

"The Hyperbole Engine is the freaking bomb. It transforms matter. You can have the most measly ship in the galaxy and this thing will turn it into a freakin' Destroyer."

"No, no, no." It's Muscles talking, and at first I'm sort of confused because his voice isn't that slow, low voice you come to expect from cartoon musclemen. He actually sounds like a normal person. "That's not what the Hyperbole Engine does at all," he says. "It warps time. It allows you to jump from one time/space reference frame to another just like this." He snaps his fingers, and I think, *Holy— Muscles knows some big words.* I'm impressed.

"As usual, you are wrong," Tycho cuts in. "It's all about firepower and matter transformation. I know this guy—" and he goes off, and I start to tune out. I take another sip of my drink (which is actually quite good) and wish I was somewhere else.

Truth be told, I don't even *pretend* to understand how the Hyperbole Engine works. I'm not even sure how many people there are in this Universe that actually *do* know, but I know one thing: it's not about being able to transform matter, it's not about speed and it's not about firepower. It's all about odds.

Einstein said something about God not playing dice. Well, Einstein was wrong. At the quantum level God plays dice a lot, and every roll starts a brand-new parallel universe running alongside this one where all of the different decision possibilities are made. If you add up all of the good decisions and subtract all of the bad decisions, you are always left with zero. This was all proven a quarter century ago by that physicist from Orion II—I can't remember his name. Cornig-something. Shit, one drink and all my grade nine physics goes to hell.

Anyway, the short of it is that God plays dice, and the Hyperbole Engine stacks those dice in your favor. It somehow twists things around so all of the good decisions happen in this Universe. *This* universe being the one the Hyperbole Engine is in.

The rest of that crap these guys are spouting? It's

just a bunch of Boontog shit. But I'm not about to tell them that. It's guys like this that have kept the Hyperbole Engine safe for this long. Hard to hit a nebulous target.

"Nobody's ever gonna find it," Tycho says. "Trust me on that one. It's tucked away somewhere good."

This is the only thing he's said so far that makes any sense to me whatsoever. I nod. "I think you're right."

" 'Course I'm right. I'm always right, hey, Gwort?" He elbows Muscles. "Anyway, you let us know if there's anything we can help you with." He gets up from the table. Gwort follows suit. Tycho looks at Sonja. "You coming, Toots?"

"In a bit," she says, her voice sultry and melodious. "Just gonna finish my drink first."

"Suit yourself," Tycho says and off he and Gwort go, folding into the shadows in search of other potential clients.

"Nice friends you keep," I say to Sonja.

She smiles. "You are an ISF Agent, right?"

I shrug. "You're empathic enough to know without asking. How about you? What's a nice blue-skinned girl like you doing hanging out in a dump like this?"

She shrugs. Alladarians aren't dumb. Give as little information as is needed.

"Well, regardless, I want to show you something." With a subtle glance left and right, I reach into my pocket and set the "thing" on the table.

"What's that?" she asks.

I lean back, scratch my nose. "That's it."

283

She looks at it and blinks. With the double eyelids, it's kind of weird, like two blinks. Two wonderfully gorgeous blinks. "That's . . ."

Crossing one leg over the other, I lean back in my chair, my thick leather jacket opening around me, revealing my white shirt and shoulder holster underneath. My weapon was checked at the door when I came in. I nod. "The Hyperbole Engine."

Her eyes narrow. "It's—smaller than I expected."

"Everyone says that," I sigh with a grin. Another double blink. Not sure if she gets the joke, but it doesn't matter.

"So it was you," she said, seemingly impressed. "You're the one who took it."

"The balance of power needed shifting, so I shifted it."

"So what're you going to do with it?"

"That's the thing," I say. "What can I do with it? I need to hide it. I can't use it, and I can't really trust it to anybody like—" I gesture my head in the direction of Tycho and his muscle-bound friend.

She gives me one of those pretty smiles Alladrians are famous for. "Must be hard. Never knowing who you can trust."

I smile. "Oh, I know who I can trust: nobody."

Her eyes take on an even deeper sadness than before. Like oceans of despair, and I feel her concern. It's real. Not the practiced concern of an Alladarian but the genuine concern of real empathy. "That's so sad. You must be so lonely." And I can't help but feel the irony of her words.

"That's why," I say, "I'm giving it to you."

Her eyes widen, and she does another double blink. And then she sits back staring, just staring at me like she's waiting for the other boot to fall. The part where I tell her she has to come home with me and get tied to a bunch of leather-clad midgets scrubbed down with oil and roll around in a vat of vanilla pudding. "Why me? Why would you give it to me? I'm the last person who—"

"That's why. Because it will be safe. Because I can tell you know how to keep secrets. I can see it in your eyes. And nobody would ever believe it was in the possession of an Alladarian. Nobody. Even if word got out, it would be written off as just another bagatelle."

She considers this. "And if I don't want it?"

I shrug. "Then I'll just move on and keep looking for somewhere else safe to hide it. It's not like I expected to find you tonight. I just saw an opportunity, and I'm following up on it. No harm, no foul."

"And what's stopping me from just taking it and selling it to those guys—" her eyes shift to the right, but the rest of her head doesn't move. She's obviously used to talking covertly, "—or any of a number of other misanthropes in this place?"

Rubbing my hand over my chin, I realize I need a shave. "Absolutely nothing, I guess, but I don't think you will. I think you understand the balance of power.

I think you understand the implications. In a lot of ways, you and I are similar, only your power lies in the fact that nobody realizes how well you play the game. How perfectly you calculate every move."

She raises her eyebrows and gives me a genuine smile. "Interesting. You say nobody, yet in the same breath, you claim to know all this."

I shake my head. "No, I only guess it. Maybe I'm wrong, maybe I'm not, but I know the safety of the Hyperbole Engine lies in it being buried under all the exaggeration and rumor. If word leaks out that it's fallen into the possession of an Alladarian—" I shrug, "—it's just more far-fetched speculation. Nobody's going to believe it."

"And if I use it? What if I want to make my life, this life in this quantum state, better? What makes you think I could knowingly have that potential and not use it?"

"I don't. I fully expect you to use it. But you're used to having power and not letting it show. You know how to use power *discreetly* and not let it get out of hand. It's how you earn your living. It's what's made you what you are today. Really, your species are the perfect guardians for the engine." I hadn't actually considered this until this moment, but as I say it, I know it's the truth.

She sips her drink, careful to show no trace of emotion, to not reveal a single card. There's no question this is the right decision. "Go ahead," I say. "Take it." I feel slightly uneasy with it sitting right here on the table, although I've always believed in hiding things in the obvious. When in doubt, just display that which you don't want people to see and they will look everywhere but straight at it.

Setting her cup on the table, she asks, "No catch?"

"No catch," I say, so quietly it's almost a whisper.

She plucks the Hyperbole Engine from the table, holding it in her palm. The light from the bar refracts and reflects through and off the crystal. In her hand, it looks almost as magical as her eyes.

"It's beautiful," she says. "But I'm not taking it."

Across the room, a waitress drops a tray. The resulting crash makes me think she was carrying bowls of nails, which is a delicacy in some parts.

"Why won't you take it?" I ask.

Her eyes flicker. "Because I don't trust you. Not one bit. I don't even know how it works." As she speaks, she places the Hyperbole Engine in front of her and fiddles with it. Before I can stop her, she gives it a spin and says, "And I think you're—"

The Alladarian takes the Hyperbole Engine from the table and lets it roll around her fingers as she examines it.

While she stares at it, my gaze is locked onto her eyes. They are magical. Captivating. She looks up and mouths something like "It's beautiful," but I don't catch the words; they are lost in the crash of a tray across the room falling from the waitress' hand.

"Sorry," I say, "I didn't hear that."

"I said it's beautiful."

"As are you," I say.

She blushes. I can't tell if it's the rehearsed blush or if, this time, she truly appreciates the comment. It doesn't matter.

She asks: "And what if I want you to come home with me, too?"

Now it's my turn to blush. "Do you?"

She takes a last look at the Hyperbole Engine before dumping it into her pocket. "I'll tell you this," she smiles, "in at least *one* universe I do." Reaching across the table, she places her hand on top of mine. "How about you buy us another round of drinks and we find out if it's this one?"

It's the single most intelligent thing anyone's said to me all night.

The Galaxy's Most Wanted

by Annie Reed

LAST TIME I COUNTED, I had two hundred fifty-seven wives and four hundred thirteen children. Five hundred forty-one nieces and nephews. A couple of hundred pistol-toting fathers-in-law. And a dog.

I'm also wanted on seventeen planets in sixteen different systems. That's not counting all the outstanding interstellar warrants against me for child abandonment, failure to support, and back alimony.

I don't look like much, at least not anymore. At least not compared to the pretty woman who brought me out tonight. Yeah, that's her. The brunette. Curves in all the right places. She's sitting on the bar stool to my right, flirting with the hunky bartender, he of the bulging muscles and piercing blue eyes, full head of blond hair and easy smile. If I had looked like Mr. What Can I Get a Pretty Little Thing Like You to

Drink Tonight, I wouldn't be in this mess. Guys like me, we have to try harder.

That's how the whole mess I'm in started, trying to get women to pay attention to me. A little lie here, an embellishment there. What's the harm? So I don't actually own a star cruiser (I am—or was—the third assistant to the second-shift lead maintenance tech on the refuse recycling scow that ran between Omicron and Zeta Sawh, but who's quibbling?) and I'm not the man who ran a high-quality bootlegging outfit on New Marris Prime (although I never said no to a decent alcoholic beverage), but a guy like me's got to have a little edge, you know? Something to get a girl to look past the receding hairline and paunchy belly, and the fact that I'm a little short. Okay, a lot short. But I do come up to at least shoulder height on most humanoid women. Not all that bad from my perspective, if you think about it.

That's my problem, you see. I just always liked women more than they liked me.

Even the ones I shouldn't have. Like the pretty brunette on the bar stool next to me.

The first time I saw her I'd just walked into a dark, dingy bar at the end of a long, uneventful recycling trip. I mean, really—how much trouble can a guy get into on a ship full of recycled garbage? Bored and more than a little bit lonely for some female companionship, I cleaned myself up, spritzed on my favorite deodorizing aftershave, charged up my tally card with the money I'd earned on the trip, and went looking to get laid.

And I found Brina.

Oh, Brina . . . Man, she lit up that dark, dingy bar. I didn't hear the grit crunch under my boots or smell the drunks passed out in the corner. Smoke from a dozen or so illegal substances didn't clog my lungs or make me cough, and I never even paid attention to the table full of loud, obnoxious cruiser jockeys I might have otherwise tried to impress. All I could see was Brina. Sleek legs up to there, shiny hair falling in curls down to there, and a whole lot of there in between. Gorgeous round face, high cheekbones, full pouty lips, and dazzling blue eyes that sparkled like the third ring of New Marris from high orbit.

I made a beeline for her, even though I knew I didn't stand a chance. If you're gonna shoot, aim high, that's what my daddy always told me. Good advice. I always expected to get the cold shoulder from the real lookers, so when they said no, I had nowhere else to go but up, you know what I mean? If you start with the ones who are merely passable and *they* shoot you down, well . . . a guy's ego can only take just so much.

So I sidled up to Brina at the bar. She sat perched on a stool, her legs crossed, one creamy thigh atop the other, her knees dimpled and tempting beneath those ultra-sheer tights she wore. Even today I can't remember what else she wore that night, except that it was red. Brina always did look best in red. I do remember that I had a hard time peeling my eyes away from all that almost-bare skin of her legs to meet the curious glance she gave me.

"Buy you a drink?" I asked in my best "I'm the coolest guy this side of Saturn" voice.

"No, thanks." Her voice was husky deep, what my daddy used to call a whiskey rasp, and damn, but it did things to me I hadn't had done to me in more time than I cared to remember.

Of course, back then I didn't know she'd had her voice enhanced. Just like a lot of other things she'd had done. Ignorance was bliss.

Maybe I should say potential bliss. I just had to get her to let me buy her a drink.

She'd been polite, at least, I had to give her that. Polite I could work with. Polite usually meant nice manners and sometimes a warm heart. Warm hearts were even better. I could definitely work with a warm heart.

I ordered myself a drink from the servo-tender. No real live humanoid bartender, not in that place. All spindly, dull metal arms and wheezing, rusty gears, the automated bartender was an outdated model. I'd probably hauled a couple hundred of the things to the recyclers over the years, so I didn't expect much from this one. I watched it spit my drink order into a semi-clean glass and then hold it hostage until I inserted my tally card into the slot in its torso. When I punched in my approval code for the drink charge, I noticed a submenu of selected services the tender offered. I tried not to grin as I ordered up fifteen minutes of Lend an Ear.

I was in.

I took a sip of my drink and proceeded to tell the tender a sad tale about my harridan of an ex-wife, a money-grubbing, self-centered woman who never gave me a moment's gratitude for taking her and her three fatherless children in before leaving me for greener pastures. The tender listened with a carefully empathetic expression on its flat, featureless, display screen face.

I got about five minutes into my story when I noticed that Brina seemed to be paying at least a little attention to me. I had seven minutes of my prepaid fifteen left—I'd just about reached the part of my story where I was combing known space looking for children I'd grown to love like my very own—when Brina actually looked at me with something akin to sympathy. By the time I was waxing poetic about my (nonexistent) baby girl, the light of my life who would never even remember her father thanks to my (nonexistent) ex-wife, Brina had her hand on my arm.

I was definitely in.

Brina let me buy her a drink after that. She let me buy her a lot of drinks while I embellished on my tale of domestic woe, and then she let me take her home. At her front door, I stretched up and she leaned down, and we shared a kiss that made my toes curl. Among other things.

Then she let me inside and I kissed a whole lot of

other things that made her toes curl. That turned out to be a night to remember.

Brina was probably the prettiest woman I'd ever taken to bed. Even the next morning, her hair still gleamed dark chestnut against white sheets that weren't quite as crisp or white as they'd started out the night before. Her eyes still sparkled that incredible shade of blue, and even her lips were still the same pouty red as I remembered from the bar. She had a birthmark on her left shoulder right below her collarbone that tickled when I kissed it, and a small series of moles that trailed down the back of her neck from her hairline to the top of her spine.

Those moles should have given her away, and probably would have if I'd been paying attention. I'm not the brightest guy in the universe when I've been deprived of female companionship for too long.

"I've got a friend who works in personal location resources," she said in her husky voice that morning after she fed me breakfast. "Maybe I can ask her to help find your children. I know how much they mean to you."

"Yeah."

Yeah, my nonexistent children.

"That would be great," I said, calculating how long I could distract her against how determined she was to help. I figured I had about a half hour before I had to bug out with some excuse and a promise to call.

I was off by about ten minutes.

"No, really, I can help," she said, one hand idly stroking my chest as I tried to catch my breath.

"You don't have to do that," I said, my mind still floating in that happy place I go to after some woman makes parts of me really, really happy.

"It's no trouble. I want to."

"Not important," I mumbled. "I'll track 'em down one of these days."

I never said I was particularly smart when I was in my happy place.

Her hand stopped stroking me. It took me a minute to register that maybe she wasn't as satisfied with me as she'd been five minutes ago.

"How many children do you have again?" she asked.

"Four," I said, absolutely sure of the answer.

"You said three last night."

"Well, three are my ex-wife's, and the baby makes four."

"You said three."

The whiskey in her voice had definitely chilled just a bit more than I liked.

"I said four." I leaned up and tried to kiss her on the tip of her perfect nose, but she backed away from me. "I guess that means it's time for me to go."

I felt those sparkling blue eyes of hers watching me the whole time I got dressed.

"You do this a lot?" she asked as I pulled my boots on.

"Do what?"

I probably shouldn't have asked that, but sometimes I don't know when to keep my mouth shut. Remember the part about not being smart? Yeah, I'm sure you've worked that out by now.

"Spin stories like that to get some woman to take you home."

Well . . .

I looked into those blue eyes and felt the truth just pulled out of me.

"Pretty much," I heard myself say, much to my horror.

What? I couldn't have just said that.

"For how long?"

I tried to clap a hand over my mouth, but it didn't help. "About ten standard years now, ever since I kind of let myself go."

"You could have gotten yourself enhanced," she said, and then I got it. About her enhancements, why she'd seemed so perfect to me.

"Like you did? That's not exactly honest either," I said, and this time it wasn't just in response to the unnatural pull of her eyes.

"What kind of stories do you tell? I mean, besides the one you told me."

The sparkle in her eyes intensified, and I found myself spilling out all the stories I'd told over the years. How I impressed space jockeys I felt inferior to—which, let's face it, a short, follically-challenged, glorified refuse man on a floating garbage scow feels inferior to pretty much every space pilot with a decent cruiser—by telling them I was wanted by whatever big badass happened to control a neighboring sector of space. How I spun differing sad sack tales of woe to woo buxom maidens to my—or more than likely *their*—beds. How I left the maidens with a smile and the pilots with a good chuckle, and managed to wheedle more than my share of free alcohol along the way.

"You're very inventive," she said when I was done. "So am I, only a little differently. An upgrade to the— what would you call it? Standard Buxom Bimbo Enhancement Package?—and a pricey one at that. Worth it, though. Why don't you let me know in a year or two if you think so, too."

I had no idea at the time what she meant. I only knew that the world had stopped revolving around those sparkling eyes of hers. Now was as good a time as any to bug out. I could think about what she meant later. Probably nothing, just a little attempt at psych out on her part.

Three weeks later I found out just how wrong I was. Another dingy bar, another dingy planet, another too-long trip hauling stinking mounds of barely recognizable recycles to their destination. And no prospects of comely female companionship in this bar either. The planetary outpost was ninety-five percent male. The other five percent of the population was home making happy with someone other than me.

Well, I did spot a table in the back corner crowded with likely candidates for my tall tales of interplanetary intrigue. If I couldn't find female companionship, maybe I'd be able to wheedle a free drink or two. Or three.

I'd just gotten really started when a bright light flashed in front of my nose, a glass exploded on the bar, and I heard a high-pitched whine about the same time I smelled singed flesh.

My singed flesh.

I fell back out of my chair onto the dusty neocrete floor.

"Gotcha!"

The voice was female, high -pitched, and grating.

I dove beneath the table, determined to stay out of trouble's way. Unfortunately, it turned out I was just the person trouble was looking for.

Another bolt of light hit the metal table I crouched beneath. The charge crackled and sparked along the frame before dissipating in the floor.

"You bastard!" I heard the woman shriek. "How dare you desert me in my hour of need!"

"Not so fast!" This voice was male, deep and authoritative. Probably belonged to someone who could bench press my body weight with one hand tied behind his back. "I've got the bounty on this one, and I'm taking him in. Alive."

Bounty? On me?

What the hell for?

I risked peeking out from beneath my table. A middle-aged woman with a laser pistol and a bandolier of extra energy packs slung across her chest stood toe-to-toe with a muscle-bound, bench-pressing soldier of fortune type, also heavily armed. Both had weapons pointed in my general direction, but they were too busy arguing about whether to take me dead or alive to actually pay me much attention. I'd become pretty good at bugging out, and I scuttled out from under the table and out the door while they began shouting obscenities at each other.

So began my five-year ordeal of running from everything and everyone who wanted my head for one reason or another. I couldn't go back to my worthless job. I spotted four more bounty hunter types and at least ten self-righteously outraged women lurking around the berth where my shuttle back to the garbage scow was docked. I hid in a dusty alcove on a street four blocks away from the docking station and watched with a pang of something almost like homesickness as the shuttle blasted off without me. Third assistants to second-shift lead maintenance techs aren't hard to replace, and apparently no one thought I was important enough to wait for.

Except all the people who suddenly wanted my hide.

And that number seemed to increase almost exponentially.

That's when I started taking even lower-tech jobs, positions that paid in trade rather than traceable money. I traded for food and places to stay, for transport from one planet to the next. I traded for disguises and simple, physical enhancements to change my appearance.

And I traded for 'net time.

No spacer used to boring, routine runs has any problem hacking into semisecure 'net sites, so it didn't take me long to figure out what had happened to me. Every story I'd ever told for the purpose of fooling someone out of his booze or into her bed had come true.

Well, not quite totally true. I reaped none of the benefits of my tales. I wasn't independently wealthy, nor did I command the respect and admiration of all the crime bosses I'd bested in my make-believe boot-legging, gunrunning, money-laundering, and cargo-smuggling adventures. None of the ex-wives who tracked after me or sued me for child support and alimony remembered any of the good times we sup-posedly had, and I sure wasn't getting laid with any regularity.

I had no home, no decent job, no prospects, and my dog had been on the shuttle I'd watch leave with-out me.

I really, really missed my dog. He'd been the only one who didn't make me feel self-conscious about my bald spot.

For the first few years I was so busy running for my life that I didn't see the connection to Brina. Running from two hundred fifty-seven ex-wives with four hun-dred thirteen hungry mouths to feed, not to mention the crime bosses on seventeen planets, takes a lot of energy and nearly more brainpower than I had. Remember the not smart part of my tale? Yeah. You try living on the run from half the known galaxy for a while. It'll sap your smarts, too.

After I finally figured it out, it took me a while to track Brina down. She'd moved a few times over the years, although not nearly as much as I had. I finally found her on the third moon of Correa, where she had herself a nice, upscale little apartment in a high-rise development.

I'd learned a few tricks over the years, so I tweaked the entry pad to her apartment and let myself inside to wait for her. A golden tabby cat watched me from a high shelf in her living room, tail twitching annoyed patterns in the filtered air. I had to reprogram her security bot to leave me alone, so I sent it to search out and destroy wayward cockroaches. The third moon of Correa is about the only place I've ever been with no indigenous cockroach population. It would be busy for a while.

It felt so good to be inside a comfortable, grime-free apartment I almost forgot why I was there. Almost. I sat down to wait in an overstuffed easy chair, pistol held loose and resting on my lap. It didn't take long until Brina showed up.

She hadn't changed much in the intervening years. She still had shiny hair down to there, sleek legs up to there, and her there was certainly all there, it just didn't appeal to me anymore. I came prepared this time, though. I had my own enhancement, my own little series of moles running down the back of my neck.

I blinked twice to activate my implant when Brina walked in her door, and this time when I looked in her eyes, the sparkle had dimmed and just looked like plain old blue sky. No pull. No control. It felt damn good.

"What the hell did you do to me?" I asked her. I leveled my pistol straight at that gorgeous body of hers.

Her eyes widened a little as she took in my gun, but all in all I was disappointed that she didn't seem more afraid of me. I actually *was* a hardened criminal now—okay, a minor-league, jaded, not-quite criminal on the run—but still, it would have been nice if she'd begged for her life just a little bit.

"Took you long enough," she said.

The door to her apartment swished shut behind her. Her security bot, hot on the trail of a life-form that might be an oversized cockroach with really good legs, pressed a sensor arm to her thigh. She yelped and swatted the bot away. It squawked and extended the sensor arm toward her clearly nervous cat.

Brina put her tally card on her kitchen counter along with a small potted plant she'd carried in the door.

"I didn't do anything to you," she said. "You did it all yourself."

"I did *not* put two hundred-fifty-seven ex-wives on

my tail," I said. "I don't even have one ex-wife, much less two hundred fifty-seven of them."

She laughed at me. "That's how many times you told that sorry story of yours? Good galaxies, you're a fool. Tell me . . ." She slipped off her shoes and curled her toes into the soft, ivory floor covering beneath her feet. "How many times did it work?"

More often than you might think, I almost told her. "Enough," I said instead.

"And you left all those women the next morning, probably without a second thought."

Her toenails were stained red, I noticed. Not quite the same shade as her lips, but close. I watched her scrunch her toes deeper into the ivory pile.

The cat yowled and leaped off the shelf, ran for the next room, tail fluffed out twice normal cat size. The bot followed, a clump of golden fur at the end of its sensor arm. Brina didn't pay it any attention.

"Not always without a second thought," I said. Damn, but her red toenails against that ivory floor covering were distracting.

"But without ever hearing from you again, I imagine."

No, I was definitely a love 'em and leave 'em kind of guy. I figured none of them would want a life with a garbage tech who was gone more than he was home. At least that's what I always told myself. I really wasn't all that callous. I just had their best interests at heart.

Really.

I did.

"Pretty heartless way to treat someone who takes you into her bed," she said. Her voice hadn't lost that whiskey rasp, only now I found it annoying.

How did she get her toes to wiggle like that? I curled my own toes inside my boots, but I didn't think I was quite as flexible.

"Least you could have done was leave a plant. Or maybe a flower. Something classy. Something that says you cared, for that one night anyway."

Okay, so I was a cad. Did I have to pay for it for the rest of my life?

"But no, you just bugged out as soon as you could. That's pretty low, even for a lowlife like you. My cat has more class."

I wondered what those toes would feel like massaging my back. I tried to remember if toes had been involved in our one night together.

"Even this plant has more class than you do," she said, her voice so low and raspy now that if I hadn't been mesmerized by her feet I might have noticed the odd intensity to it. "You know what you are?"

Could she please just be quiet so I could concentrate on her feet? At that point I would have agreed to anything to get her to shut up.

"I get it already," I said. "I'm the lowest of the low. Lower than your cat, lower than even a cockroach. I'm dirt, okay?"

And that was the last thing I ever said.

I wonder sometimes why she takes me everywhere

with her. Sure, there's less of me to carry than there used to be. Take away the water and people don't weigh all that much. She did buy a hand-thrown pot of emerald green Correa clay to keep me in, and she drenches me every few months with fertilizer for the plant that shares space with me. That was an odd feeling at first—having the plant's roots growing in and through me, but I've gotten used to it. In fact, it's kind of nice, not being all alone in the world.

I wonder sometimes what happened to all those bounty hunters and pistol-toting ex-wives. It's not like I can wish them out of existence. I can't even wish myself out of this pot. Not that I'm sure I would. It's relaxing not having to duck laser fire all the time.

I still miss my dog, though. I'm not as fond of Brina's cat as I was of my dog. Every now and then the cat leaves me a present I could do without.

I don't think the cat's ever forgiven me for the cockroach-seeking bot incident. You'd think a cat wouldn't be quite so sensitive about a bald spot.

AUTHOR NOTES

Loren L. Coleman is the author of over twenty novels, including *Blood of the Wolves,* which led to the relaunch of fiction novels for the world of Conan, and *Sword of Sedition* for the Mech Warrior: Dark Age line. He also writes a great deal of short fiction for http://battlecorps.com/ and is working on a new original novel. When he isn't writing, Loren coaches local sports and collects DVDs. He holds a black belt in traditional Taekwon Do, which he considers mandatory for any father with a daughter. His personal website can be found at http://www.reqal.com.

It's been almost exactly ten years since Sarah A. Hoyt sold her first short story. In the interim, she's sold over three dozen short stories to magazines such as *Amazing, Asimov's, Analog* and *Weird Tales* as well as an assortment of anthologies. Alongside the short stories, she's sold a dozen novels. The most notable are her critically acclaimed Shakespeare Fantasy series, her Musketeers Mysteries series beginning November 06 with *Death of a Musketeer* written as Sarah D'Almeida (http://www.musketeersmysteries.com), her new Urban Fantasy Shifter's series (http://www.shifter series.com) which started with *Draw One In the Dark.*

307

Over the next couple of years there will also be a historical fantasy trilogy. Sarah lives in Colorado with her two teen sons, her husband and a varied pride of cats. She's hard at work on her next dozen novels. Catch up with her progress toward this goal at http://www.sarahahoyt.com.

When not writing, Steven Mohan, Jr., works as a manufacturing engineer in Pueblo, Colorado, where he lives with his wife and three children. His fiction has appeared in *Interzone, Polyphony,* and *Paradox* (among other places), and his short stories have won honorable mention in *The Year's Best Science Fiction* and *The Year's Best Fantasy and Horror.*

After a third-place win in the first volume of the *Star Trek Strange New Worlds* anthology, Phaedra Weldon has written other *Star Trek* pieces including an S.C.E. novella as well as fiction and source for *Classic Battle-Tech.* After several short story sales in various anthologies, she is looking forward to the publication of her first novel about an astral-projecting investigator.

Greg Beatty is recently married. He and his wife live in Bellingham, Washington. Greg has a B.A. from University of Washington and a Ph.D. from the University of Iowa, both in English, and attended Clarion West 2000. Greg's work has appeared in *3SF, Absolute Magnitude, Abyss & Apex, Andromeda Spaceways Inflight Magazine, Asimov's, Fortean Bureau, H.P. Love-*

craft's Magazine of Horror, the *Internet Review of Science Fiction, Ideomancer, Oceans of the Mind, Paradox, SCI FICTION, Shadowed Realms Strange Horizons, Star*Line,* and *The New York Review of Science Fiction,* among other venues. Greg won the Rhysling Award in 2005 (short poem category).

Michael Hiebert is an award-winning writer of novel length and short story fiction. Recently, he was short listed by Joyce Carol Oates for *America's Best Mystery Stories.* His work has been published world-wide. A self-described geek, Michael lives in British Columbia on the west coast of Canada with his unbelievably supportive wife-to-be, Candice. He has ten computers, two cats, and two wonderful children. Michael can be contacted via mythmaker@mac.com.

David DeLee is a native New Yorker who now resides in Central Ohio with his wife, two daughters and too many cats. His previous short fiction has appeared in the annual anthology *Strange New Worlds,* vols. 8 and 9. He is currently hard at work on several new writing projects.

After experimenting with numerous occupations, Louisa Swann, a native Californian (ack! She admits it!) settled on writing as her long-term mental aberration. During her excessively loud oral dissertations (proved integral to her writing process as evidenced by numerous short story sales, including *Star Trek: Strange New*

Worlds V, VI, VII and *Tales From The Captain's Table*
anthologies) husband and son shake their heads and
mutter something about "the muse." In the interest
of survival, husband Jim acquired an eighty-acre compound complete with coyotes, frogs, and screech owls
to serve as nightly backup band for a raving writer's
rants. Now neighbors wave and smile as the Swanns
drive by instead of casting sidelong glances that cause
hubby to wonder when the Men in White will be
showing up. Luckily dog, cat, and horses understand
Louisa perfectly; she often goes to them for grooming
when the outside world bares its claws.

Leslie Claire Walker hails from the lush bayous and
urban jungles of the Texas Gulf Coast. Her short fiction has appeared in *L. Ron Hubbard Presents Writers
of the Future, Volume XVI, Hags, Sirens, and Other
Bad Girls of Fantasy*, and *Fantasy*. Leslie is at work
on a novel about a seventeen-year-old boy trying to
balance school, friends, and family with his part-time
night job as the Grim Reaper. She is thrilled for
"Hanged Man," to appear in *Cosmic Cocktails*.

After twenty-five years working in the corporate
world, Dan C. Duval had enough, retired from high
tech, sold his horse ranch, and moved to the Oregon
Coast, where his cat sits on the back of his desk chair
and continually reminds him that he should be writing
more and that he has not given the cat a pet in the last
few seconds. Currently working on writing thrillers, he

has sold short stories to a number of anthologies and online magazines.

As a former news director, magazine editor, and radio comedy show host, Allan Rousselle has enjoyed practicing different types of writing for a wide variety of audiences. He finds that all compelling writing is ultimately about story, whether describing news events or setting up a comedy sketch, delivering a marketing pitch or exploring the human condition. He particularly enjoys writing where humor and tragedy intersect. In this story, he presents a dark take on "A man walks into a bar. . . ."

Daniel M. Hoyt aspires to be *that* Dan Hoyt—you know, the one who writes those cool stories and books. Realizing a few years ago that rocket science was fun, but unlikely to pay all the bills, Dan embarked on a new career choice—writing fiction for fun and profit. Since his first sale to *Analog*, he's sold several stories to other magazines and anthologies. In addition, Dan is particularly pleased to announce his upcoming DAW anthology, *Fate Fantastic*, edited with Martin H. Greenberg. Curiously, after a few short years, Dan's mortgage is still outstanding, but he remains hopeful. Catch up with him at http://www.danielmhoyt.com.

Peter Orullian is the author of *At the Manger, the Stories of Those Who Were There,* as well as being a talented editor and book reviewer. These days, he spends his writing time on his current novel, as well as on developing content for Xbox.

Annie Reed is an award-winning writer whose short fiction has appeared in *Ellery Queen*, three volumes of *Strange New Worlds*, and two previous DAW anthologies—*Time After Time* and *Hags, Sirens, and Other Bad Girls of Fantasy*. She writes mystery and science fiction as well as women's fiction.